WORDS
ON FIRE

JENNIFER A. NIELSEN

WORDS ON FIRE

SCHOLASTIC INC.

This book was originally published by Scholastic Press in 2019.

All rights reserved. Published by Scholastic Inc., *Publishers since 1920*. SCHOLASTIC and associated logos are trademarks and/or registered trademarks of Scholastic Inc.

ISBN 978-1-338-27578-0

10 9 8 7 6 5 4 3 2   22 23 24 25 26

Printed in the U.S.A.   40
This edition first printing 2022

Book design by Christopher Stengel

For Logan. Because when you join the family,

a book gets dedicated to you.

Also, we think you're awesome.

To be without learning is to be without eyes.

—Lithuanian proverb

CHAPTER
ONE

My name is Audra.

In my language, Lithuanian, it means *storm*.

But my language had become illegal. If the soldiers we passed on the roads heard us speaking it, we could be whipped on the spot or arrested. Or in some cases, we might disappear. That happened sometimes.

So I avoided saying my name in public, but I often wondered: If my language was forbidden, then my name was forbidden. Which meant I had no name.

Which left me perfectly free to do everything I could to defy the Russian occupiers.

I redoubled my grip on the sacks slung over my shoulder, braced myself against the wind coming at me, and continued down the path.

I'd come this far. No matter what was ahead, I could not stop now.

I *would not* stop now.

Too many lives depended on me. Starting with those of my parents.

June 1893

My father was made of magic.

Not real magic, of course—I knew magic wasn't real—but if it ever might have been, then it was inside my father's quick hands and lively voice. He was born with tricks and effects and a talent to share them with others, delighting audiences wherever he traveled.

How I wished I could be more like him, bold and adventurous, always ready with a joke or a story. Instead, I was the girl who ducked into the shadows when we had visitors, the girl who watched life from afar but rarely participated. The girl who wanted to be more than she was but knew such a thing would be the kind of magic even my father couldn't achieve.

Mama's magic was different. Since Papa's work took him away so often, she found ways to fill our home with the smells of fried sweet bread, with the music she sang as we worked the garden, and with her tender good-night kisses on my cheek.

Those times were special, but nothing replaced the moments when we were all together. I loved to sit at Papa's feet by the fire, watching him prepare for his shows, letting him test his tricks on me to see if I could guess the secrets. By now, I could, of course—I'd seen every trick a hundred times and could do many of them myself, but never in public, never like him.

"You can be like him in other ways," Mama often said on the nights Papa was gone. "Be happy like him, be smart like him. But do not travel like him, that's not for you."

I had no wish for that either. Lithuania was a dangerous place to live. My parents had often explained that as their reason for keeping me on our little farm.

Our country was occupied by Cossack soldiers from Russia, the empire that claimed Lithuania as its own. Lithuanians disagreed, of course, but we were a small country of farmers and simple peasant folk. What were we supposed to do against such a vast empire?

"We're supposed to keep our heads down and obey their laws," Mama said whenever my father broached the question; then she'd steal a glance at me. "For Audra's sake."

"All of this is for Audra's sake" was always Papa's answer.

Those conversations continued late into the night, long after they thought I was asleep, and those were the moments when I realized that something about my father's work had begun to make Mama nervous.

"Has this gone too far?" she'd whisper. "Have we risked too much?"

It wasn't the first time she'd asked that question, but lately, Papa was taking longer to answer.

On this night, he finally replied, "Everything is fine, my love. This work is more important now than ever."

Then his work wasn't magic shows, not really. My father must have been involved in something more serious when he traveled, something that made Mama anxious.

Then she offered another question. "Do you think Audra suspects something?"

If I did, then that was all I had, a suspicion of *something*. And Papa's assurance that I didn't know what they were doing began to feel like an itch I couldn't scratch. I needed answers.

To get them, I began secretly listening in on their conversations, becoming so good at it that I could sneak up close enough to touch them and they wouldn't realize I was there. One scrap of information at a time, I began to understand that something in my father's travels was illegal and dangerous, and that Mama feared one day he would make a mistake and we'd all be in trouble. Every discussion they had ended in the same way—with their agreement to keep me out of their business.

That is, until the summer after I turned twelve. On the evening of the summer solstice, Papa said to my mother, "Audra should come with me tonight."

I immediately sat upright, wondering what might have made him suggest such a thing. He was seated in his chair at the table and had been reviewing a card trick for tonight's performance. Laid out on the table was his brown leather shoulder bag, the one in which he carried most of his tricks. At his side was a tall canvas sack containing extra clothes and provisions for his travels from one village to the next. He wore that on his back and rarely traveled with anything more.

"Did you hear me, Lina?" Papa asked, giving me a wink as he did. "Audra should come—"

Mama didn't even look at him to answer, "You're going on to other villages after the show. Audra won't know how to get back home." Mama was stirring a stew for the night, making extra for Papa to take with him. Her voice was usually soft and gentle, but I heard the warning in her tone tonight. There was no chance of me going.

But he wasn't giving up. "We'll stay in our own village square, and there will be festivities all around. She won't be in any danger tonight."

"How do you know that, Henri? People have disappeared from our village. We both know why!"

"Audra is still young—"

"Will the soldiers care about that?"

My father set his cards down. "She must learn to see our world the way it is."

"The way our world is, Audra is safer here."

"Ignoring danger does not protect us from danger. Let me teach her." His voice lowered almost to a whisper. "I've been giving this a lot of thought. She's better off if she knows."

Mama crossed the room to face him directly, standing at my side. "Henri, we have an agreement."

By then, I was sitting up even taller, trying to figure out what they were talking about. "What is the agreement? Mama, I want to know."

Mama folded her arms. "You don't understand what you are asking."

I lowered my eyes, considering her words, while Papa said, "But we do. We cannot refuse to teach her any longer. We agreed to do everything we could—"

"But no more than that. Nothing that puts Audra in danger." She glanced at my father's canvas sack. "Is everything packed and ready?"

"Yes, including the most important part."

My curiosity sparked. "Can you show it to me, Papa?"

He opened his mouth to answer, but Mama took his hand instead. "Help me carry in the milk," she said, pulling him outside. Which meant they intended to finish talking where I couldn't hear.

I hated when they did that, when they made it obvious how little they trusted me with their most serious conversations. If they couldn't trust me, then I figured there was no need to be trustworthy.

Papa was carrying something away from here in secret. I had to find out what it was.

As soon as the back door swung shut, I tried to lift his bag, but it was so heavy, I could barely make it budge. I unbuttoned the top and wondered why. Nothing I saw should have made it so heavy. There were only clothes and blankets and a few tin pans for cooking. What was beneath all of it?

I started to dig deeper into the bag, but everything was stuffed in tight, making it difficult to maneuver around. I wanted to get to the bottom of the bag, but my parents' voices were getting louder, coming closer.

I had just buttoned up the top when Mama walked into the house, picked up her spoon, and began stirring the pot of stew again. After a long sigh, she said, "I suppose the midsummer festivities only come once a year. If I go, too, then Audra and I can return home together."

From where he stood in the doorway, Papa's eyes twinkled—they often did. It was one of the ways I knew magic was inside him. I wanted my eyes to sparkle just as bright.

And Mama tried her best to smile, though all I saw in her eyes was worry, a glimmer of sadness I noticed more and more often, especially when Papa was away for his shows. And last winter, he'd been gone quite a bit, though he'd left his bag of magic tricks behind. On those trips, she did more than worry. Sometimes I heard her cry in the nights, long after she thought I was asleep.

Rubbing his hands together, Papa returned to the table and faced me. "Even with your mother there, you must follow our rules."

My heart leapt with excitement. Whatever the rules, whatever the conditions, I intended to agree to them all. Anything so that I could go.

"I know the rules," I said. "Avoid the Cossack—"

"There is one policeman in particular you must avoid. His name is Officer Rusakov and he is new to this district. He must have something to prove to his superiors, for he is strict with the law, all laws. We speak Lithuanian here at home, but out there tonight, it must be Russian, even if you believe you are surrounded by friends. Rusakov has spies, informants."

"I never cause trouble, Papa, you know that." I wasn't a rock thrown into the pond; I was a leaf that fluttered onto the water where even the breeze wouldn't notice me.

"And if anyone asks about school, tell them you are not interested."

I wasn't interested. I had enough to do to help around the farm. School could not offer me anything better than the life I already had.

"Also, if you should get lost—"

"I can find my way home, Papa." I wasn't allowed in the village, but in the daytime, after I'd finished my chores, I sometimes wandered the forest behind our home, and I knew the trails well. My parents didn't know that, not even my father.

Mama began stirring the stew again. "If you want to go, then finish your chores."

I immediately grabbed a basket to gather the eggs and went outside, lingering in the doorway long enough to hear Mama's whispers to Papa. "I think we're being watched. I passed a package to a woman in the market last week and felt a shiver run up my spine."

The door closed behind me, but I froze in place there, unable to fully understand what I had just heard. Mama was not a bystander in my father's work—she was part of it! When she spoke to Papa of the risks and the danger, she was talking about her own safety too!

And now they were speaking of sharing their secrets with me. I had spent months trying to find out for myself, but suddenly, I didn't want to know. I wished I hadn't even overheard my mother just now.

But I had. Which would change everything about attending the midsummer festivities tonight. I needed to tell them that I knew more than they realized. Then at least we could talk openly.

I turned to enter our home again, but instead I pressed my ear against the door in time to hear Papa say, "We're making a difference, I can feel it!"

"The Russians can feel it too," Mama said. "They've occupied our country for decades. Nothing we do will change that."

"At least they might acknowledge that this is *our* country! We are not Russians. We will never be Russians. Don't you see how important this is?"

"I know it's important. That's the only reason I'm coming along tonight, to help with this delivery, and to be sure we're all safe by morning."

"Audra can help," Papa said. "She is quiet, but she listens and watches and she is smart."

"She is not ready, Henri."

"Because we haven't prepared her. Let me teach her, let me show her all there is to know!"

"Another year," Mama said softly. "Another year and then we will teach her. Please."

After a brief moment, Papa agreed, "Another year," then whispered his love to Mama, and at least for the moment, everything became right again in my world. Tonight would be better if they believed their secrets belonged only to them. I would tell them tomorrow, and we could enjoy this evening. Mama had described the festivities to me every year, but this was the first time I'd be allowed to go.

This night, the twenty-third of June, was the shortest night of the year and was said to be a night of magic. Herbs gathered from the meadows on this night would have special healing powers, and the grasses could be woven into wreaths that could predict the future husband of the girl who wore it on her head.

I knew such things were nonsense, an entirely different kind of magic from my father's, but that didn't matter. I was so excited to go that my parents' secrets became pushed to the back of my mind—they were too serious for such a beautiful day. I was saving all of that for tomorrow, after the festivities.

After supper, I went to my room to change into my finest clothes, a white linen skirt and blouse with a green vest and matching plaid apron, finishing it off with a white woven sash around my waist. Then I rebraided my hair, careful to brush out the long blond strands first so they'd be neat and shiny in the moonlight. I wanted everything to go perfectly tonight.

Which was why when I emerged from the room and saw a basket of wet laundry, I offered to hang it for Mama so that she could get ready.

I walked out the rear door with the basket in my arms. The clothesline was at the back of our house but enough to the side that I had a wide view of the land around us. I began hanging the clothes, starting with a long bedsheet that took some effort to get over the strings. As I bent down for a towel, my breath caught in my throat.

At least ten soldiers on horseback were riding up the gently sloped hill toward our home. They wore blue uniforms with red bands on their caps and shoulders and two columns of gold buttons down their fronts. Each man carried a rifle and many appeared armed in other ways. They were only two or three minutes away, and I had no idea what to do.

This was what my parents had warned me about for all these years.

The Cossack soldiers were here. And that could only mean trouble.

CHAPTER
THREE

I left the basket where it was and scrambled back toward the house, crying, "Papa!"

He must have already seen them, for he and my mother were frantically moving about the kitchen, placing small wrapped packages inside Papa's traveling sack. Why should they care about that right now? The soldiers were almost here!

"Did they see you?" Papa asked.

"I—I don't know."

"Go with your mother out the back door. You've got to run!"

I stared at him, barely understanding his words. "Run? Where?"

"Get to the forest. Hurry!"

I grabbed his hand, my fingers trembling . . . No, that was *his* hand shaking in fear. My father wasn't afraid of anything, had never been afraid before, not until now. He steered me toward the back door, but I kept pulling him with me, crying, "Let's all go together!"

"I can't, Audra." He drew in a sharp breath. "I'm going to stall the soldiers here, give you and your mother a chance to get away. Don't you come back, don't you even look back. Now go!"

He grabbed his shoulder bag from the table and gave it to my mother. She slung it over one arm, then put a hand on my back and pushed me forward, running behind me.

We had a small yard and our farmland lay beyond that. It'd be a long run across those fields before we reached the forest. My father couldn't possibly stall long enough for us to make it all that distance.

Even as I ran, I heard the soldiers break down our front door and shout orders in Russian. But before I heard my father's reply, Mama and I were already crossing the farmland.

I was faster, so I didn't realize at first that Mama had fallen. When I heard her call my name, I turned to see her foot had become tangled in some low-hanging wire for our climbing plants.

"No, Audra," she cried. "Keep running!"

Nothing could make me leave her, not as Papa had just forced us to leave him. I hurried back to her, my heart pounding in my chest so forcefully that I hardly could think.

"You must get to the forest," Mama said.

"I can untangle you." My trembling fingers were working at the wire that had somehow twisted around her leg.

How could this have happened? How could the wire be gnarled like this?

I knew the answer. This was a job my mother had asked me to do a week ago, to straighten these wires from where our cow had trampled over them. I'd completely forgotten about this chore . . . until now.

"Take your father's bag," Mama said. "Take it and go."

"No, I can do this!"

"I'll untangle myself," Mama said. "But you must get to the safety of the trees. I'll follow you."

"No!"

Mama thrust the shoulder bag into my hands. "Keep running!"

I started to protest, but she waved me away. I got to my feet, but stood there, unsure of what to do.

"If I can't . . . if I don't follow you, then inside that bag is a package. You must take it to a woman in Venska named Milda Sabiene. Promise me you'll get that to her. Only her."

"Mama, I don't know where—"

At that moment, the sound of a loud crash came from our home, followed by the tinkling of breaking glass. I jumped and Mama briefly closed her eyes, then in a low voice said, "Audra, you will obey me now. Run and don't you stop."

This time, I did as she said, though tears were streaming down my cheeks. I was barely halfway across the field, each footstep crushing the tender shoots of potato plants in the earth, when Cossack soldiers burst from our rear door, shouting for me to stop.

I raced toward the forest, looking back only when I heard my mother call for me to keep running. A few of the soldiers had already surrounded her and were tying her hands behind her back, arresting her.

The others pointed at me and began to give chase. If I could get into the trees, I would be safe. I knew the area directly behind my home better than anyone, certainly better than these soldiers. I could hide in there, if I was fast enough.

Before crossing into the forest, I turned back at a sudden *whoosh*, just in time to see my home explode into flames. What had they done? Had my father been inside? Had they brought my mother back to the home as well? I couldn't see her anymore.

My parents could have been inside. What if they were inside? My chest burned with horror and despair . . . even as my home burned.

Flames continued to rip through the back of our small wood home, consuming first the corner that served as my bedroom. I had nothing in there of value, but the fire was spreading fast, taking with it my peace, my comfort . . . my family. Everything that mattered to me in the world was engulfed in flames. I swallowed down the pain that was destroying me, too, then turned again to run, almost blind with panic. Fully aware that the soldiers weren't far behind me, and that whatever had happened to my parents could happen to me next.

The Cossacks were fast, but I was more nimble in jumping over the low-hanging branches to enter the woods. I dove into the thicket and took a sharp right toward what I knew was a steep slope down into some dense underbrush. When I was near it, I clutched the shoulder bag against my chest and leapt into the air, then fell through nothing until my body caught up with the slope and I half slid, half rolled the rest of the way to the bottom.

By that time, I heard the first soldier enter in the same way I had come, shouting orders to the others to join him in the search. I crawled as deep beneath the thick leaves as I could, praying they would see the slope and go around it. Praying one of them wouldn't accidentally take a tumble and end up falling right beside me. This was a good hiding place but not a secure one.

I didn't dare look out, but from the voices around me, I believed there had to be thirty or forty soldiers here now, rather than only ten. It wasn't possible for there to be so many, I knew my fear was exaggerating their numbers, but what did it matter if there were forty men brushing through the leaves, or ten? They were looking for me. I barely dared to breathe, and before I knew it, thick tears were rolling down my cheeks. It was everything I could do not to sob aloud.

What had happened to my father, to my mother? Were they even still alive?

Mama had warned me once that drawing the attention of the Cossack soldiers could cost a person their life.

Her life. Papa's life.

I curled into a ball, burying my head in my arms so that if I did cry out, if I screamed out the pain I felt at what had just happened, no one would hear me.

By now, my home was surely engulfed in flames, though nothing I could imagine explained why they had burned it, or why they had even come.

Except that maybe I could explain it.

My father had hidden a wrapped package inside his shoulder bag. My mother had chosen to pass it to my care rather than to save her own life. I had just lost my parents because of that package.

Whatever it was, the soldiers considered it valuable enough that they were after me now. I had to deliver it to this woman, Milda, or else my parents' sacrifice would be for nothing. But once it was in her hands, I wanted nothing more to do with it. Whatever *it* was, it had just cost me everything I loved.

CHAPTER
FOUR

I wasn't sure how long I'd lain in the underbrush, but the soldiers seemed to have left the forest some time ago, and the air around me was dark now except for a partial moon that hung low in the sky. I didn't know this Milda Sabiene, nor had I ever been to Venska where she lived, but I knew I shouldn't stay here. The soldiers would return, probably in greater numbers. They would find me. Then I would be captured too.

Besides, I *couldn't* stay here, watching my home, my family, my life turn to ashes before my eyes. I was already broken and empty, hollowed out to nothing. If I stayed any longer, I'd lose the will to move ever again. I would die here.

Tentatively, I crawled out from beneath the brush, though when I tried to stand, my right foot crumpled, bringing a sting that made me gasp for breath. I must've injured the ankle when I jumped off the slope and was only now realizing how bad it was. I gritted my teeth together and hobbled forward. An injured ankle was the least of my worries now . . . unless the injury created worse problems. Was I headed toward Venska? I didn't know. What would I do if I got there? I didn't know that either.

I limped along for some time before I saw lights in the distance and heard the playful sounds of laughter and music. I froze and squinted at the lights, trying to understand them. Then I remembered what it was and shook my head in disbelief.

This was Midsummer's Eve, an all-night celebration for Lithuanians. The night of magic.

If my father was gone, then magic was gone as well. I wouldn't believe in it any longer; I couldn't.

Nor could I believe that the midsummer festivities were still continuing. Didn't they know what had happened to my parents? How could all these people dance and sing and laugh with one another on a night as horrible as this had been?

The voices were coming nearer to me, and once again I ducked beneath the undergrowth, burying myself inside the summertime foliage. I had to. My eyes would be swollen and red from crying, and my clothes were filthy from the tumble I'd taken. I'd stand out from the group for certain. If the Cossacks were still looking for me, I couldn't take the chance of anyone here turning me over to them.

I'd no sooner hidden myself than the party filled the clearing around me: what sounded like dozens of happy people without a single serious thought on their minds.

"It's not yet midnight!" a boy called. "It won't do any good to look for the fern blossom now!"

More laughter followed his statement, with girls calling back that they had plenty of grasses to gather until midnight.

"Weave your wreaths, then," he replied. "I will set mine out on the river with any of you pretty girls!"

They giggled and shooed him away and I tried to smile, thinking of the fun I would have had if the night had gone as planned. At exactly midnight, two people in love would set their wreaths out on the water. If they floated together, the couple knew the fates wanted them to marry. And if the wreaths separated, they were also warned to separate. That was nothing to smile about.

"Pardon our intrusion," said a deep Russian voice, "but we are looking for a fugitive."

I caught my breath in my throat, recognizing the voice of the soldier who had followed me into the forest earlier. I heard the snort of a horse. Perhaps the soldiers had returned to my home for their horses and ridden around the forest to this place.

There were sounds of more horses, so I knew this soldier wasn't alone. It didn't matter how many more had come. I couldn't outrun a single soldier on my injured foot.

"My name is Officer Rusakov and I am new to this district," the man continued. "The fugitive is a blond girl in braids wearing a white blouse and skirt."

"Sir, you've described most of the girls in Lithuania tonight," the boy who had spoken before said.

His comment wasn't taken kindly. I heard him gasp as he was hit, perhaps with the butt of a soldier's rifle, and he fell to the ground.

"This girl was a child, perhaps no more than twelve or thirteen," Officer Rusakov continued. "She is the daughter of Henrikas and Lina Zikaris. They have just been arrested."

My heart skipped a beat as I absorbed his words. My parents were alive, both of them? For the first time since I'd seen those soldiers come up the hillside, I felt a sliver of hope.

Then Rusakov added, "We wish to see to the safety and care of the girl."

I nearly scoffed aloud at that. They had chased after me with weapons drawn, terrified me, and left me to believe that if I did not give up this package in my arms, something terrible would happen. I doubted that had anything to do with my safety.

"Naturally, we will report her if we see her," someone said. "But the Zikaris family kept to themselves. I doubt any of us even know this girl."

"She will be carrying something wrapped in twine, perhaps inside a brown leather shoulder bag," Rusakov said. "Her clothes will be dirty from hiding. I am confident that you will recognize her . . . and can promise you a fine reward for turning her in."

Turn me in? Hardly the words someone would use if their only wish was to see to my safety and care. None of the people here should know me, even from the few times I'd been to the markets. I knew how to blend in with the shadows, how to not be noticed. I was more comfortable that way.

A different girl spoke now. "With your permission, sir, the hour is creeping closer to midnight. We beg you to allow us our traditions."

"Your foolish Lithuanian stories," Rusakov said. "They'll be gone soon enough." After a heavy sigh, he added, "But you may carry on for tonight, as long as you do not get in our way. We will remain in the area to continue searching."

Slowly, the people who had been laughing and singing minutes ago began moving about among the trees. I was sure all of them wanted to get as far from the officers as possible, but nobody wanted to be the first to leave the area. Maybe they figured they were safer here, together in one group, for it seemed impossible that the officers would attack so many people at once. But for all I knew, they would.

I looked around me and silently groaned. I was hiding in a thick patch of ferns. Of all nights and of all places to hide, I had made the worst possible choice.

"Perhaps the fern blossom is here," a girl said, her voice coming closer to where I was, more quickly than I could figure out what to do about it. "Perhaps . . . oh!"

I knew she'd seen me and I turned to look up at her, then

silently shook my head, pleading with her not to turn me in. She had every reason to do it, including a reward that would probably be a great help to her family. If the officers discovered that she had allowed me to stay in hiding, my punishment would also become hers.

She stared down at me, then her eyes darted away as she decided what to do. I recognized this girl. Her name was Violeta and she sold pastries on market day from her father's bakery.

"What is it, Violeta?" a friend called to her. "What have you found?"

"Yes," Officer Rusakov called, his tone dripping with suspicion. "What have you found?"

CHAPTER
FIVE

Time seemed to freeze while Violeta made her decision. No matter what choice she made, there would be rewards for it . . . or consequences. Officer Rusakov would be here soon, and it would be so easy for her to point me out, so easy to gain the favor of the soldiers by doing them a favor now.

His heavier footsteps crunched over the twigs and old autumn leaves as he came closer, and my heart crashed against my chest. It was possible I was in the last few minutes of my life.

Almost instantly, Violeta pasted a smile across her face and leaned over. "It's a fern blossom, I'm sure of it. Everyone come see!"

My eyes nearly leapt from my head with horror. It wasn't enough for her to turn me in alone; she wanted half the village to help her do it?

Excitedly, she motioned to her friends, who came running over beside her, enough of them hoping to see the magical blossom that they seemed to have forgotten about Officer Rusakov.

One by one, they gathered around the ferns where I was hiding, and one by one, they saw me, their eyes widening as they realized what Violeta had truly discovered.

I did not dare look at any of them, though I wished I could. It would be harder for them to report me if they saw my face. I only crouched there, wondering which of them would betray my hiding place, which of them would be the first to call out that they had found me and demand their reward.

I cringed when I heard the first person draw a breath to speak. She called out, "It is indeed a fern blossom, Violeta. Do you feel its magic yet?"

I peered up at her, just barely. She hadn't turned me in at all.

A girl beside Violeta asked, "Can you understand the language of the birds yet?"

Violeta glanced behind her toward Officer Rusakov, then back at me, saying, "There are no birds out this late. Perhaps tomorrow, I will."

The group pushed in tighter around the fern, and a boy said, "Violeta, surely you know all secrets."

Her eye fell on me again. "I'm afraid the greatest secrets are still a mystery to me. There is at least one thing about which I have many questions."

Then a third person asked, "And what of the third promise of finding the fern blossom? Can you read our thoughts?"

I finally looked up, and Violeta's gaze locked on mine. She nodded. "Yes, I can. I know the thoughts of everyone in this circle, and perhaps you all have been touched by the magic, too, for I am sure you know everything I am thinking."

Perhaps they did, for the group moved in even tighter around the fern, so many of them that unless the officers forced them apart, I would not be seen. They were protecting me. I almost couldn't believe it, but in some unspoken pact, they were keeping themselves close enough together to shut out the moonlight and bury me in their shadows.

"There are no fern blossoms!" Officer Rusakov shouted from somewhere outside the group. "You illiterate peasants don't know how foolish you are!" Anger was thick in his voice as he issued orders to the other officers still searching in the area. "We'll search the village, and if we find any of you have taken this girl into your home, you'll pay dearly for it."

The soldiers left with him, and the people around me casually moved about the area, perhaps so they wouldn't draw any suspicion our way, if the officers were nearby spying on us. When a boy ran back to say that we were safe, Violeta reached into the ferns and offered me a hand up.

By then, my ankle had stiffened worse than before, and without her holding my hand, I might have fallen. With my other hand I still kept my father's shoulder bag close against my chest, hiding the package inside it along with its other contents.

There must have been twenty people around me, mostly older teens or people in their early twenties, all looking me over as if I had leeches on my face. I looked down at my white blouse and skirt, which were so stained with dirt that they were anything but white now. I'd lost my woven sash somewhere in my walk here, and my green apron had a rip in the side.

"I've seen you before, in the market," Violeta said.

"What's in that bag?" a boy near her asked.

"That's not our business, Filip," Violeta said sharply. "I'm sure we don't even want to know."

Nor could I tell them. I merely pulled it tighter to myself.

"You need to get as far from this village as possible," Filip said. "You'll want to stick to the forest. The Cossacks will look for you in the villages next."

I glanced up, forcing myself to speak. "Venska. I need to go to Venska." Then I immediately looked down.

Filip pointed northward. "Follow the path there and cross the river, then continue for about twenty kilometers; the path will split, one to the left and the other to the right. You'll go to the right, and eventually it will empty out into Venska."

"Twenty kilometers? So far?" I couldn't hide the concern in my voice. As dark as the rest of the night would be under this thick canopy of branches and leaves, I was likely to wander off the path and never know it.

"If you need help—" a girl behind Violeta offered.

"I don't." I wanted to be clear on that. Any of them could have been arrested tonight, just like my parents, for allowing me to hide in the ferns. Or it could go worse for them. I knew how much they were risking. I would crawl to Venska on my own before I accepted any more help from these people.

"Here, take this." Violeta removed her shawl and wrapped it around my shoulders. Then someone behind Filip passed forward a basket with some cakes in it. With my eyes lowered, I mumbled a thank-you as I accepted both gifts, then hobbled toward the path.

Minutes later, as the path wound into the deeper part of the forest, I glanced back, hoping to see my parents there, beckoning me home again. When they weren't there, when filtered beams of lantern light from the party created long shadows among the dark trees, I turned around again. There, I faced thick brush and a winding dirt path that led to a tomorrow I could not predict. One step later, I was officially the farthest from my home that I'd ever been. And I was certain I'd never come back again.

Which was the worst thought of all.

I'd probably only walked a couple of kilometers before I became too tired and sore to continue on any farther. I tucked myself into a copse of trees far off the path and pulled the shawl tight around my shoulders to sleep, using the package from inside my father's bag as a pillow. I doubted I'd get any real rest this way, but I didn't care if I did. If I slept too deeply, I'd have nightmares.

I dug into my father's bag again and pulled out a blanket he sometimes used in a trick to make a person disappear in front of a crowd of onlookers. The blanket itself wasn't much for warmth, but it might offer me some bit of comfort tonight as I cuddled it to my chest. My eyes became sleepy, and as I closed them, I wished my father could've had the kind of magic to disappear when the Cossacks had come for him.

More than anything, I wished magic were real. Which made me hurt even more to know that it wasn't—that without him, it never could be real.

I stayed curled up in that position, drifting in and out of an empty sleep that left me more tired than when I'd begun. Thankfully, it was a warm night, but still I shivered through it, out of fear and loneliness, I supposed. Finally, the sun began to rise, and with it my mood began to improve. Maybe the worst was over. Maybe the soldiers would realize it had all been a mistake, and my parents would be released, wherever they were.

I sat up, stuffed the blanket back into the shoulder bag, and ate one of the cakes, saving the rest for later, for I had no idea how long it would take to walk the rest of the way to Venska. I grabbed a nearby stick and pressed it against the side of my ankle, then used Violeta's shawl to tie it tight to my leg. I hoped that would brace it and lessen the pain of walking. So far this morning, I'd done well for myself.

That was, until I picked up the package. The forest floor must have been a bit damp, for the cloth around the package had soaked up some moisture overnight. If the moisture had gotten to whatever was inside, I didn't care. My mother had been right in all her pleas and protests to my father, that it would end badly. I cared nothing for whatever was in that package.

Except that my father had cared deeply about it, and my mother had, too, despite her worries. They had sacrificed their freedom for it and may yet lose their lives for it. What could possibly be so valuable?

Then something exciting occurred to me, a thought that lifted my spirits once again. If this package was so valuable, then surely it could be useful in getting my parents back! I had something the Cossacks clearly wanted, and they had my parents. Maybe we could make a trade.

My heart pounded with anticipation, with hope . . . but then it almost immediately sank into nothingness.

I couldn't make a trade with the Cossacks. I didn't know any of them personally and certainly couldn't trust them. If I presented them with the package, they wouldn't agree to a trade. They'd merely arrest me and take the package for themselves.

Maybe Milda could make the trade. Maybe that's why my mother wanted this package to go to her, because she would be able to use it to get them back.

My eyes fell upon the wrapping again. I had promised to get it to Milda but never promised it would arrive *unopened*. I set the package on my lap and tugged at the knot, but somewhere behind me, a branch cracked. Maybe it was only an animal or a whisper of the morning breeze, but maybe not. I grabbed the basket of cakes, checked quickly to be sure I'd left nothing behind, then ran as fast as my ankle would allow.

My entire foot throbbed worse than it had last night. I didn't think it was broken, or else I couldn't have walked on it at all. But I was sure whatever damage I'd done to it was made worse by so much walking, which meant by the time I got to Venska, I'd be lucky if I wasn't dragging myself to Milda's front door.

Along the way, I passed a small river straddled by a bridge as wide as only three planks of wood and suspended by weathered rope. I hoped it was safe because I needed to cross it, so I held my breath, held even tighter to the rope, and took my first step forward. When I'd crossed, I looked back and felt a swell of pride. That hadn't been nearly so difficult as I'd expected.

I paused at the river's edge for a long drink. Where the water had pooled and become still, I stared at myself in the reflection and gasped. I looked horrible. Streaks of dirt lined my cheeks where I'd brushed tears off my face. Both my braids looked like something had clawed bits of hair loose to stick out in all directions. And my eyes were still red, though there was nothing I could do about that.

I washed my face, which already helped me feel a bit better, then undid my braids, finger combed my hair the best I could, then braided it again as neatly as possible. While I rested, I ate the second of the three cakes in the basket. I knew I shouldn't have. It would surely take at least the rest of the day to walk to Venska, and I was bound to get hungry. But I was hungry now too.

Once I'd finished the cake, I decided I had better keep walking and get as far along the path as possible before my stomach rumbled for more food.

By mid-morning, I reached the fork in the path that Filip had told me about, or at least, it seemed like a fork. I didn't think the trail that led to the right had gotten much use, but maybe few people ever went to Venska. Maybe just me and an occasional squirrel.

However, it became clear within the hour that I had taken a wrong turn. The worn path beneath my feet had faded into young summer plants and old autumn leaves so thick I knew nothing else had passed this way, not even a squirrel.

At least there was no evidence of soldiers passing this way either. So if I was lost, it could be worse.

But I was lost, and I'd been lost for long enough that I wasn't even sure how to retrace my steps back to where I thought there'd been a fork in the trail. I would have to hope that if I continued, I would eventually come to Milda's village or to any village where I might receive some help.

I limped forward while the sun rose in the sky and continued on even as it began to sink again. With it, my spirits sank too. For all I knew, I'd passed Venska hours ago and was halfway to Russia by now.

My mood worsened further when I first heard the sound of a river. Filip had said nothing about having to cross a second river, so I knew now that I was very far from where I ought to be. I rounded a bend and came upon it, then sighed. This river was much too wide to jump across, and if I tried to wade through it, I'd be soaked for the rest of the day and probably into the evening.

I searched upstream until I found an area with enough rocks that I could step from one to the other to cross. And it worked perfectly . . . at first.

Halfway across, my injured foot teetered on an uneven rock. One arm held on to the package while the other arm flapped wildly in the air, trying to keep my balance. For the first time, I was glad to be alone because I must have looked ridiculous. Nor did it work. I fell bottom-first into the water, landing on a sandbar a half-meter deep. Instinctively, I'd held up my father's bag, so it was only splashed, but it had cost me the last cake to protect it. That had fallen from the basket in my arms and was now sailing down the river, sinking lower until it was out of sight. Tears filled my eyes, but I fought them back. It was absurd to cry for the loss of a cake when I'd lost my parents less than a day ago, and their loss was far worse. Maybe these tears weren't for the cake at all.

"Why didn't you cross on that log?"

The words were in Lithuanian, not Russian, but I still froze in place. I turned to see a boy downriver, standing beside a donkey, allowing it to drink from the water. Between us was a sawed log, nearly flat for crossing the river. How had I missed that? Worse still, how had I missed this boy? He looked older than me by a year or two but was about my height, so either I was a little tall for my age or he was a little short, I wasn't sure. His brown hair was tousled and in need of a cut, but I gathered from the unkempt look of his clothes that his appearance wasn't a priority. He had a nice smile, though, or he would have, if his smile wasn't so upsetting. Was he laughing at me?

"I prefer crossing on rocks," I told him, which was a stupid thing to say.

"Ah. Round river rocks with slippery moss on the sides." He grinned. So he *was* laughing at me. "Excellent choice."

I stood, but my ankle hurt worse than ever, and with the current pulling at my legs, I began wobbling.

The boy left the donkey and ran for me, catching me beneath the arms just as I was about to splash in again.

"It's no crime to ask for help," he said, putting an arm around my shoulder. Then he smiled again. "Unless you ask in Lithuanian, of course. Then it's a very serious crime."

I tilted my head as I looked over at him. What a strange boy he was.

He nodded at the package in my arms. "May I carry that for you?"

"No." I pulled it to my chest. I wouldn't hand it over to anyone other than Milda, or maybe the Cossacks if Milda wouldn't help me bargain with them for my parents.

He shrugged and led me the rest of the way to the riverbank, then let me sit on the grasses to rest.

"I'm Lukas," he said. "I haven't seen you around here before." He hesitated, waiting for me to say something, and when I didn't, he added, "Are you lost?"

"I'm trying to get to Venska," I said.

Lukas grinned again. "Then you are indeed lost." He pointed behind me. "Venska is about a half kilometer behind us now, once you get out of these woods. Be careful to spot the path leading into the village. It's easy to miss."

I grimaced and got to my feet again. I'd only taken a few steps forward before I braced myself for greater courage, then said, "Can you show me the way?"

Lukas hesitated and looked around him. "No, I'm sorry, I can't."

"Please."

He shrugged. "I'm not someone you want as a friend, trust me."

I didn't need a friend. I only knew that I was hungry and tired and my emotions were wrung out. I couldn't risk missing the turn and ending up walking straight back into Rusakov and his men. It wasn't in me to ask for help, or really to ask for anything at all, but I had to convince this boy to help me.

I considered offering him some sort of bribe or payment, but when I looked in my father's bag, hoping a few coins might have magically appeared, I saw nothing . . . except for magic. Papa had let me practice with his tricks all I wanted, though I'd never tried the tricks on anyone but him and Mama. Did I dare to test a trick on Lukas?

No, but I also didn't dare to return to the woods without him as a guide. That would be far worse.

I reached into my father's bag and pulled out a deck of cards. "What if we make a bargain? You can pick any card from this deck, and if I guess what it is, you have to take me to Venska."

Lukas grinned. "And if you don't guess it?"

"I'll show you what's in this package."

He cocked his head. "You'll give me what's in the package, you mean."

I nodded, trying to look as if this were a fair game. It wasn't.

"Any card I choose?" Lukas asked.

Technically, it'd be the exact card I wanted him to choose, but this was a trick my father had taught me years ago. I could do it in my sleep, and as tired as I was, I might almost be doing that very thing.

I fanned out the cards facedown so that neither of us could see them. Lukas pulled a card from the deck.

"Look at it," I instructed him. "Then return it to the pile."

He did, and then I shuffled the cards back together. He watched me carefully, thinking he had gotten the better of me. I held up one random card for him, a jack of spades.

"It isn't this one." Then held up a second, a red seven. "Nor this one."

Lukas smiled. "Are you going to tell me all the cards it's not, or the one it is? Because our bet—"

I held up a third card, the ten of clubs. "It was this one."

Lukas's smile turned to amazement, and when he recovered, he bowed low. "I don't know how you did that, but you win. Where in Venska would you like to go?"

I opened my mouth but realized I'd forgotten the full name of the woman I was supposed to find. "Er, I'm looking for Milda . . ."

"Sabiene?" Lukas grinned.

"You know her?"

"I do. She always has a treat for Pasha when we come."

I couldn't help but smile. "Pasha?" In Russian, it meant "small and humble."

Lukas nodded toward his donkey, then added, "The name is to remind this animal who is in charge." He tugged at Pasha's rope again but to no avail. "It obviously is not me. My father is away on business. I suppose he won't know that I'm not going to be home tonight . . . again." He cocked his head at me to follow him. "Let's go."

I began following him away, then asked, "What do you mean 'again'?"

Lukas chuckled to himself. "You've heard the story of the fool son?"

I shrugged. "No."

"Ah. Well, the name tells you all you need to know. My father considers me a great fool, and he may be right. I don't need to go home to be reminded of that every time he speaks to me."

"I'd give anything to go home," I whispered, too low for him to hear. Which was a good thing, because I could never explain to him that I understood exactly what he'd meant. I would not be going home tonight either. I would likely never go home again.

CHAPTER
SEVEN

I'd ridden my father's horses before, of course, but always with a saddle. Lukas's donkey was bareback, which made riding him somewhat like staying balanced on two logs floating down a bubbly river. By the time we reached Milda's home, the bruises on my backside would match those on my ankle and I'd neither sit nor walk for a week.

"Where did you come from?" Lukas asked.

I shrugged, which was all the answer he was going to get. I didn't want to talk to him any more than was necessary, and certainly not to tell him anything about me. If he were one of Rusakov's spies my father had told me about, then I wouldn't be foolish enough to give myself away.

Or at least to make things worse than they already were.

"You know, there's a story for a girl like you," he said. "Once upon a time, there was a girl named Rue—"

"Rue! That's what my father calls me!" Then my shoulders sank. "Used to call me."

"Yes, but this was actually her name." Lukas cleared his throat, then continued. "Rue was the daughter of a wealthy man, and a very special girl because she could do magic. For this reason, the snake that lived on that same land wanted the girl for himself so she could do magic at his bidding. One day the wealthy man was injured when his cart overturned on him. The snake said, 'I will save you, but you must give me your daughter.' As it was the only way to save his life, the man reluctantly agreed."

I found myself smiling as Lukas spoke. I'd heard similar stories from my mother all my life, though never one quite like this version.

"The snake went to a bear that lived in the nearby forest and threatened to bite the bear if the bear did not help him free the trapped man. 'I will help you, snake,' said the bear. 'But when the man gives you his daughter, you must let her choose between us, choose which of us she prefers.' The snake agreed, for he was certain the daughter would never take the side of a bear."

"I wouldn't choose either one," I said.

The expression in Lukas's eyes warned me to let him finish the story. "The man was freed and the next morning he brought his daughter into his fields to choose between the snake and the bear. Like you, Rue wanted nothing to do with either of them, but her father warned that if he did not keep his promise, the snake might bite them and the bear might eat them."

I screwed up my face. "How awful!"

"Well, it would be, if Rue weren't so clever. She told the snake to swim up the longest river in Lithuania, and if he were her choice, she would meet him at the end. She told the bear to run to the deepest part of the forest, and if he were her choice, she would meet him at the end. The snake immediately began swimming, farther and farther north, until one day he swam right out of Lithuania."

"And what of the bear?" I asked.

"He waits there still, hoping one day she will come." Lukas glanced back at me. "He knows he was tricked, but he believes if she comes, she will be a most valuable friend."

"That's a lovely story," I said. "I've never heard that one before."

"There are many more stories to be told of Rue's adventures," Lukas said. "Perhaps I can tell you more of them one day."

"You won't have time, I'm sure," I said. "You must have a family who needs you, or someone you work for."

Lukas only shrugged. "My family doesn't want me and certainly doesn't need the sort of help I might offer them. And I work out here for Ben, though he doesn't exactly pay me. Making money is hardly my concern, though. If I have a bite of food each day and I'm on my feet each morning, then I have enough."

So he was a sort of thief, then, maybe living on his own for some time considering how comfortably he moved about these woods.

I said, "Someday you'll have to learn to work a proper job instead of wandering through the forests on some mysterious errand for a person named Ben."

He snorted. "So says the girl who I found wandering through the forests carrying a bag of tricks and a mysterious package."

I rolled my eyes but remained silent. He'd made his point.

Lukas stopped and turned around to face me. His eyes flicked between my bag and my confused expression. "So what's in that package?" When I hesitated, he added, "Oh, you don't know what you're carrying! Where did you get it?"

My eyes darted away. Officer Rusakov had called my parents criminals, and this package was obviously evidence of their crimes. Evidence of my crimes now, I supposed. Before long, Lukas continued walking again, whistling a tune as we went.

"You shouldn't do that," I said. "The Cossacks—"

He stopped again, and this time the expression in his eyes was far more serious. "Have you had trouble with them?" Again I refused to answer, but he said, "I make a point of traveling where the soldiers do not. But they'll come if they believe you have something to hide." He glanced back. "Do you?" Another pause, then, "Was your trouble with the police, or with the border guards?"

"Border guards?" I sat up straight. "I've never gone near the border."

"Well, you should sometime. It's beautiful there. Even prettier across the border in Prussia."

"I have no papers to cross the border."

"Why should papers matter?" He chuckled again, but it sounded forced this time, as if too much truth was hidden behind his words. That made me suspicious. If talk of the border made him nervous, there was good reason for it. Although my home was far from the border, that was another of my father's rules: Never get close to the border. The only people there were either challenging the law or, worse, they were the law.

Hundreds of years ago, the borders of Lithuania had been very different. Many of the countries around us now used to be one kingdom known as the Grand Duchy of Lithuania. But one bite at a time, chunks of our land were conquered or claimed by other countries, including Lithuania Minor to the west. That area had been absorbed into Prussia and was now controlled by the German Empire. The rest of our land was controlled by Russia, under the rule of Tsar

Alexander III and whichever governor he'd installed lately to keep his thumb on us.

This was done through the enforcement of his Cossack soldiers who patrolled the land. Get in their way and the luckiest thing that might happen was a stiff beating. It only got worse from there. Just the week before, my mother had spoken of people from my village who had disappeared, their last known act being some small defiance of the Russian laws we all hated. Our priest had disappeared a year earlier for having preached his sermon in Lithuanian. Now both of my parents were gone as well.

Lukas had become silent again, and I was grateful for it. After a while, he reached into the satchel at his side and pulled out a handful of fried cheese curd cakes. My mouth immediately watered for them. I liked mine best when they were fresh out of the pan and served with a little jam, but they were delicious any way I could get them.

Lukas ate three before he turned around and held one out to me. "Want one?" I shook my head, but he only smiled and tossed it onto my lap. "Of course you do. They were made last night."

I picked up the ball of cheese and popped it into my mouth, closing my eyes to savor the taste. When I'd finished, I asked, "Where did you get them? You don't look like you have any money to buy them."

"Not a ruble to my name, but it doesn't matter. The cheese was a . . . gift."

"A gift?" My eyes narrowed. The way he'd said it suggested it wasn't a gift in the traditional meaning of the word.

Now Lukas was the one who preferred not to answer. He merely shrugged and turned forward again. But he didn't need to say anything. He obviously didn't trust me any more than I could trust him.

"Are you a thief?" I asked.

He glanced back and his smile returned. "Not exactly, though I'll steal if necessary. But I'd think that of anyone, you'd understand."

My spine stiffened. I didn't know him and he didn't know me . . . shouldn't know me. I assumed he was thinking of my card trick and wondering if I used that skill for criminal activity. Which, of course, I never would.

Other than using it just now to make Lukas help me deliver my illegal package.

Lukas seemed to know the package was illegal, too, which meant he was making guesses about me that simply weren't true. And if any of my guesses about him were correct, then I had to be on my guard.

As soon as this package was delivered to Milda's home, I would get as far from Lukas and his dangerous life as I could, and as quickly as possible.

CHAPTER
EIGHT

We entered the small and scattered village of Venska by dusk, and Lukas pointed out Milda's home to me soon after. It was made of stone and seemed to be one of the larger homes in the area, although half of it had been converted into a sort of shop . . . or bakery . . . or something that sold things people might need, I wasn't sure. The few windows were crowded with various goods—anything from bolts of fabric to tins of baking goods to farm tools. A sign in the window probably explained the place further, but my eyes only glossed over it.

"I assume you don't know her," Lukas said as he helped me off the donkey.

"I assume you do," I countered. My legs had become so wobbly on the trip that, combined with my right ankle, I barely could walk.

"Milda's a bit odd," Lukas said. "But don't think about it too much." He grabbed my arm to pull me back. "And don't stare. It makes her uncomfortable."

"Don't stare at what?" I asked.

"Well, she might be perfectly *normal* right now, but again, she might not. The Cossacks think she's crooked in the head, so they leave her alone, which is just how she wants it."

I was more comfortable alone. I'd spent most of my life alone. Even with my parents, there was always so much work to be done in running a home and chores on our farm, it was easy to find an excuse to be somewhere that people were not.

"Why does Milda want to be left alone?" I asked.

Lukas's only answer was to flick his eyes down at the package in my arms, then give me a wink. I drew back, nervous. Did he know why my parents had been called criminals? Lukas had admitted that he would steal if necessary, so he probably knew other thieves and criminals. Maybe Milda was one of them.

If so, then why had my mother sent me here?

At her door, Lukas knocked twice, paused, then knocked twice again, much more slowly. Seconds later, the door creaked open, like it was heavier than the entire home. An elderly woman peered around the doorframe. She had tangled white hair beneath her head scarf and wrinkled skin that appeared crusty. She was heavily bent over with a hunched back, leaning on her cane for support, and she seemed to have exhausted herself simply by coming to the door. I sincerely wondered if she would live long enough to invite us inside.

Lukas clicked his tongue and, with a nod of his head in my direction, said, "This one seems all right. I think she's Henri's daughter."

I turned so fast to look at him that I nearly lost my balance. He knew my father but had said nothing to me?

"Is that true?"

It took a moment to realize Milda was speaking to me. I said, "My name is Audra. Henri Zikaris is my—"

"Hush." Milda frowned at me, then widened the door. "Better come inside."

I followed Lukas in, but by the time I'd turned back to Milda, she had leaned the cane against the door, fully straightened up, and was removing a white-haired wig, leaving gray-flecked hair in a bun beneath it.

"Be a dear, young lady, and get the pillow," she asked me, untying the sash from her vest.

I stepped forward, unsure of what to do until Lukas motioned toward her back. I put a hand at the bottom of her vest and felt upward until I touched a small pillow. I pulled it out and her hunched back instantly disappeared.

Meanwhile, Lukas had wet a cloth at Milda's sink and handed it to her. She began wiping at her face, removing the crust that had seemed like her skin.

"Flour and water and a few other ingredients," she explained when she saw me looking. "I'll keep working on the recipe."

"Maybe add some ground oats next time," Lukas suggested. "For texture."

Milda smiled, and when she lowered the cloth, I saw a woman who was old but still seemed half the age of the near corpse who had answered the door. She had a pleasant smile and a pointy nose, and once she removed the thick glasses, she had intelligent eyes.

They settled on Lukas first. "I saw you coming from a distance, but you're shooting up so fast, I barely recognized you!" She threw her arms around him for a hug, then stood back and looked at me, her tone becoming solemn. "I do recognize you. Your father's hair, but your mother's daughter in every other way."

My eyes widened. "You know my mother too?"

"Of course. She was the bravest of women."

"Is." I'd spoken so softly, I was sure Milda hadn't heard me, but when she tilted her head at me, I whispered, "My mother *is* the bravest of women. She's been arrested, but she's alive. Both of my parents are."

Milda nodded. "I see. And what is that you're carrying?"

I held out the package to her. "Mama wanted me to bring this to you. She gave it to me . . . before the arrest."

Milda's brows pressed together, and she accepted the package. "You poor, sweet girl, you must tell me everything that happened. Have you come all this way on foot? You must be exhausted."

"Lukas helped me get here," I said.

"Well, he probably only did it because he's hungry and he knows I always cook extra. Are you hungry too?"

My eyes might've popped out of my head because she nodded and moved toward her fireplace before I could answer. Above it hung a pot of what I thought might be stew, but she grabbed a plate and dished out at least a dozen dumplings.

Lukas practically dove for them and I would have, too, but for my injured ankle. Milda merely pushed past him to set them on the table nearer to me, then gestured for me to have a seat.

I wanted the dumplings. My mouth was watering for them as it never had before. But I nodded at the package I'd brought to Milda.

"Can you at least tell me what it is?"

"Supper first." Milda lowered a knitted afghan over the stool where the package was lying, then sat with me and Lukas to eat. She must have already eaten, because she took nothing for herself, but simply watched as Lukas and I devoured one dumpling after another.

I glanced over at him as we ate. If he was this hungry, then either he wasn't a very good thief or else he didn't steal food.

I finished first, and as we waited for Lukas to finish,

Milda asked me about my parents. I opened my mouth, then looked again at Lukas.

"It's all right," she said. "You can trust him."

I didn't see how, but I started with the disagreement between my parents ending with their decision to take me to the midsummer festival, then the soldiers who had come, and the fire, and once I got past that, I spilled out the rest of the story, right up until meeting Lukas.

Milda sat quietly as I spoke, occasionally dabbing at her eyes with the corner of her apron. Lukas seemed to have forgotten his food and merely stared at me, slack-jawed.

Before I finished, I added, "Milda, I only came here because . . . well, I have an idea. The Cossacks want whatever is in that package, and I want my parents back. Will you help me make a trade?"

Milda's expression fell. "Oh, my dear child, I'm afraid that won't work. They'd take the package and use it to convict your parents, not save them."

My heart sank, leaving an empty hole inside my chest. I hadn't wanted to hear that. Maybe this plan was far-fetched and built on little but hope and foolishness, but I had nothing else left. I couldn't let it go like that, like these ideas were nothing more than smoke in my hand.

Except maybe that's all they were.

"Then what did they give me?" I asked. "Can I see it?"

"I think you must see it." Milda reached over to the package and carefully undid the twine around it. She unfolded the fabric and held it so I couldn't see the object until she lifted it up. And when she did, my fists curled and I felt nearly ready to explode with anger.

It was a book. Just a stupid, ordinary book.

CHAPTER
NINE

Several seconds passed in which none of us said a word. I couldn't speak. My chest was heaving and my insides were knotted with anger.

Finally, Lukas asked to see the book, and when Milda handed it to him, he turned it over in his hands. It was thick and bound in black leather but looked heavily worn. A brass band was attached to both ends of the book with a lock on top to keep it closed.

"Do you have the key?" Milda asked while Lukas shook out the bedsheet the book was wrapped in to see if it had fallen loose.

I shook my head. I'd never seen that book before. How could I possibly know about any key?

Milda took the book in her hands again. "It's a little damp on one side."

"She fell in the river," Lukas said, though that wasn't the reason it had absorbed some moisture. He didn't know that

I'd used it as a pillow on the dewy forest soil. Nor did I care that I had. It was only a book.

Sometimes I had wondered if my father was not truly a traveling magician, that those tricks were only games to distract from his true missions, perhaps as a spy, passing coded messages to confuse our enemies. Or maybe he traded in gold and silver, hiding the wealth of Lithuania as part of his magician disguise. Or perhaps he was working on a secret plan to free Lithuania from Russia's control. I'd dreamed up a thousand scenarios of heroism and courage. Not one of them had involved my father spending night after night away from home, all to deliver a few stupid books.

This one, at least, had to be special, or else the Cossacks wouldn't have come after me the way they had. If Milda believed it couldn't be traded for my parents' return, then it was nothing to me. I was glad it was in her hands and my problem no longer.

"She doesn't know about the books," Lukas said, offering Milda a wink that bristled against my temper.

Milda nodded, then smiled. "Come, child."

We followed her into a bedroom at the back of her house where a little stairway led to an upstairs loft. I started up the stairs, but she pulled me back, then knelt down and picked up the lower step, folding each plank of wood like a fan until three full stairs were open, each plank connected by a hinge. I peered into the gap she had created, but it was pitch-black until she leaned past me with a candle. Even that didn't help much. Now all I knew was that a ladder led into that darkness, and, I feared, I was expected to go down there.

Milda led the way, followed by Lukas, and I went down last, a dozen questions already in my mind. A hundred more instantly popped into my head as soon as I turned around in the room where I now stood, for I hadn't expected this.

Milda's underground room was the size of our root cellar, where we stored the winter vegetables. It was equally cool, though Milda's wasn't damp like ours. Instead, the room was lined with shelves, and every shelf was packed with books. I'd rarely seen any books at all, and certainly never so many in one place.

I let my fingers brush along the spines of the books as I walked a circle around the room. Some were soft and smooth while others were stiff and even scratchy. They were all sizes, and there were nine or ten copies of some of the books along the row.

Milda smiled. "This is a bookstore, but a very secret bookstore. And it's only half of my underground home. Follow me."

She led us through a wood door into another room that was a little larger, directly beneath her home. The walls here were papered in a pattern that had long ago faded and were covered with maps and charts of letters and numbers. A small table stood in the front of the room and eight or nine stools were scattered about.

I looked over at Milda, too confused to know where to start for a question. I simply had no idea what this place was, or why it should be hidden.

Lukas answered for her. "This is Milda's school. Obviously, you can never tell anyone about this. Or at least, you can never tell the Cossacks."

"A secret school?" I ran my fingers over the table at the front of the room. A book was laid out there, and a small stack of chalkboard squares was in a crate beside the book with a cup of chalk sticks worn almost to stubs in the corner of the crate. Last night, my father had warned me against joining any schools, and now I understood why. It would only bring trouble.

Just thinking of that conversation put a stab of pain in my heart. I missed my parents. It felt like years since I had seen them. It couldn't only have been a single day.

Milda put her hand on my shoulder. "If you'd like, you can stay here with me. You can come to this school, learn about the books."

"No . . . thank you." My chest tightened. I refused to learn from a school that taught from books that got my parents arrested. Nor *could I* ever learn from something that had nearly gotten me killed. I'd return to the forest alone before I opened the pages of any book.

Now Milda folded her arms, and her tone became stern. "Let's make an agreement, then. You don't have to go to the school, but you cannot tell anyone about it, either, or about the books you saw."

I nodded my acceptance. Who was I going to tell, anyway? The Cossacks? We were hardly on friendly terms.

"But you also need food and shelter," Milda added. "Try living out on the streets and by the end of summer they'll have some reason to arrest you."

"What will happen to my parents now?" I asked. Even the question sent shudders through me.

Milda frowned. "I'm afraid it's not good, Audra. They're not likely to be released. If they're lucky, then they'll be sentenced to a prison here in Lithuania."

Prison? That was if they were *lucky*? A lump formed in my throat. "And if they're not?"

"Siberia," Lukas breathed.

I turned to him. "Where is Siberia?"

"You don't want to know," Lukas said.

"Hush!" Milda scolded.

But Lukas didn't seem to notice Milda's warning expression. He said, "Siberia is on the far eastern side of Russia. It's cold on a good day and below living temperatures all other days. Even if you escape the prison, you'll soon realize the place itself is a prison. There'd be nowhere to go."

I had to force myself to swallow that thought down, and

it landed in a deep pit in my stomach. Siberia sounded so awful, and so far away. I'd never be able to find them, nor would they ever escape, if they even could survive such an awful place. "They might send my parents there?"

Milda put a hand on my shoulder. "At least they'll be together, to take care of each other. And if you want to stay with me, we can take care of each other too." I must have nodded at that, because after a brief pause, she added, "If you'd like to stay, then I have an errand for you."

I groaned, already suspecting what it must be.

Milda led us back into her room full of books and plucked one from the shelf. "Your father promised that the next time he passed this way, he would deliver this book for me. It's a simple delivery, and I wonder if you might be interested in finishing the job he would have done."

I shook my head. If she knew what I'd gone through to carry the book here, she never would ask such a question. I said, "He can still deliver it, *when* he returns. Until then, let me stay until my ankle is healed, and then I'll find somewhere else to stay. Somewhere . . . with fewer secrets."

Milda's face fell. "Very well. I should not have asked."

She looked so disappointed, and so did Lukas, that I felt I ought to apologize to them. But for what? Wanting to stay alive, to stay out of Siberia? Wanting to go back to the life I'd known with my family, one that was simple and slow and sheltered? It wasn't much, but at least what I'd had before was familiar.

And I'd hardly get back to it if I agreed to do what Milda wanted. And for that, I would not apologize.

TEN

I slept at Milda's that night, and for another week while my ankle healed. Every day, people came to the small shop attached to her home to buy butter or honey or whatever excuse they might have invented to visit Milda. Who, by the way, never attended her shop unless she wore a disguise of some sort. Today she wore a head scarf and darkened spectacles, and felt her way around the shop like a blind woman, doing a terrible job at it. She found whatever she needed far too easily and addressed people by name as they passed through her door. I was hardly an expert in disguises, but I was sure I could do better than that.

Nor were the people who entered her shop particularly good at hiding their true purposes for coming. The first time I suspected they made excuses was when a woman had slapped some money onto Milda's counter with an order for "anything you're selling today."

Milda had smiled back. "Can you be more specific?"

More meaningfully, the woman had replied, "Something for my children perhaps. They're growing up so fast." Then they'd laughed together. I'd rolled my eyes and groaned. Why didn't the woman just say, "Sell me an illegal book!"

And that woman wasn't the only one. Nearly everyone who walked into Milda's shop came with a hushed request for something from Milda's book collection. She'd tell the customer to wait, then go into her bedroom and close the door, returning minutes later with a wrapped package that she'd help the customer slide into a sack covered with fabric or bread loaves or whatever might keep the package out of sight.

After one particularly busy day, a rainy day when people should have been better occupied at home than coming out onto the muddy road, Milda poked her head into the kitchen where I was cutting potatoes for a pan of *kugelis*, one of my favorite foods. "Audra, I've gone up and down the ladder so often today, my legs are worn out."

I had no doubt that she was. It was a new day and a new disguise, so naturally she was experimenting with faking illness. She had applied powder to her face and a little grease beneath her eyes to seem pale and hollow. She'd done a fine job at least—much better than the blindness. Up close, the powder appeared to be an attempt to improve her complexion and the shine of the grease looked like sweat. However,

I wondered if all of her trips up and down the ladder were adding to her look of exhaustion too.

Milda added, "Do you mind going downstairs for me?"

My eyes darted. "To get a book?" I hadn't been down into the secret room since Milda had first shown it to me, and that wasn't an accident. That room was a reminder of all that I'd lost, and all that I still might lose.

Milda shook her head. "Not a book. This time it's a newspaper, *Varpas*. The latest edition."

"I won't know where to find it."

"I keep them in a bin right by the door. Make sure it's *Varpas*, though, and not one of the others."

I sighed but set down the potato and walked to the back of the home, opening the stairs and descending the ladder. I'd never minded being in small, dark places before, but this room felt haunted to me, as if hundreds of spirits lingered here, hoping to find an open book so that they might peruse its pages, for whatever good it might do them. The book I'd carried all the way from home was in here now, lying on its side high on a shelf, mixed in with so many others but somehow still alone, as if it didn't truly belong in here.

As I truly didn't belong in here. Not among row after row of books, some of them stacked in front of another row of books, and for all I knew, another row behind that, endlessly burrowed inside this secret cavern of words and pictures. I didn't know how Milda kept track of them all.

I turned to find the bin with the newspaper she had wanted, but the problem was, she had two bins with different writing on each. I didn't know which to grab, and I figured since this was supposed to be a secret place, the last thing I ought to do was bring up both newspapers and let the customer pick from them.

Besides, I'd feel stupid doing such a thing. Or more stupid than I already felt.

Varpas. The titles in the bold lettering on the top had about the same number of letters in each bin. I recognized the *A*'s in both titles since I knew I had *A*'s in my name, but that didn't help, either, since I didn't know the letters that would be in *Varpas*, nor did I know any of my letters other than the *A*.

This was humiliating.

While I stared between the two, I heard a quick hiss that might've been Milda saying my name, then the opening above me slammed shut and I was left alone with nothing but the single flame in the oil lamp I'd taken down with me.

I started up the ladder, certain that it must have been some sort of mistake and ready to call out to Milda about why she had closed the opening. Then I heard men's voices speaking almost directly above me. Speaking in Russian.

I froze in place on the ladder, worried that even moving my foot might cause a creak in the wood. Here, I was so close to the stairs. Could they hear me breathing, or the pounding of my heart? It seemed impossible that they wouldn't have heard Milda slamming the lid shut for this little room, and then they'd realize she was in disguise and as healthy as ever. Surely they would search the home until they figured out what had made that slamming sound.

Until they found me.

Maybe that was why they had come, to arrest me, or to take the book I'd given Milda. If I dared to move, I would've slid that book behind the others. My parents were in prison or on their way to Siberia because of that book. I wouldn't let them take Milda for it too.

If I listened carefully, I could barely make out the conversation happening almost directly above me. In her false voice of sickness, Milda was trying to list off her many ailments for the men, but they told her to stop or her ills would hardly be the worst of her problems. Their tones were sharp, sounding impatient. In Russian, they demanded to search the home, and Milda laughed, telling them they were welcome to look anywhere they'd like.

It was a lucky thing I'd come to Milda's home without any possessions, only the clothes I was now wearing and my father's shoulder bag. It was always at my side, except for when I slept. Milda had offered to find me a change of clothing when she had more time, but I was glad she hadn't done so yet.

If only there were something in my father's bag powerful enough to help Milda, who I knew was in grave danger upstairs. I knew how hard the Cossacks had looked for me, and that was for a single book. Milda had hundreds down here. What if it wasn't simply my father's book they wanted? What if they wanted all these books?

As the Cossacks moved into another room for their search, I crept down the ladder and used the oil lamp to look over the different volumes, wondering what their titles said. All these books had somehow come to Milda. Some of them must have been carried by my father. She said she'd been expecting him.

This was my parents' work, these books. I was surrounded by their secrets, their risks. How many times had I wished that my father would just tell me the truth of where he went at night? How often had I wished to be as brave as him, as determined as my mother?

And when Milda had asked for my help, I'd refused her. I wasn't brave like Papa, and my only determination had been to refuse the very work my parents had literally dedicated their lives to doing. I'd failed my parents.

I wandered into the secret school room and picked up a square piece of chalkboard, then used the chalk to scrawl the letter *A* onto the black surface. It wasn't as elegant and straight as the *A*'s I'd seen on the books in the other rooms, but it was recognizable.

I didn't know how to write the letter for my mother's name—I'd never seen her do it. I assumed she could because

I knew she could read. I'd asked her once if she would teach me, but she'd told me it would bring trouble into my life. Obviously she was right.

My father could write too. He used to record the secrets of his tricks into a brown leather notebook, but I didn't know where it was. Certainly not in my shoulder bag.

His shoulder bag.

My father's name, Henri, started with two straight lines standing beside each other like twin trees in the forest, then connected by a shorter line. I didn't know the name of the letter, but my *A* was almost the same as his, only the tops of the trees in my *A* touched, like the branches had decided to grow together and become one.

I drew his letter next to mine, then made a small forest of the letters. Papa would say to avoid the forest, that it was full of thieves like Lukas, and villains like the Cossack policemen who hunted them. But I thought it was a nice picture anyway.

Then a loud sound clattered overhead. Glass shattered with it and I froze, wondering what had happened. Was Milda all right? Was she hurt or arrested? Would they do to her what they had done to my parents and then light this place on fire? I'd be trapped!

As quietly as possible, I looked around the room. A curtain hung against one wall, likely concealing some storage, but at least I could hide in there. I pulled it aside and was surprised to see a small passageway leading away from Milda's home. More secret places?

I started down that way, then jumped when I rounded a bend and saw a girl a year or two younger than myself crouched in the corner. Her arms were wrapped around her legs and tears streamed down her face. As frightened as I was, she looked so much worse that I immediately forgot my own worries and knelt beside her.

"It's all right," I whispered. "What's your name?"

"Roze."

"Like the flower?" I forced a smile to my face, hoping to calm her. "My father used to call me rue, another flower, but my name is Audra. What are you doing here?"

"I forgot something earlier today."

"You were here at the school earlier?" When had Milda found time today to teach down here?

Roze added, "We're not supposed to come if we see soldiers, but they weren't here when I came."

My heart pulsed with anticipation. Roze hadn't come through Milda's house . . . which meant there was another entrance. An escape for us!

"Can you show me how you came in?" I asked.

"They'll see me," Roze said. "They'll see this." She lifted a book, then tucked it beneath her legs, as if to hide it.

"They won't see us," I said, lifting her to her feet. "I'll protect you, but you must show me the way out of here."

Roze sniffed, then stuffed the book inside the sack she was carrying, carefully covering it with a shawl. Then she took my hand and led me through the corridor and up another ladder. I went first and came through a door on a hinge attached to a floor. When I passed through it, I was in a tiny room surrounded by garden tools.

A shed! Milda's shed in the back of her home. This was how her students came and went from her secret school.

I pushed the door open but couldn't tell if the Cossacks were still in Milda's house, so I closed it again and crouched on the floor, my back against the door should they try to come search in here. At least if they burned Milda's home, we wouldn't be trapped beneath it.

"How long will we be here?" Roze asked.

I shrugged. We'd stay here until I was certain it was safe to leave, and the way my heart was still pounding, that wouldn't be anytime soon.

Roze folded her legs up to her chest. "I'm scared, Audra."

She looked so near to crying that I began to worry she would make noise and call attention to our presence here. I was about to cry myself, but that would make things worse. For both our sakes, we needed something else to think about.

I dug into my father's bag and pulled out a Russian coin that Milda had given me that morning, holding it flat on my open palm. "See this?"

Roze nodded, looking slightly confused.

"Watch it carefully." I closed my fist around the coin, then moved it around in a circle. At one point, as she was distracted, I secretly transferred the coin to my left hand and held it safe. I stopped rotating my right hand and said, "Do you believe in magic, Roze?"

Her eyes widened. "Yes!"

According to my father, it was the answer that children always gave. He once said he felt bad about asking that question because he knew they were only tricks. I understood that now. But I had to keep up the ruse.

So with a smile, I opened my fist, and she saw the coin had disappeared.

"Where did it go?" she asked, her smile beaming with surprise.

I reached for her ear with my left hand, letting the coin rub for just a moment against her skin, then pulled it to where she could see it. "It was hiding in your ear!"

Roze touched her ear, likely checking for other coins, but delighted by such a simple trick. "It is magic!" she said.

I put the coin in her hands. "It is. Because this is a special coin, full of powers. Whoever holds it gets extra courage."

"To be quiet while the Cossacks are outside," Roze whispered.

I nodded, watching Roze close her own fist around the coin and bring it to her chest.

Several minutes later, Milda knocked on the door of the shed in the same patterned knock Lukas had used when we first came to her home. I stood and opened the door and Roze rushed past me to give Milda a hug.

Milda's dress had a tear in the sleeve, but she seemed all right otherwise. I decided to ask her about it later, when it was just the two of us.

"Audra kept me safe," Roze said, then whispered, "and she has magic that kept your books safe."

Milda eyed me, but I glanced away, embarrassed and hoping she wouldn't ask me to explain myself.

"Magic?" she asked. "Same as your father, I assume."

I took a deep breath and spoke as quickly as possible to ensure I got through the sentence.

"That book my father promised to deliver. I think he would've wanted me to say yes, that I'd carry it for him."

Milda tilted her head. "What changed your mind?"

My heart began pounding at what I'd just agreed to do, but I'd made the offer and wasn't about to back down from it. "If I cannot trade a book for my parents' return, then I'll deliver a book in their honor. Just this once."

While Milda smiled at me, Roze touched my arm, then gave me back the coin. "Here," she whispered. "It gives a person extra courage. I think you're going to need it."

CHAPTER
ELEVEN

I'd expected Milda would send me out with the book right away, but she didn't. Instead, after my ankle was fully healed, she set a *spurgos* in my hands. Freshly baked, it smelled of fruit and was covered in powdered sugar. I lifted it to my nose and the warm scent made my mouth water. Then she folded her arms, waiting to see what I'd do with it.

What was I supposed to do? I wanted to eat it, but when I started to, she clicked her tongue and said, "I've got to be sure you're ready to transport a book for me."

I showed her the pastry, wondering if this was another of Milda's false acts of insanity, or if she really was a bit unbalanced. "Milda, this isn't a book. You can't eat a book and I definitely want to eat this."

She smiled. "This spurgos is not for eating. It's a test, to see how you will do in getting past the Cossacks."

"Why do they want the books?" I asked. "What do the books say?"

Milda frowned. "Don't you know?"

I blinked back at her. Papa used to say that whenever I did that, he knew I was finished with a conversation, and the same was true now. Rather than answer Milda's question, I held out the spurgos. "What should I do with this?"

"Go to the end of this village and back again. If anyone asks what you are carrying, you must give them the pastry. Come back and tell me how far you got."

I didn't see why it mattered, but I did as Milda asked, folding my hands over the dessert and walking onto the street. It was market day so the streets were full. I'd no sooner reached the road in front of Milda's home before I happened to see Roze, the same girl who'd been hiding in Milda's secret school. Recognizing me, she ran forward, sniffed the air, then said, "Something smells so good. What is it?"

I sighed and opened my hands to show her what I had. "You can have it."

Her eyes brightened. "Really?"

"I suppose." Once she'd accepted the spurgos, I turned back to Milda's home, where she was already waiting at the door with another one.

"Try again."

"Milda, these smell wonderful. Too wonderful!"

"Don't they? To the end of the village and back again. Now go."

This time, I tucked the pastry inside the folds of my dress and made it halfway down the road from Milda's home before I was discovered by the trail of powdered sugar I was dropping and had to return empty-handed.

My third pastry was fully wrapped inside my apron. I even sniffed it to see how close I'd have to be to smell anything. That much of my plan worked fairly well, except a gentleman passing by asked what I could be carrying that was so valuable as to hide it in my apron. He walked away with a warm spurgos, and I trudged back to Milda's home, thoroughly discouraged.

"I can't do it!" I told her. "I can't hide something like this."

"Then you cannot carry a book," she said, putting another pastry in my hands. "But I hope you'll figure this out soon, before I feed the entire village."

I sighed and turned around again. This one was larger than the others had been and, if possible, smelled better than any of them before. But this time, I was determined to complete the task, simply to prove to Milda that I could do it.

Milda had said I had to get to one end of town and back again, but she'd never said that I had to take the roads. So this time, I cut around to the back of her home and snuck from one yard through another, careful to be sure no one was outside at the time. When I couldn't go any farther, I waited to be sure the road was clear, but I wasn't about to take any chances. I lifted the pastry to smell it again, but another scent filled my nose, that of mint.

Looking down, I saw a patch of mint in the garden at my

feet. Milda had said that if anyone detected the spurgos, I'd have to give it to them, but she'd said nothing about them detecting a little mint. I reached down and plucked a few leaves, rubbing them over my arms and then folding them around the fried bread.

It wouldn't do to wrap it in my apron—that was too obvious. Instead, at the edge of the road, I saw a patch of lavender flowers. I picked as many of them as I could and formed them into a bouquet, bundling it around the pastry.

Then I walked toward the center of the market, smiling as passersby complimented my flowers and sniffed the fresh mint dangling in the air behind me. If they talked of a lingering smell of sugar as well, I wasn't there to hear it. I didn't wait for them to notice it, I simply moved on.

Twenty minutes later, I returned to Milda and presented her with the spurgos. She arched a brow as I showed her the flowers and the mint, then she smiled down at me. "Audra, my girl, have a seat. I would like to tell you about the books."

She placed a cup of tea and a pastry of my own in front of me, then sat at my side, keeping her voice low. "If your parents never told you about our books, then it was because they believed that would keep you safe, and maybe they were right. Are you sure you want to know?"

I pressed my lips together and nodded, intensely curious.

She reached to the center of the table, where a tiny chest was placed. I'd always assumed the chest was a decoration and nothing more, but she opened it and withdrew a knife with a beautiful carved handle, handing it to me with a clear reverence. "This belonged to my father," she said. "Thirty years ago, he joined an uprising of Lithuanians who attempted to overthrow the Russians and bring freedom to our land. It wasn't the first uprising, but it was the largest and most well organized. They fought hard and they fought well, and for a short time, we had hope for their success. But in the end, what can our small country, most of us untrained peasants, do against the entire Russian Empire? We were crushed."

I ran my finger along the handle of the knife. "Then your father must have been arrested, too, just like my parents, or sent to Siberia."

"Oh, no, child, as awful as Siberia is, the fighters weren't allowed even that much mercy. A governor was sent in from Russia who was nicknamed the hangman. And with such a name, what else could be the fate of nearly all those who were captured? But their deaths didn't satisfy the tsar. He wanted a way to ensure that there never would be another uprising again."

"So he banned our books?" I asked.

"Worse. He banned the idea of Lithuania. We were all to become Russian. To speak like Russians, and especially, to think like Russians. Lithuania was to be erased from the map." Milda grimaced a moment, then picked up the knife and turned it over in her hands. "How do you destroy a people? You take away their culture. And how is that done? You must take their language, their history, their very identity. How would you do that?"

I pressed my lips together, then looked up at her. "You ban their books."

Milda nodded. "I believe you are ready to carry that book for me. And for that, you deserve a gift." She reached behind her to a bundle on the floor and put it in my hands. It was a new apron, embroidered in lines of bright green, yellow, and red, and far nicer than the plaid one I'd had before.

I passed it back to her. "I can't accept this."

"I insist—look!" Milda turned the apron over, revealing several small pockets in the lining underneath. "These may be helpful when you have a lot to carry, or to hide."

"Such as a book?" I held out my hands for it, but Milda shook her head. "In a few more days. We must wait for Ben to return."

I arched a brow. "Ben?" That was the same name Lukas had given me when I'd first met him in the forest. "Who is Ben?"

"A few more days."

And that, apparently, would be my only answer.

CHAPTER
TWELVE

A few days passed before Milda said everything was ready. I awoke before dawn, eager to be on the road with only the farmers and bakers for company, and, I hoped, no soldiers. When Milda heard me stirring about, finishing up tying the new apron she had given me, she peeked from her room, her eyes half-open. "Goodness, child, you can't leave yet. What reason would you possibly have to be on the road this early?"

"This early, no one will see me."

Milda frowned. "The Cossacks are always watching, Audra, always with someone on patrol. Be one of dozens on the road, not one of two or three."

My brow furrowed as I was reminded again of Officer Rusakov and all that I'd lost since my parents had given me that book. I took a deep breath before asking, "Is it all Lithuanian books the empire hates, or only certain ones?"

Milda padded out from her room and began stirring the ashes from last evening's fire to warm some coffee. As she did, she said, "All Lithuanian books. Some might be tempted to overlook an early reader book as harmless, but it is with the young that these ideas first begin." Milda placed a book into my hands. "What is in this book, do you think?"

The cover had some letters printed on it, and when I opened its pages, I saw more shapes for letters, few of which I recognized. There were no pictures, only page after page of words. I closed it again. "It's nothing to me."

"Perhaps one day, you will think differently." Milda placed her hands over mine as I held the book. She pointed to the lettering on the front and read it for me: "*The History of the Ancient Lithuanians*. This, Audra, is a very important book, for how can we know who we are if we do not know who we were? Succeed with this delivery and you will give someone knowledge, and with that knowledge, you'll give them greater power in their life."

I smiled up at her. "And I thought I was only giving someone a book."

Milda's laugh quickly became somber. "Being caught with even one book is dangerous, so pay close attention. You must follow the lane from my house up to the neighboring village, and in the market square, you will meet a man named Ben Kagan. This book is for him. No one else must see it, or even suspect you have it." Then she took the book and slid it into the bottom of a deep canvas sack with straps to carry it on my back.

The sack was light brown and similar to the one my father had traveled with, only slightly smaller. She began filling it with scraps of fabric. "Avoid all Cossack officers, and anyone who looks at you too carefully, but do not make it look as if you are avoiding them. Guard this as if it were your most precious possession because books *are* our most precious possessions." When she had finished stuffing the sack with the fabric, she looked me directly in the eyes. "Can you do this? It is all right to say no."

I wanted to say no, because I had begun to understand that this would not be a game, as it had been with the spurgos. This was real, and very dangerous.

And that was more than enough to get me to tell her I wouldn't go, except that since the moment I'd agreed to transport this book for Milda, something had come alive in me, the feeling that my parents would have wanted me to do this, that from wherever they were now, they were cheering me on, and maybe saying to each other, "I suppose Audra is braver than we had thought."

I hoped I was. I hoped that despite my pounding heart, the sweat on my hands, and my unsteady legs, there was a small spark of courage. I needed to find it. I needed to prove to myself that it existed.

So I nodded at Milda, placed the pack with the fabric scraps on my back, pulled on my father's shoulder bag over that, then turned and walked out the door without looking back. Maybe if I pretended to be brave, I would become more brave.

Near the same spot where I had encountered Roze with the pastry, I found her waiting again. She ran up to me, and I was sure she hoped I had another pastry for her today.

"Where are you going?" she asked.

"On an errand for Milda," I said.

She lowered her voice. "Delivering books?"

I turned sharply toward her. "Hush, Roze!" She stepped back and her eyes welled with tears. So more gently, I added, "It's just an errand, nothing of interest."

I began walking again. Roze stayed at my side. "I heard your parents are being sent to Siberia."

I stopped in my tracks, facing forward. That was the last thing I wanted to talk about right now, or think about. Through a clenched jaw, I said, "We don't know that. Maybe they're only in a prison."

"Or Siberia." Roze shifted the weight on her feet, then said, "What if you end up going there too?"

"I won't."

"You might."

Yes, I might. But I couldn't dwell on that or my journey would end right here, without me daring to take another step forward. I tilted my head toward her and, with little patience, said, "I need to go now, Roze. Alone."

Roze wiped a stray tear off her cheek, then said, "Good luck on your errands!"

By the time I reached the center of Milda's village, a few of the markets had begun to open for the day. I remembered Lukas saying he only went places that the soldiers did not, but an officer was already here this morning, and I feared if I turned back, it would look suspicious. He called to me in Russian, and I waved back as if I didn't understand, hoping that would be enough.

He called again, more sharply this time. From the tone of his voice, I understood he wanted me to stop.

I turned toward him so he could look at my face rather than at a sack for which I could be arrested, then did my best to smile, all the while reminding myself to speak to him in Russian. And hoping he would not ask my name and interpret that as me speaking an illegal language.

"Little girl," he said. "Why are you out so early?"

I shrugged. *Speak in Russian. Speak in Russian.* "The sooner I begin my chores, the sooner I finish them."

"All chores? No school?"

I wasn't sure how to answer him. I knew there were public schools designed to make its students good Russian citizens. My father would've hidden us in the forest before allowing me to go there. The only other school I knew of was the secret school beneath Milda's home, and I'd never tell him about that.

"No school," I told him.

He walked a circle around me, tugging on one end of a fabric scrap that had sprung loose out the top of the bag. "You work for a seamstress?" he asked. "Bringing her pieces to be made into a quilt perhaps?"

"Perhaps." Whatever he wanted to believe, I'd agree with him.

"Here or the next town?"

I didn't know any seamstresses here, so I said, "The next town." Hopefully he wouldn't ask for the woman's name, and if he did, hopefully he wouldn't know that I was lying.

"Wait here." Then he walked back to his horse and began digging into the saddlebags. My legs went numb and I considered dropping my sack of fabric and making a run for it. I even loosened my grip on the handle so that if he turned back around with anything threatening, I could be halfway to the woods before he knew how to react.

Except Milda had said to protect that book as if it were my most precious possession. At the moment, my life was the most precious thing I owned, the *only* thing I owned, really. Surely she had not meant I should give my life for this book.

No, Milda would have known that might be necessary. That's why she'd given me so many warnings.

When the officer turned around, I was surprised to see something familiar in his hands: another book, only this one with very different lettering from what was written on the books in Milda's secret library.

"You may have this if you want it," the officer said, holding it out to me. "It's for you, a gift from the tsar."

I tilted my head, instantly suspicious. The leader of the Russian Empire didn't know me. He didn't know any of the peasant citizens of Lithuania, and even if he did, he'd never have sent gifts to us. No one gave us gifts unless they wanted something in return.

My loyalty perhaps? I tried not to squint back at him, or to look as anxious as I was.

"You may take this book, and if it interests you, maybe we can see about enrolling you in school. Teach you to read and then you can learn how to become something more than a peasant who sells fabric scraps. Teach you to be—"

"A Russian?" I'd spoken before I thought better of it, thinking of my parents and wondering if this man in front of me had been there the night they were arrested. He probably hadn't been, but I still couldn't help but wonder. And I instantly knew it was a mistake. My tone had been too sharp, too angry.

To cover, I quickly reached for the book he'd offered me. "Thank you. I'd like to learn to read."

His suspicion cooled, even as my cheeks heated. Not because I was frightened, or because I'd made an enormous error, but because I'd just spoken aloud a truth that had stayed at the back of my mind for years, even when I'd denied it to my father.

Papa had asked me that very question once as we sat together at the supper table. I'd begun to answer, but before I could, Mama told Papa she needed his help outside, and they remained out there until long after our supper was cold. When they returned, my parents quietly continued eating, as if they hadn't been gone at all. Finally, hoping to ease the tension in our home, I said, "I have no wish to read, Papa. Another time perhaps."

That other time may have finally come. I wanted to learn to read.

"Don't waste time with a peasant girl!" The officer who shouted to the Cossack I was speaking to must have been his superior, for this soldier quickly straightened up and saluted. "We're going to monitor all roads north of here. We heard there might be trouble that way."

That way happened to be the same direction I was headed, which meant I needed to avoid all roads from here on. My head had been ducked low while he spoke, and it was only after he left that the soldier I'd been speaking to sent me on my way.

I kept the book tucked under my arm as I walked. I figured it made me less suspicious to any other soldiers who might notice me—or at least, they'd see I already had a

Russian book, so what would I ever want with a hidden Lithuanian one?

By midday, I'd made it to the next town, just as Milda had instructed. I hoped I was in the right place since she hadn't given me its name, nor did this small village appear to have one. I ducked my head inside a blacksmith's stables. Just to be safe, I asked my question in Russian, "Do you happen to know a Ben Kagan?"

The blacksmith looked me over like I was a bit of mold to be scraped off his bread. "Who are you?"

I drew back, unprepared for that question. Finally, in my scrambling to say something coherent, I mumbled, "A friend of his sent me here."

"You're no friend of his, speaking as you do, and holding that Russian book. Go away." The blacksmith returned to his work, making it clear he was finished with me.

I sighed and immediately felt someone tap on my back. With a start, I looked and saw Lukas behind me, arching his brows as if I'd done something to amuse him.

"Not bad, Audra, really, for your first try."

I balled up my hands into fists. "You followed me?"

"Not followed you exactly. I only walked here on a separate path that allowed me to observe your actions without you, or that Cossack soldier, ever seeing me. Milda asked me to be sure you were safe." He smiled and glanced down at the Russian book. "But what are you doing with *that*?"

I held it up. "It was a gift—that soldier gave it to me. I didn't ask for it."

"Why do you think it was a gift? Because no one will buy these little hatchets!"

My brows pressed together. "Little hatchet?"

"Their books are their weapons, meant to swallow us up if we allow it." He took the book from me. "I know you're supposed to meet Ben, but before you do, we must make sure this book is put in a safe place, somewhere special where no one will ever bother it." He walked across the road and I followed.

An old farmer happened to be passing us by, pulling a load of manure. Lukas ducked in immediately behind the cart, then shoved the Russian book into the center of the foul-smelling load. Then he turned back to me with a wide smile. "Now it's just where it belongs. Come with me and I'll introduce you to Ben."

CHAPTER
THIRTEEN

Lukas and I had taken no more than three steps forward when a wagon barreled down the street straight toward us. Its driver had a patch over one eye, and the other was zigzagging in wild alarm. His white hair stuck out in every direction and his clothes seemed so much a part of him that I suspected he might've grown into them from birth, and simply slept, bathed, and prayed in them year-round. He held the reins with one hand and, with the other, tossed a long piece of canvas fabric behind him, letting it flutter in the wind to spread out its folds.

Lukas muttered to me under his breath, "Audra, meet Ben. You've caught him on one of his better days."

I gasped and started to dodge out of the way, but Lukas took my hand and pulled me with him toward the wagon, stepping aside barely in time to clear the horses.

Ben slowed long enough to direct his attention to Lukas. "Get on or get run over, I don't much care which!"

"She has to come," Lukas said.

I protested, but Lukas must not have heard me. Instead, the instant Ben flicked his eyes at me and nodded, Lukas grabbed me by the waist and half tossed me onto the back of the wagon, then jumped on himself almost at the last minute as the wagon burst into full speed.

I scrambled deeper into the wagon, which was filled with bundles of hay. I pushed through them and felt something hard at my feet—books, I assumed. Of course they'd be books. No wonder I'd seen so few of them in my lifetime. Milda and Ben must have hoarded all the books in Lithuania. Lukas raised the back of the wagon's gate and latched it, shutting us in.

"Grab a corner," Ben said. I had to stand to catch the canvas, but a burst of wind tossed it out of my reach, and I stumbled, nearly losing my balance as our wagon tilted on two wheels around a bend in the road. Then Lukas caught an edge of the fabric, which brought my corner into control. Together we tucked the ends around the straw, and Ben tossed us some rope to tie everything down.

"Now sit down like you belong there," he said. "And whistle if we're being followed."

Of course we were being followed. Why else would he have rushed us out of town like that?

"Who's the girl?" Ben asked. Lukas started to answer for me but Ben said, "Doesn't her voice work?"

I rolled my eyes at being forced to speak when Lukas was doing a fine job of it. "My name is Audra."

"No last name?"

Milda had warned me against using my last name, and even if Lukas knew Ben, I didn't, nor did I particularly trust either of them—not yet.

"Just Audra," I said.

But the driver only looked me over and said, "She looks like the daughter of Henri Zikaris. Same eyes."

My head whipped back at him. "You know my family too?"

"All book carriers knew your parents."

"They're still alive." When I got no response, I repeated that, then added, "And I'm working on a plan to get them back again."

He shrugged. "It'll never work. Even if it could, you won't be involved. I'm dropping you off at the next town, as a favor to your father."

"I'm supposed to stay with her," Lukas said.

"Then I'll drop you both off," Ben said without missing a beat. "You're too young for this as well." Then he glanced back at me. "Why are you here anyway? Your parents wanted you kept out of this business."

I closed my eyes, wishing he wouldn't talk about them as if they were dead. They weren't. And I didn't appreciate him brushing off my talk of a plan to get them back as if it was just the silly idea of a young girl.

Unless it *was* just a silly idea. No single book could possibly be as valuable as my parents' lives.

"So you never knew?" Lukas asked. "Until now, you never knew about your parents' work?"

"I knew a little," I said, which wasn't quite true. And I wasn't at all happy that Lukas and Ben seemed to know far more about my parents than I ever had.

"Well, no matter," Lukas said, smiling. "I think you'll be quite good at smuggling."

I had no plans to smuggle long enough to become good at it—I had only agreed to this one delivery in honor of my parents. I sat up straight, for the first time remembering the book I carried. It was still in the sack slung from my shoulders. "We've got to hide this one too."

"Agreed." Lukas looked around. We'd left the town behind and were headed north. Where had the soldiers said they were going to search for any signs of trouble?

Here. They were searching here.

"Something's wrong," I whispered.

Maybe the trouble was Ben's doing, or mine, or maybe it had nothing to do with us, but we would be swept up in it anyway. The Cossacks would be happy to nab anyone they considered in violation of the law.

When it didn't appear that Ben had heard me, in a louder voice, I said, "We've got to go back."

"Can't go back," Ben said. "Somewhere behind us is an entire regiment of Cossacks."

"Then get off the road!"

"This wagon wouldn't get far through the woods." Lukas's brow pressed low. "If you're afraid—"

I was plenty afraid, but that wasn't the reason I wanted off this wagon. No, my fear came from what I was about to do, what I had to do if we were going to get through the next few minutes.

Before Lukas could finish his thought, I pulled the book out of the sack of fabric and tossed it at Lukas, then jumped from the side of the wagon with the sack in my arms. Alarmed by my sudden actions, Ben pulled up on the reins, but I said, "Let me go on ahead. After three minutes, you can follow me."

He gave me a quizzical expression but halted the horses. I slung the sack over my shoulders again, with my father's shoulder bag beneath that, then continued on down the lane. I'd only rounded the second bend before a voice called out in Russian for me to stop. And I did.

Six soldiers on horseback were waiting by the roadside. I scanned them from one end to the other, increasingly certain that I'd made a terrible mistake. By the time I reached the final man, I knew this was worse than a mistake. It was a disaster.

Officer Rusakov was staring at me, brows pressed low. It hadn't yet been even two weeks since he had arrested my parents, burned my home, and chased me into the woods. Would he recognize me? Ben had known who my parents were on his first glance at my face; was it that obvious who I was?

Rusakov had already seen me coming, and his eyes narrowed as he directed his horse to the center of the road to intercept me. Maybe he didn't know who I was. Maybe he looked at everyone that way—like they were a criminal. A fugitive. Was that what I was now?

He'd only seen me from behind as I ran from him, and only for a brief moment.

But he had seen me.

My knees went wobbly, but if I tried to run now, that would be an absolute admission of my guilt. And besides, less than three minutes behind me, Ben and Lukas were about to pass along this very road with a wagon full of books. I thought again of my parents, and especially my father, who I guessed had done the actual transport of books. What would he do right now?

Magic. My father would do magic. I wished I knew a disappearance trick, either to make the soldiers vanish or me, I really didn't care which.

Rusakov addressed me in that same low voice that had haunted my dreams every night for the past two weeks. "Do I know you?" His brows were pressed low, already suspecting I intended to lie to him. That had been the plan, but I was so nervous, I'd give myself away if I lied. I'd have to play carefully with the truth.

"We've never met," I said. And if we had met, I'd be dead right now.

"Which village are you from?"

I tilted my head back to where I'd just been. "That one." Whatever its name. I felt foolish for not having bothered to ask for the place's name.

He was staring at me so closely that I wished I could melt away to nothing. Could he hear the pounding of my heart? Did he know the true reason my breaths were coming in such quick gasps? Rusakov dismounted and walked a full circle around me with his arms folded.

"Your blouse has dirt stains . . . perhaps from the forest?"

"It's the only dress I own. I'm sure it's stained from many things." At least I had the new apron from Milda. Otherwise, he'd have been sure to recognize me.

"And what are you doing out here?"

I slid the sack off my shoulder and dug into it, pulling out a handful of scraps for him to see. "Would you care to buy these? I'm not allowed home until I've sold them all."

Rusakov frowned and yanked the sack out of my hands. He pushed one arm downward through the fabric while with the other hand he felt around the outside of the bottom of the bag. He could search all he wanted—the book wasn't there anymore. When he failed to find anything, he shoved the sack back at me.

But it hardly meant I was out of trouble. "You say you're not allowed home until all of these have sold? Where is your home?"

"Back in the—"

"Who are your parents?"

My mind went blank. I had no idea what to say or do. Nor did he need my answer.

"You are Miss Zikaris," he said. "You used to live on a farm near Šiluva."

I began trembling, so much that he surely could see. The corner of his lip curled.

"Your parents have been given a life sentence in Siberia," Rusakov said. "They'll leave on the next train, in two days, and you will never see them again."

"Please, sir—"

"What would you give to bring them home? What would you do?"

"Anything. Please."

He arched a brow. "Anything? I wonder if that's true." His eye flicked past me to the road. Ben's wagon was only around the bend now. Within seconds, he would come into view. Rusakov crouched down to look directly at me. "Are those your friends coming? Did they send you here to distract me?"

"I . . . I don't know who's coming," I said.

"If that were true, you would not look back with such fear." I realized I'd been doing that very thing and forced myself to turn to Rusakov again as he said, "I am going to let them pass, I'll let them think I've been fooled by a silly girl like yourself. And I'll do this because you are new and need time for what I'm asking. I am looking for a boy near your age, a smuggler like you. He has given me a great deal of trouble."

Lukas. He was looking for Lukas, who was headed directly our way right now!

Rusakov continued, "Within two days, I want you to meet me here with that boy's name and any information you have on how to find him. Do this and I will release your parents. They will come back to you and you can be a family again. If you are not here to meet me in two days, then you will spend the rest of your life wondering how long they were able to survive in Siberia, if they even made it there alive. Or you will get the answer for yourself when I arrest you for book smuggling and give you the same punishment." Ben's horses rounded the corner. "Do I make myself clear?"

I couldn't speak, so I merely nodded and tried to hold back my tears.

By then, Ben's wagon itself had come into view, but I only saw Ben, whistling a tune and smiling as if he hadn't a care in the world. If Lukas was still with him, then he must have been hiding beneath the fabric to throw off any suspicion about the books. Either that, or he knew Officer Rusakov was after him.

"Halt!" Rusakov ordered, walking to the center of the road to stop Ben, who pulled up on the reins and tried not to look at me from his unpatched eye. "What are you carrying?"

"A delivery of straw for a farmer in Šiauliai." Ben spoke as if he was bored, as if he'd been through searches like this many times, and maybe he had. But never exactly like this.

Rusakov put a hand on my shoulder. "This poor girl is attempting to sell fabric scraps. Would you take her as far as Šiauliai with you? I think she may have some luck there."

Ben's head tilted, surprised at the luck he thought he was receiving. If only he knew. If only he knew.

Ben offered me a hand to climb beside him onto the wagon seat, though I couldn't even look at him. Once we left these soldiers behind, he'd congratulate me on creating a story that turned their suspicions, when in reality, I'd done just the opposite.

Instead, I'd have to tell Ben the truth, that Rusakov had offered me a way to save my parents.

Or . . .

I'd tell him a lie, let him believe that I had created a story so that the soldiers let us pass by without being searched. I'd lie, at least until I figured out what to do about Lukas.

Ben dipped his head humbly toward the Cossack officers. "As you wish, sir."

I kept my head down as we drove away, completely drained of any strength I might have had and exhausted from the effort of pretending to be brave for so long.

A full kilometer ahead, Ben finally stopped the wagon so that Lukas could come out from beneath the canvas. They both faced Ben and me gave me a deep nod of respect. "You have your parents' blood indeed. Perhaps one day, when you are much older, you can become a book carrier."

I lowered my eyes, deeply ashamed of myself for considering Rusakov's offer. Ben was praising me for saving books, even as I was deciding whether to turn in a person who smuggled them. It was wrong; I knew it was wrong. But wasn't it also wrong to refuse to help my parents—even to save their lives—when it was possible to do so?

Yes, it was still wrong.

This was horrible, and I had no idea what to do about it.

Lukas grinned over at me, but said to Ben, "I prefer the term 'book smuggler.' Anyone can carry a book, but smuggling is an art."

"Smuggling is a crime," Ben countered. "Carrying is noble."

"Then let Audra be noble with us. She's good, Ben. I've seen her and she's got good instincts."

"She'll have those same instincts when she's older." Ben turned around to face the road again. "After this delivery, we're taking her back to Milda's. This is too dangerous for a young girl."

"It's too dangerous for all of us," Lukas said. "But we have good reasons for doing it."

I had my own reasons for continuing to smuggle—within two days, I could bring my parents back home.

And I had better reasons for jumping from this wagon and running as far away as I could from the books, from Lukas, and from that cruel Officer Rusakov. That's what I should do. Run from a decision I didn't want to make because any decision I made would be awful.

But I didn't run. Instead, I lowered my eyes and said, "Let me keep smuggling."

If Ben heard me, he said nothing. I took his silence as a yes.

FOURTEEN

As we continued on our ride that afternoon, Lukas seemed to sense my thoughts were heavier than usual. He leaned forward. "There's a story for when you're in a mood like this."

"No, there's not."

"There is, trust me." Lukas smiled and began, "Do you remember the story of Rue, the beautiful daughter of the wealthy man who was injured by the overturned cart?"

"Of course."

"Well, because of his injuries, the man was confined to his bed for a very long time, so much that Rue had to take charge of his estate. Her father had a great deal of land and she knew nothing of how to manage it all. Finally, she thought of the bear and wondered if he was still waiting in the forest for her to come. The bear had seen her father manage the estate for years, so she was certain he must know what to do."

"Was he there?" I asked.

"Yes, because he hoped if he was patient, that Rue would eventually come." Lukas leaned in. "The bear knew of a peasant boy who lived on the land, a boy who had worked on that estate for his entire life. He told Rue to trust the boy, which, naturally, Rue could only do if she also trusted the bear. But the bear had saved her father, so Rue decided to trust them both."

I sighed. "And the boy saved the estate for her?"

Lukas grinned. "No, the boy had his own troubles. But he taught Rue everything he knew so that she could run the estate until her father returned."

My eyes narrowed. "'Returned'? You mean until her father recovered."

"If you wish."

I nodded at him, then looked away, ending his telling of the story. I was pretty sure he had made up all of it, and if he had hoped to make me feel better, it worked, maybe a little.

Thankfully, there were no more problems that afternoon, and by evening, we ended up in front of a church in Šiauliai, a beautiful white building with a tower in front that seemed to stretch to the sky. As if he had been expecting our arrival, almost immediately a priest in long black robes walked out front and followed my gaze. "It's impressive now. But probably around the time you were born, it was struck with lightning. Destroyed a most precious clock, so few people in this town ever know what time it is. Except we all know it is time for the Cossacks to leave, no?"

He started to laugh at his joke, but Ben only grunted. "Enough talking. We need to get inside."

"Of course." The priest pointed to some stables near the church. "I believe your delivery of *straw* belongs there." He winked at me as he spoke.

"The church is smuggling too?" I was genuinely surprised that men who preached of honesty and obedience on the Sabbath day would spend the other days of the week breaking the law and encouraging others to do the same. The priest gave me a knowing smile, then walked ahead of us.

Once we had ridden into the stables, Lukas began tugging at the canvas covering the straw, preparing for us to unload the wagon, so I did the same. As we worked, he said, "It was the priests who started the book smuggling. When their prayer books were banned and burned, what else could they do? It wasn't about breaking the law; it was about protecting the right to pray."

I closed my eyes and whispered a prayer of my own. Maybe Lukas was a thief and he certainly was a smuggler, but he was also a nice person who seemed to have a good heart. Whatever he had done, it couldn't be awful enough to deserve the punishment Rusakov surely had in mind for him.

But nor did my parents deserve their punishment.

And I could not save them any other way. There was no other way.

Lukas dug through the books below us and found a thin one with a large printed *A* on the cover, the same as my name. "You take this book—it's yours."

"It's for the priest." I wouldn't accept a book from Lukas even as I was considering turning him in for handing out books.

But Lukas pushed it toward me again. "This book is for someone who wants to read in her own language. Someone like you."

"This is an illegal book! Doesn't that bother you?"

"Just because it's a law does not make it right. This is how we fight the Russian Empire, Audra. Words are our weapons, and protecting these books is a noble defense of our country. Join us, or don't, but at least understand what we're fighting for, and why." He dropped the book in my lap, then jumped from the wagon.

He and Ben began hauling books where the priest directed them, covering each stack with the straw so that it would blend in with the stables. I merely sat in a corner of the wagon, turning the book from Lukas over in my hands, unsure of what to do.

Since coming to Milda's, I'd tried to figure out what made these books so important. There wasn't much to them, merely a stack of pages with letters scrawled onto them, bound into a soft leather or fabric cover.

For books like these, the tsar of the Russian Empire condemned people to death or to a lifetime of imprisonment. I wondered how many hundreds—maybe thousands—of smugglers he'd punished.

And despite that, year after year, the smuggling continued. I couldn't understand why.

Nothing in these pages could be that wonderful, that satisfying. If it were, then of all the books my parents smuggled, why had they never kept a single copy in our home? If it was so important, shouldn't they have enrolled me in a school like Milda's? Shouldn't my parents have allowed me to work with them?

I knew the answer, of course. They'd already told me why. They wanted to keep me safe. "One more year, Henri." That had been my mother's plea. One more year before telling me the truth about anything. One more year before putting a book in my hands and explaining why it mattered to them, why it should matter to me. Always one more year. All to keep me safe.

And now, here I was. Could I do what was necessary to make them safe again too?

The priest rested a small stack of books on the side of the wagon, getting my attention. "Thinking about your parents?"

I nodded. There were no words in my language, or the Russian language, to describe how much I missed them. The closest phrase we had was *aš labai pasiilgau tavęs*, which failed to express my utter emptiness without them.

The priest continued, "I never met them, but I've heard stories of their work. Your mother collected orders for books and passed the information to your father, who would secretly cross the border into Prussia. We have printers there who gladly take our money to make the books for us. Then your father smuggled the books back here into Lithuania. Their work was exceptionally dangerous, but if they were anything like Ben and Lukas and the other carriers I work with, then I understand why they did it."

I stared back at him, hoping he would explain further. Because I desperately wanted to know the answer. Yes, I had felt the rush of excitement in getting a single book past that soldier in town, but what did that matter? I'd failed in my attempts to smuggle since then and it had left a horrible pit in my gut all day.

The priest smiled. "Your parents must have loved you very much to care so deeply about your future. They hoped to give you the chance of growing up in a Lithuania that was free, that belonged to our own people."

I glanced down. Maybe that was true. But if my parents loved me so much, why couldn't they have made choices to keep us together? Of course I wanted my country to be free, as much as anyone, but no matter whether Lithuania was free or occupied, I'd still rather have had the chance to grow up with my family at my side.

The priest must have sensed my feelings because he added, "Your parents couldn't stand by and watch our light be extinguished by the occupation. If our country ceases to exist, then who will you be? An orphan to a nameless people, not Lithuanian, not Russian, not anything."

That was exactly the problem. I would become an orphan . . . unless I helped Rusakov. Helped him destroy the very thing my parents had worked so hard to protect.

"I found a book in our home once," I said, keeping my eyes down. "Years ago, but I still remember it. Mama snatched it from my hands and told me books were dangerous."

Lukas was passing by to get another load of books. "Your mother was right. Books can be exceptionally dangerous."

Now I looked up. "How?"

The priest picked up a book from the wagon, one in a simple leather binding with letters on the cover that meant nothing to me. "This book speaks of what Lithuania might have been now if we'd been left on our own. Read it and you will see that what the Russians have stolen from us is so much greater than simply our land and our lives."

"What good does it do to wish that things were different?" I asked. "The Cossacks are here to stay. A few words of protest in a book won't change that."

Lukas took the book from the priest and widened it to show me the pages inside, as if that would matter. "It's not just wishing, Audra. This is a book of ideas. Someone thought the idea and put it into words on paper. That became a seed, and every time someone reads those words, the seed is planted in their mind, too, and it grows and spreads and soon that tiny seed of an idea becomes belief, and belief becomes a plan, and those plans begin to change the world. Control the books and you will control the people."

I smiled as I began to understand. "Give them books, and the people will control themselves."

"Control their own future!" Lukas added.

He started to leave, but I said his name, and when he turned back to me, I asked, "With enough books, could we control our future enough to get the Russians out of Lithuania? Isn't that the purpose of the book?"

Ben had been listening to us and now ducked in. "The book gives knowledge, but don't expect freedom from it. The Russians have been here a very long time now."

"But *could* it happen?"

"In other words, is there any chance for your parents to come home again?" Ben frowned. "I already answered this. In my lifetime, I've never once seen anyone come back from Siberia."

A tear escaped my eye, leaving a wet trail down my cheek. If that were true, then I really had no choice. I couldn't let my parents die in Siberia, not for a few books. I knew what I had to do.

Lukas had been gathering another stack of books in his arms and now lowered them again to face Ben. "That's not what you've told me before. You've said—"

"Don't get her hopes up. We're not doing this to make Lithuania free. We do this just to preserve the idea that Lithuania exists at all."

"No, Ben!" Lukas shouted the words, then calmed himself with a deep breath before adding, "I know what you've always said, what you really believe. That books themselves are freedom. Freedom to think, to believe, to dream."

Ben had been nodding as Lukas spoke, then said, "Put a thousand more hosts of Cossack soldiers on our roads if that's what the tsar commands, but if I have a book in my hand, I am free. Now, I'd appreciate it if you'd get several books in your hands and help this old man unload the wagon."

Lukas grinned playfully, and as he began piling a stack into his arms, he glanced over at me. "I warn you that once you start carrying, you won't be able to go back to who you were before. Will you help us, then?"

His simple question seemed to choke me, too much for an honest reply. Whatever I did next, it would feel to them like I was helping, but the truth was just the opposite. I had to meet Officer Rusakov in two days and tell him how to find Lukas. I just had to. Slowly, I nodded.

"No, she won't help," Ben countered, then faced me directly. "A book carrier's work is dangerous, her life is at risk at all times, even in the moments when she's not carrying books. Just as it was for your father." I winced, and Ben continued, "You'll sleep in cold ditches, run when your heart threatens to burst from your chest, go hungry, and be lonely and more afraid some nights than you can possibly imagine. And more than once, you will ask yourself why you are doing all of this."

On the other side of me, Lukas said, "Smuggling is in your blood, Audra. Adventure is in your blood. If all you want is a simple life, then forget everything you have seen and everything you've already done. You can grow up without ideas or dreams or knowledge of a world any bigger than your own home. Do you want that, a life of small, safe dreams?"

"She wants to live!" Ben scowled. "Stop filling her head with hope. Her parents kept her away from all of this for a reason and we should respect that."

I stared down at the book in my hands, the one with the *A* on the cover. Was that all I'd ever be, just that single scrawled letter? Perhaps the simple life I had laid out for myself wasn't really the life I wanted. "That's the first letter of my name," I mumbled. "The only letter of my name that I know."

"The rest is inside that book." Lukas smiled as if he had won some sort of contest against Ben, when in fact, it wasn't about either of them. It was about me.

Was it enough for me to simply be a letter *A*? Maybe it had to be enough. I wasn't ready to risk my life to know the letters that followed it.

"You can finish the job we're on now," Ben said. "But this life isn't for you. If your parents had taught you better, encouraged you to read rather than hiding information from you, then you might have made a very good book carrier. As you are now, I do not think you are up to the task."

"I am," I mumbled. And when he didn't seem to hear me, I looked up. "I can do this, Ben."

Or at least, I had to. Just until I got my parents back.

After that, I could return to the life I'd had before. The one where my mother insisted on protecting me from the world beyond my home, where my father believed I knew and understood less than I truly did. I could return to being a girl who stared at the first letter of her name and wondered if there was anything more to her.

And that was the problem. More than anything in the world, I wanted my parents back. But I did not . . . could not . . . return to being the same girl they had left behind.

I closed my eyes and tried to contain the emotions rising in me. I'd seen a glimpse of myself as I wished to be, a reflection of who I might become if I allowed courage to enter my heart, or ideas to enter my head. I saw myself as the girl who defied any hold on her future because she refused to acknowledge the limits others placed on her.

When I imagined the girl I wanted to be, it was the girl who smuggled books.

I looked down at the book in my hand.

"What do you think?" Lukas asked Ben. "We really could use her help, and she was good back there on the road, you know she was."

"She was," Ben grunted at me. "But I still don't like this one bit." He hesitated a moment longer, rubbing the scruff on his chin as he considered what to do, then said, "Until I can get you back to Milda's, I suppose you're a smuggler now."

FIFTEEN

We slept in the church that night, each of us taking a separate pew with a blanket and a bundle of my fabric scraps for a pillow against the hard wood seats. Ben fell asleep immediately, but I rolled until I caught an angle of my book against the moonlight streaming in through the church's tall arched windows.

My book was meant for a much younger person, but I was unable to sleep and had nothing better to do, so I began thumbing through the pages. They listed thirty-two letters, each letter making a different sound. Combining the sounds completed a word. So all I had to do was figure out the sound associated with each letter, and the word would unfold before my eyes.

Each page had a series of pictures and the words to describe each one below it. Well over an hour later, I had made out the first three words on the page.

Vaikas. Child.

Namai. Home.

Motina. Mother.

I stopped there and closed the book, my heart pounding as if I'd just finished a race. My mother was so much more than a series of six letters. It didn't describe her enough, didn't identify her in any way that contained the uniqueness of how she spiced a beet soup, the warmth of her smile, the tender touch of her hand on my back when I needed her most. Ben was wrong. There was no power in a word that failed to encompass who my mother really was.

I looked over to the pew where he slept to ask him about that, and only then noticed how low the candle had burned. I should have been asleep myself. I dropped the book on the floor, frustrated by how those words simplified the clash of emotions inside me when I thought about my mother. How I missed her, loved her, desperately wished for any news of whether she was safe, whether she was afraid of going to Siberia. But I was also angry that she had kept a secret life so separate from her life with me, never once letting on what she was doing, never once trusting me to help her, or now, to save her.

And for all those thoughts, the only word the book offered me was "motina." Little comfort as I finally closed my eyes.

I couldn't have been asleep for long when the doors of

the church burst open and a man ran through the door, call-ing, *"Kunigas, Kunigas!"* for the priest to come.

Both Ben and Lukas bolted straight up from their benches and Ben tore off his blanket to rush over to the man. Although he asked the man to lower his voice, the tall open ceilings of this room created an echo, making it easy to hear their conversation.

"A search is coming," the man said. "They're looking for you. By morning, the Cossacks will be here. Are there any books in this church?"

Ben glanced at Lukas. "Get the priest." Then to me he said, "Gather up our blankets. We must leave at once."

I began stuffing the fabric scraps back into my sack, then folded up the blankets, pulled my boots on to my feet, and followed Ben and the man who'd come out of the church and into the stables.

Ben began hitching up the horses while I started loading books back into the wagon as quickly as possible.

"No." Ben held up an arm, but it was the tension in his voice that stopped me in my tracks. "They know a wagon brought the books into the town. They'll watch for wagons to be leaving the town. We must go other ways."

"I have a cart with me," the man said. "If you and your carriers will take the extra books and leave town, I'll take all the books that were meant to be distributed here and get them delivered by morning."

By then, Lukas and the priest had joined us. The priest helped load books into the man's cart while Ben gathered me and Lukas around him.

"How many can you carry?" he asked Lukas.

Lukas looked over the pile. "A dozen, I think."

Ben nodded at him, then turned to me. "How many?"

"A dozen." Ben started to object, but I added, "If Lukas can, then I can." I began pulling the fabric scraps from my sack to make room for the books. Ben counted out twelve books and handed them to me, though I noticed they were thinner than what he handed to Lukas. I stuffed them deep within my sack, pushing the fabric scraps around the edges so that my sack would look rounded rather than square.

"Fabric scraps won't do." The priest held a finger to his temple. "Wait a bit." He hurried back toward the church, returning a few minutes later with some maroon tube-shaped flowers that somehow smelled like raw meat. I cocked my head away from them as he stuffed them into the top of my sack. "*What* is that?"

He smiled. "Birthwort. If you don't like the smell, then neither will the occupiers. Tell them it was your mother's favorite and you're going to lay them at her grave."

I stiffened. "My mother is still alive."

The priest drew back. "Oh, yes, of course! But that is a good excuse for why you might be carrying them."

"If I'm stopped, I won't use that excuse."

"Tell them anything you want," Lukas said, stuffing a canvas sack with his own books. "Better yet, don't get stopped."

"We're leaving together." I looked from him over to Ben. "Aren't we?"

Ben shook his head. "Three of us together will draw too much attention. We should take separate routes toward Šiluva. Have you heard of that place?"

Of course I had. That was the closest town to where I'd lived my entire life. But I barely knew where I was now, so I had no idea how to get back there. I desperately wanted to return to Šiluva, though, just to see what was left of my home . . . if anything was left of it.

"I don't dare to draw you a map," Ben said. "If you're caught, it will lead them to all of us."

"Do you have any paper?" I asked the priest. "And a little milk?"

The priest's brows knitted together, but he nodded and excused himself, returning a minute later with both items I'd requested, which he gave to me.

I passed them to Ben and said, "Dip your finger in the milk and draw me a map on the paper."

"With milk? No one will be able to see it."

"Exactly!"

"Not even you, Audra. What good—"

"Please, Ben, just trust me!"

I doubted Ben had the capacity to trust me, but hopefully he'd decide it was easier to do as I asked so that we could all get on our way. Whatever his reasons, he drew the map and passed it back to me with a huff. I waited for the paper to dry, then carefully folded it and put it in an inside pocket of my apron. If I was caught, all they would see was a blank paper. It occurred to me that maybe we should print all our books this way.

When I'd finished, Ben said, "You've had a little practice at smuggling, and you've done well, but this will be more difficult, for we're headed into a city where there are more watchful eyes. Our people will not trouble you—if anything they will greet and protect you as a hero—but there are Russian civilians in the cities. Speak Russian to everyone you meet, for they will expect that, and keep these books hidden until I find you in Šiluva."

"Where should I go there?"

Ben smiled. "If your invisible map works, then you'll end up at a secret school hidden in a barn near the church. It has a large Russian flag painted on the east side. Go inside there and wait for me."

"Ben, we need to leave," Lukas said, prodding his arm.

Ben stood but took one last look at me. "I would like to have trained you more, but trust your instincts. Get yourself to Šiluva, Audra; promise me you will."

Papa had taught me never to make a promise I didn't know I could keep, and yet Ben looked so desperate, and in such a hurry, I needed to calm his worries so he could do his job. I stood and hoisted the heavy, smelly sack over my shoulders. "I promise, Ben. I will get there."

After all, I was going home.

CHAPTER
SIXTEEN

We set out immediately, each of us from different parts of the city. Ben assigned me what I was sure was the simplest, safest, and most direct route toward Šiluva, but I accepted it without complaint. The faster I got back home, the better.

I took a path off the main road, making my own way toward the forest but keeping my eyes on the road to be sure I didn't start doing circles. Mama had once said that with so much of Lithuania was covered in forests, I ought to learn how to pass through them, but in her next breath she'd told me not to leave our farm and wander about on my own. How I wished she'd have let me explore.

For five exhausting hours, I kept to the edges of the trees, walking as fast as I could. When I crossed deeper into the forest, I finally breathed easier, even if my chances for getting lost had just increased significantly. In fact, a couple of hours later, long after dawn and when I was sure I had become lost, I knelt on the ground and built a small fire, then withdrew Ben's note from my pocket and began warming it over the flames. Papa had taught me how the milk would heat slower than the paper, leaving the map slightly darker than the rest of the paper. Once it had warmed, I checked Ben's directions against my current location, then memorized the rest of the map and burned the paper.

I couldn't be too careful. If the man who had burst into the church was correct, then the Cossacks had probably come by now, and if they found nothing at the church—and they wouldn't find anything, Ben and the priest would both make sure of that—then they'd likely continue on this way. I knew I had to be cautious, and I was being more watchful than I'd ever been in my life. But it was a beautiful morning with birds chirping overhead and fluttering happily from one branch to the other, without a care in the world. Fully unaware of the larger troubles in our country.

So I might've been, had I stayed in my little home, a softly chirping bird of little use or consequence to anyone. I would have been miserable, too, without even realizing why.

Tucked on top of the other twelve books I was carrying was the alphabet book from Lukas. I'd wanted to hide it beneath the rest, for it was my own, but I figured if the first twelve books were found, the alphabet book would be too. The order really didn't matter.

I paused to hoist the heavy sack higher on my shoulders, and as I did, I heard the crunch of dry leaves somewhere off to my right. At first I froze, but I wondered if that made me look guilty. So I angled away from the noise and kept walking, faster than before.

And the noise followed, still out of my sight. By midsummer, Lithuanian forests were lush and somewhat darkened by a thick canopy of leaves overhead. They were breathtaking in beauty but also full of shadows and tricks.

If only the noises I heard could be explained away so easily. I was being followed, I knew I was.

For most of the morning, I'd been working on an explanation for why I was out here alone, for why I was carrying the smelliest flowers in all of Europe, and for where I was really going. But my mind emptied. What was I supposed to do?

If I ran, it would be a sure sign of guilt. I'd be chased, and with my sack weighed down by thirteen books, I'd surely be caught.

I could try to lose them, but every time I moved away from the noise, it followed my shift in direction.

Not far ahead, a stick lay on the trail, thin enough to lift, to swing, but thick enough to be useful for protection. I hurried forward and picked it up, using it like a walking stick, but with both hands on it so that if anyone tried to grab me, I'd be ready for them.

Then I continued walking, listening for the noises, but they'd gone quiet. Immediately suspicious, I walked a few steps more, hoping to detect the sound again, but heard nothing. Perhaps whoever had been following me had seen me pick up the tree branch for a weapon and decided to leave me alone.

Or maybe they hadn't. I heard another crunch of leaves, coming closer. I angled the stick over my shoulder, ready to defend myself.

"Hello!" Lukas darted out from between two trees, a friendly smile on his face. I tried to stop myself, but I was already swinging the stick. It hit him across the chest, and he staggered backward until he tripped on a log and the books from his canvas sack scattered across the ground.

"I'm so sorry!" I cried. "Why'd you scare me like that?"

Lukas lay flat on the ground, trying to catch his breath. "I thought you knew it was me, that our paths had crossed. I waved at you awhile back."

"I didn't see that. Are you all—"

"Shh." Lukas put a finger to his lips and sat up. "Audra, get out of here."

"Your books—"

"Get out of sight! Now!"

I scrambled off the road and slid behind the nearby bank of a little stream just in time to see two Cossack soldiers on horseback emerge into the clearing and stop directly in front of Lukas. He'd been trying to gather up his scattered books but had been too late.

"What have we here?" an officer asked. The markings on his uniform identified him as a sergeant, but it was the cruel smile on his face that filled me with dread. "Are these Russian-language books?"

"They don't appear so," a man with the markings of a private replied. "But how can that be? Wouldn't books in this dead language be illegal here?"

The sergeant said, "I do believe they are." Then he dismounted and addressed Lukas directly. "Do you know what happens to book smugglers?"

"They are remembered as heroes of Lithuania!" Lukas shouted defiantly.

"There is no Lithuania!" the sergeant said, marching toward Lukas. "You are Russians and you are part of Russia. When will you accept that?"

"When will you accept that we cannot be crushed, and that we will not go to our knees for invaders!"

"Oh, you will go to your knees," the sergeant said. "Do it, or else."

A slight movement from the corner of my eye caught my attention. I jumped at first to see a long snake slithering up the side of the stream toward me, but it was only a grass snake. We had these near our home all the time. They were harmless.

These soldiers were not.

I peeked out from the bushes to see Lukas swallow hard,

then sink to his knees. The private had dismounted by now and directed their horses toward a copse of trees nearer to me than I would've liked. He broke off a branch from a fallen tree, then stood behind Lukas and said, "Count."

From his position on his knees, Lukas lowered his head and got his first lash across his back, receiving it with a grunt of pain.

"I didn't hear you," the sergeant shouted. "If I don't hear you, it didn't happen."

"One!" Lukas shouted back. It sounded as if his teeth were gritted, but his tone remained angry and defiant.

Another snap against his back, then, "Two!" in greater pain, as if he was holding back tears.

By the third snap, I'd had enough. I couldn't sit here and listen to this, wouldn't sit here and let it happen.

I left my sack tucked in the bush where I'd been hiding, then reached down and grabbed the snake from directly behind its head. I carried it up to the horses, releasing it beneath the restless legs of the private's horse. Eager to escape me, the snake quickly slithered forward, startling the horse, which bolted forward. The second horse followed, though I was out of sight by then and didn't get to see either of them run.

I heard the sergeant order his companion to chase after their animals, then he followed. The instant they were out of sight, I grabbed my sack and darted toward Lukas, taking him by the arm. "Let's run!"

Holes had been sliced into his shirt from the stick and through them I saw lines of blood. He was still bent over and tears streaked down his cheeks.

"Gather the books."

"They could be back at any minute!"

Lukas spoke more sharply this time. "Then gather the books, Audra! Or else what just happened here is for nothing."

While Lukas slowly forced himself to his feet, I gathered the books. He took as many as he could carry in one arm pressed against his chest, then wrapped his other arm around me to prop himself upright, and we hurried away into an even darker part of the forest.

Sometime later, I stopped. "I recognize this place."

Indeed, I would never forget it. This was the clearing where I had hidden on Midsummer's Eve two weeks ago. In this very spot, Officer Rusakov had announced to a gathering of young people a reward for turning me in to him, and he seemed to have been pursuing me ever since.

Me, and Lukas as well. Perhaps he was after all young book smugglers, hoping to suffocate the next generation of smugglers from existence. The old would pass away in time, but if they crushed the young, they would crush the movement.

Beside me, Lukas let out a soft groan and fell again on his knees. "I'm all right," he said when I reached for him, more in a whisper than aloud, and probably more as a reminder of it to himself than for me to hear. "I just need to rest."

"My home . . . the place where I've lived my entire life . . . is not far from here," I said. "Can you make it that far?"

He looked up at me. "Maybe . . . maybe you should go check on it, then come back for me if it's safe."

That wasn't really the reason. Lukas had obviously been holding back his emotions for most of our walk and needed time alone. So I agreed to his suggestion and left. As soon as I rounded a bend, I heard his first sob.

It broke my heart, too, and I was determined to find some way to cheer him up or to comfort him after I returned.

Which might've been a fine idea, if there had been anything happy inside me once I saw my home, or what was left of it.

I peered out from the woods behind where my home had been and drew in a breath I didn't know how to release.

The entire back half of my home was gone, nothing left but a burnt frame and mounds of ashes. Most of the front was destroyed as well, except for the area around our brick chimney and a few scorched items of furniture that were beyond saving.

Just as Lukas had done back in the forest, I fell to my knees and finally gave in to the sobs that burst from inside me.

CHAPTER
SEVENTEEN

I wasn't sure how long I sat there, staring at the remains of my home, the blackened shadow of what had been my innocent childhood, but it must have been a long time, for when I bothered to look, the sun had noticeably shifted in the sky.

Even then, I was so absorbed in my thoughts, in my pain, that I failed to hear the shuffling footsteps behind me at first. When I did, I turned to see Lukas walking up beside me, dragging his sack of books at his side. He looked at me, then at my home, then sat beside me, putting his arm around my shoulder.

It shouldn't have been this way. I should've been comforting him. My heart hurt, it was true, but Lukas was so much worse. He couldn't move a whisper in any direction, nor suck in a breath from the pain his back caused him.

Finally, I nodded at our barn in the distance. The word itself was perhaps too grand for the small shed it really was, but it was large enough to house some winter feed for our cow, or the cow itself on the coldest winter nights.

"We can rest in there."

Lukas agreed, though he needed my help to get up again, and I carried both our sacks of books with me, one on my back and the other in my arms. Inside the barn, I patted down some hay to make a sort of bed for him, and once he lay on it, he was almost instantly asleep.

I sat with my back against one wall of the barn, staring at his stack of books, a jumble of thoughts in my mind at what he had just suffered for them, of what my parents had sacrificed for books like these.

And what would likely happen to me one day if I continued to smuggle.

I already had some idea. Tomorrow morning I was supposed to meet Officer Rusakov. He'd expect me to betray Lukas and probably wouldn't let me go until I'd betrayed Ben and Milda too.

But I would not be there. As awful as it was to have ever considered Rusakov's offer, after seeing what the Cossacks had done to Lukas, I knew now that I could never turn Lukas over to them.

Sometime tomorrow, Rusakov would figure out that I wasn't coming, and he'd order my parents aboard the train to Siberia.

They were gone for good.

Tears welled in my eyes, even though I knew I'd made the right decision. It had to be, for how could I ever explain that I'd traded away the lives of my friends in exchange for their return? How could I ever face them again?

But of course, that was the point. I never would face them again. I never would see them again. Books had taken my family away and were keeping me from bringing them home.

The pain of such thoughts swelled inside my heart, so much that I knew I'd either burst with sadness, or begin running and not stop until I either reached Siberia or collapsed of exhaustion somewhere along the way. These were my last thoughts as I fell into a restless sleep.

And my first thoughts when I awoke. It was barely past dawn, I could tell that from the angle of the light seeping in through the cracks in our barn roof. Nearby, Lukas was still asleep, and I hoped he'd remain that way as long as possible. But until he awoke, I need some way of diffusing the deep sadness within me.

If Papa used distraction to create magic, then I needed a little of that magic to heal my heart too. Which meant I needed to distract myself. Anything. Just anything but having to sit here thinking of all that I had lost because of books.

Which, ironically, were the only things available for a distraction. Life was full of ironies lately.

In the sack, beneath those foul-smelling flowers, was the simple alphabet book.

Lukas mumbled something in his sleep, tried to roll over, then grimaced and remained where he was. I wondered what books were in Lukas's pack, what he had taken a whipping for. Curious, I reached inside it to find out.

A thick book on top seemed to be a religious text of some sort, and two or three other ones seemed to be prayer books that the priest likely would have urged me to read for the sake of my soul. I figured that risking my life to bring these books to my countrymen had to be better for my soul than simply reading about good things. So I opened another book, but this one confused me. The words were arranged in short lines running down the side of the page like the letters themselves were art. It might take me time to read it, but Lukas was asleep, and I wasn't going anywhere without him. I had plenty of time.

I wasn't sure how many minutes it took simply to read the title of the book, but I finally deciphered the letters enough to understand that it was about a forest, such as the one where we'd just come from. I thought about the thick lush trees there, and the brilliant green foliage and grasses. I could imagine the forest as if I were still there, its crisp smell of pine, the spongy dirt beneath my feet. This was a waste of time. Why should I struggle to decode the words when I saw these images so clearly in my mind?

"I know that poem." I looked over and saw Lukas was awake, though his face was twisted with the pain he must have been feeling. "That's called a poem, Audra."

"Oh." I stared down at the book for a moment. "What is it about?"

Lukas reached for the book, and when I handed it to him, he described a forest that had once been thick and green, but now the tall trees had been cut to their stumps and the grasses were gone, leaving black, barren soil behind; life had abandoned it. "What do you suppose happened to this forest?" Lukas asked. When I couldn't answer, Lukas read the words of the poem, "Long since destroyed, though no one knows wherefore."

"Destroyed?"

Lukas closed the book and gave it back to me. "We've transported many copies of that poem, and for a reason. It's about a forest, but it's not *about* a forest. Do you understand?"

How was I supposed to understand that? Either it was about a forest or it wasn't. Then my eyes brightened as the deeper meaning I'd been searching for took shape in my mind. "The tree stumps, bare slopes . . ." I lifted a page, feeling the crisp paper between my fingers and turning it over to a new page. "They've destroyed our country, like this barren forest."

"The poem was written thirty-five years ago, before the press ban, before the ban on our language, our words. Imagine how much more true those words are today. Especially because the poem itself is illegal now."

"Milda told me why our books are illegal," I said. "Punishment for a failed uprising."

"The uprising didn't fail," Lukas said. "It's still happening, and is stronger than ever. That's what we are doing each time we transport a book, and why we are doing it. You'll see—one day the tsar will have to admit that he cannot control us, cannot crush us, and certainly cannot force us into his Russian mold. You are now as much a part of the uprising as those who fought all those years ago. But our weapons today are cleverness, and courage, and words."

"And you really believe our small country, full of peasants and farmers, will win against the Russian Empire?"

"I believe the day will come when Lithuania owns its borders and all the land inside it. I believe we will be free one day, and I can only hope I'll still be alive to see it."

I stared at him, wondering why he'd said it that way. Did he think this occupation might outlast him, even if he lived to be a hundred years old? Or did he believe he might not live much longer, not as a book smuggler?

"Ben fought in the uprising too," Lukas said. "He was much younger then, of course, but every bit as grumpy, from what I'm told. He was the leader of a group of fighters near Šiauliai, where you first met him. Even when it was clear the uprising would fail, Ben refused to give up, so he and his group continued fighting until one day they were captured by the Russians. The governor of the region sentenced them to hanging, but Ben had an escape plan in mind. On the day they were to be transported to the gallows, they would fight back and overpower the soldiers . . ."

Lukas's voice drifted off then. Finally, I said, "Ben's still alive, so it must have worked."

"Ben thought it had worked. They did fight the soldiers, and they ran. But Ben was the only one who got away. The rest of his group was executed that same day. Ben will probably never tell you this story—I had to hear it from someone else. He's ashamed of himself for running when the others couldn't. He's ashamed for having survived when no one else did."

"But that wasn't his fault! Nothing would've been gained if he had surrendered."

"I know that, and you know it, but Ben doesn't see it that way. That's why he continues to smuggle: because he feels he owes it to the friends he lost that day. But it's also why he's so protective of you now, and of me too. He's terrified of being in charge of anyone again who doesn't make it out alive."

I sat with that thought for several minutes, pondering Ben's gruff, distant nature and finally understanding him. It wasn't that he didn't care. It was that he cared too much.

"We shouldn't wait here any longer," Lukas said. "Let's get back on the road."

"Your back—"

"My back will hurt whether I'm lying down or walking upright. We have books to deliver." I stood to help him, but he hesitated, pointing upward. "What's that?"

The sun had shifted angles enough for Lukas to see what I hadn't been able to from my position. Holding my breath with anticipation, I grabbed a nearby stool and reached up to a beam overhead. On it was a notebook covered in brown leather.

I pulled it down and blew off the thin layer of dust that had settled on its surface. "This is my father's notebook, where he keeps all the secrets of his magic tricks!"

I crouched beside Lukas so that he could see the notebook, too, but when I opened it, my shoulders fell.

"What's wrong?" Lukas asked.

"I can't read it."

"Let me help you."

He reached for it, but I pulled it closer to myself. "No," I said. "I can't read this . . . yet. But I will. Let's go."

While Lukas steadied himself on his feet, I tucked my father's notebook deep inside the shoulder bag that had been his once. Then we set out again in the early morning light to meet Ben. The walk was far more difficult for Lukas than he would admit. We had returned to the forest, and with every stumble over an exposed root in the road or a low-hanging branch, he had to stop and make himself breathe until the worst of the stinging had passed.

I'd added half his load of books to mine, and now with nineteen books in a sack slung over my shoulders, I was feeling an ache from my neck down into my legs. But I didn't complain. Things were worse for Lukas.

Hoping to turn his mind elsewhere, I said, "When we first met, I accused you of being a thief. I'm sorry about that."

He smiled over at me. "Don't be sorry. In fact, your accusation reminded me of the story I've been telling you of Rue. Well, not Rue, but the boy I told you about when we were back in the church. You may not know his story, but I do, for it was told to me from the very mouth of the frog who lives in a pond near the boy's home."

My eyes narrowed. "A frog?"

"A rather special frog, as you may have already imagined. For I have spoken to a thousand frogs in my life, and this was the only one who answered."

I giggled. "Does the boy know of this talking frog in the pond near his home?"

"Of course he does! In fact, the boy has never told the full truth of his life to anyone but this frog. You see, the boy has lied about himself for so long, that sometimes he forgets why he started working on Rue's land in the first place."

"Oh? Why did he start?"

"Do you remember the snake, the creature who first bargained for Rue in exchange for her father's life?"

"Yes."

Lukas shrugged. "Well, the boy knows certain things about the snake, about why he wants Rue's land. It isn't because the snake cares for Rue or her family—he doesn't. He only wants the land, and whether Rue gives it to him or he has to take it from her, it's all the same to him. The boy sees that and knows it is wrong and knows he has to help Rue and everyone on her land."

"Why did the boy care so much?"

Lukas didn't answer for a while, but finally said, "Because he understood that he had to make a choice. He had to fight the snake, or one day he might become the snake. So he began living in the forest, determined to start a new life on his own." Lukas paused again, briefly licking his lips as he stared down at the ground. "But it's nearly impossible to survive in the forest on your own. The boy met the bear, and they became friends. The boy knew that if he truly was friends with the bear, and with Rue, and all those she cared about, then he would have to help them fight against the snake."

My smile over at Lukas had changed to one of sympathy and warmth. "I don't think there was ever any worry of the boy becoming like the snake."

Lukas's eyes momentarily widened before he said, "We're all at risk of becoming the snake one day. The moment we start to choose what's easy or safe, instead of choosing what's right, we start to become like the snake."

"Maybe. But Rue would never do that. I'm sure in your story that Rue is looking forward to the day when her father recovers and the land is theirs again."

"When her father recovers," Lukas said softly. "Or when he returns."

EIGHTEEN

After an hour of walking, we arrived in Šiluva. Ben dashed out from the barn where we were supposed to deliver the books, his face nearly as white as his hair and his eye patch on crooked, from what must have been a terrible night of worrying.

"Where were you—" he began, then noticed Lukas hunched over. Gingerly, he lifted Lukas's bag off the one shoulder where he'd been carrying it and set it on the ground, then stood behind Lukas and pulled his shirt back enough to see what the soldiers had done to him. "Mercy upon you," he breathed.

"It would've been worse, if not for Audra," Lukas said.

"He wouldn't have been caught, if not for me," I said. "I'm no good at smuggling."

"Let's get these books inside," Ben said. "Then we'll decide what to do next."

I followed Ben and Lukas into what appeared to be an

ordinary barn, like any other that might be found in the countryside.

Ben directed Lukas to sit on a hay bale to rest, then glared back at me. "You say that you're the reason Lukas was caught?"

I lowered my eyes at the same time that Lukas said, "I made the mistake, not her. And her quick thinking probably saved my life."

"This is why I don't want either of you smuggling."

"I know the risks, Ben! And you've had your encounters with the soldiers too!"

That didn't help. Ben was becoming more upset, his face reddening as he spoke. "Neither of you should've been there in the first place! We should've stayed together. Or I should've sent you on different routes—"

I touched his arm. He hadn't seen me come so close to him, but now he looked down at me with eyes that were widened by fear. "Ben, we made it here alive, and we're both still on our feet. Everything will be all right. Can we finish delivering the books now?"

He drew in a slow breath and nodded. "Wait here," he mumbled to Lukas, then walked to a nearby stall and led the horse out. He gave me the reins with a gesture to tie it off to a post while he grabbed a rake to muck out the stall. Sure enough, beneath it all was a door cut into the floor, large enough for a single person, probably leading to an illegal bookshop like Milda's.

"Careful as you go down," Ben said as he descended. "It's a steep ladder."

"They're always steep," I said, putting my feet on the rung and smiling down at him.

"Too steep for me today," Lukas said from above. "I'll keep watch up here."

He sounded disappointed, and of course he would be. But the climb would be hard on his back. I was excited to describe to him how many shelves of books there were, to estimate the number of books and whether we'd brought any that weren't already down here. I'd describe it so well that he would feel he was seeing it for himself.

Except that when I reached the bottom, Ben was just lighting a candle, and instantly, all my anticipation vanished. This was a much larger room than what Milda had, with at least a dozen shelves for books. A dozen wide shelves that had been intended to hold hundreds of books. But only two shelves were partially filled.

If this were a pantry, the family would starve. If this were a shop, nobody would have any reason to bother coming in. At most, there were only fifty books in here.

No one would take the trouble to come down here for so few books. Ben was already loading the ones Lukas and I had brought onto a shelf. There weren't enough to make any difference at all.

I shook my head in frustration. "That's it? You were

right before, Ben—none of what we're doing matters. We came all this way, carried the most that we could, and it doesn't even fill a shelf!"

"Every book matters," Ben said.

"A single taste of bread matters to the man who is starving, but it won't save his life. We're not making any difference." My heart ached.

"Someone is coming!" Lukas called down, at first in alarm, then his tone calmed. "But I think it's mostly young people."

"Let them come," Ben said. "They were watching for you to arrive."

"Who was watching?" I asked.

My question was answered seconds later, when I heard the suppressed sounds of laughter and excited footsteps thump across the barn floor. Lukas's warnings to climb down carefully were ignored as, one by one, boys and girls near my own age began descending the ladder as quickly as possible, each of them rushing over to the shelves. They peered over one another's shoulders, pointing at the various titles and beginning their negotiations over who would get which book.

"Why, it's you!" I looked up to see Violeta, the girl who had pretended to find the fern blossom on Midsummer's Eve in order to save me from Officer Rusakov.

I smiled shyly, unsure of how to react. I had so much to thank her for, but how could I do that without explaining about everything else?

So I was relieved to see another familiar face, Filip, who had given me directions to Milda's village that same night. He took Violeta by the hand, then noticed me and said, "You're the girl who . . ." Then his voice became more somber. "We heard what happened to your home, to your family. We wondered what had become of you."

"But never expected this!" Violeta nudged Filip's arm with her elbow. "Didn't I tell you later that I thought we had saved someone important?"

"I'm not—" I began.

"You brought us books," Filip said. "If you ever wanted to thank us for helping you that night, you just did."

"And if *you* want to thank us," Ben said irritably, "you will choose a book and let us be on our way."

Violeta and Filip laughed uncomfortably but hurried to the shelf to choose their books before the best titles were gone. Already half the ones we'd brought had been taken away.

"What about grammar?" one girl said. "I want to write!"

"Any newspapers?" Filip asked, looking over the mostly barren shelf.

"Only one left," Ben said, handing over a copy. "Share it with anyone else who might ask."

"Of course," Filip said, then turned to me as he and Violeta left. "Thank you again, for all you do."

By the time the last person left, the shelves were emptier than when we had first arrived. But rather than feeling discouraged by that, I was now filled with excitement. The room felt like a kind of magic of its own had swept through here, leaving a spark I almost could see lingering in the air.

I leaned against the wood-enclosed wall and sighed with contentment. "I feel like we just experienced a whirlwind. Did you see how happy they were?"

From above us, Lukas said, "They always are."

I paused, then said, "The girl who wanted the grammar book so she could write . . ."

"Barely reading, and you want to write now?" Ben asked.

I stepped back. "No . . . I can't write. I wouldn't know what to say."

"Everyone has something worth saying," Lukas said.

I shook my head. "Not me."

"We'll find you some paper and let you discover that for sure." Ben shoved a hand into one pocket and looked around the room. "In the meantime, we have more shelves to fill. These books do matter, Audra."

I understood that now, as I hadn't before. I practically leapt up the ladder, eager for the next adventure. Lukas turned to us and smiled, even if his once-carefree grin was still full of too much pain.

Ben followed up behind me. "Lukas, we have a place nearby where it'll be safe for you to stay and recover. I'll borrow a wagon and get Audra back to Milda's home."

"No!" I said. "Ben, I did a good job!"

"You were better than that," Ben said. "And so was Lukas. But I won't let what happened to him happen to you too."

And so, despite my protests and frustration, it was arranged. An hour later, Lukas was settled in at the home of the same girl who had requested the book on grammar. Ben must have mentioned my interest in learning to write to her, because before we left on the wagon, she handed me a small tablet of paper and a pencil.

I tried to give it back to her. "This is too much."

But she pushed it toward me. "For what you did, this is too little a gift. Please, take it."

I tucked it inside a pocket of my apron for safekeeping, then settled in for the trip back to Milda's home.

"I want to carry books again," I said to Ben.

He glanced over at me. "It's not safe. The Cossacks know that Lukas escaped, so they'll be extra watchful of our usual routes."

"And when they find nothing, they'll go into the villages and search there," I said. "We need a safe place for the books."

Ben sighed. "Nowhere is safe, Audra. Not for the books, not for those who read them. And certainly nowhere is safe for a book carrier. It's not a question of when we are caught, only how much good we can do until it happens."

"Will you be caught one day? I can't believe that would ever happen to you."

Ben frowned and shook the reins of our horses to go faster. "I'm getting old and I'm not as quick as I used to be. Lukas is the next generation of book carrier, maybe you too, so your lives matter more than mine. I'll never be caught, but this is the work I'll be doing right up to my last day on earth."

CHAPTER
NINETEEN

I stayed with Milda for another three months without a word from either Ben or Lukas. Three long months during which people came to Milda's shop for baked goods and left with books tucked deep at the bottoms of their bags. Three months in which nothing new came in and her crowded shelves began to dwindle. Milda started offering trades on books rather than selling them, but that only slowed the problem, not solved it. She still held school, and for three months I sat in the back, watching the other students pore over the books as if nothing else existed but the words on the page.

I sat in the back . . . at first.

Roze was there every single day, having finished whatever book Milda had loaned to her the day before and eager for a new one. She invited me to sit beside her in school but I always declined. I didn't want her to know how dim I felt trying to decipher a single word in the same time as she finished an entire page.

Gradually, I began to understand that if I wanted to read, I needed to study the books for myself, not simply watch as others did it. So after school hours, when no one was looking, I returned to the secret schoolhouse and opened the same pages. At first, they were only words, just as before. Words I could speak and think, so why was it necessary to read them? But slowly, almost without my realizing what was happening, the words came to mean more because of how they were combined with other words. Words became ideas and thoughts, and it was just as Lukas had said—those thoughts were seeds that sprouted new ideas in my mind, growing and taking me to places I'd never even known existed.

Words!

They weren't simply a formation of letters to identify an object or an action. How could they be so little when one sentence set my heart pounding and another caused me to gasp with delight? How could they mean nothing when they lingered in my mind, followed me into my dreams, and challenged everything I'd always believed?

The Russian Empire wasn't afraid of a country that spoke a different language. They were afraid of a country whose language denied Russia's right to control it. The words wouldn't lead to our independence—words themselves, their very existence, *were* our independence. If we surrendered our books to them, we'd surrender our minds, leaving us hollowed-out puppets, ready to be controlled.

That's what Ben and Lukas and Milda and the kind priest and everyone else I'd met so far understood. If we lost our books, what was there left to live for?

"Did you write this, Audra?"

I turned with a start, realizing Milda had come into the secret school. It was nearly suppertime, and she was usually upstairs in the kitchen at this hour, so I hadn't expected her. I must have been so lost in my thoughts that I hadn't heard her approach. She was in a rather clever costume today, wearing a pair of crocheted shoes, one significantly longer than the other and stuffed with bits of fabric, and a pair of glasses with the lens in one eye particularly thick, making that eye seem almost double the size of the other. She removed those glasses now to focus on me properly. In her hands were a few papers I recognized.

"Did you write this?" she asked again.

I shrugged. "It's only a story."

I was attempting to write a fairy tale, adding my own thoughts to Lukas's story of Rue. Except in many ways, Rue was simply me . . . or the me I wished I were. I wanted to be her, and somehow, writing about a strong character made me feel stronger too.

Milda smiled and sat down in one of the chairs near me.

"Do you imagine stories in your head? Tales of adventure and danger and friendship?"

Slowly, I nodded, not sure of why she was asking such an odd question.

Milda glanced at my papers. "These characters in your story—do you hear them speak to you, a voice in your head that wishes to come alive on paper?"

Ashamed, I lowered my head and nodded again. Milda only pretended to be mad, to keep the soldiers away. But in admitting this, I was sure she would think I was truly as unbalanced as she pretended to be. And maybe I was.

I knew the characters who spoke in my head weren't real, of course. But thinking of them kept me company at night before I fell asleep, and sometimes they would whisper the words they wanted me to put into their stories. Sometimes I'd wake up in the night and search my alphabet book for the way to write those words. And then the characters would whisper even more.

Milda seemed to understand that. "You are a writer, Audra. You are meant to create with words, not simply absorb them."

I shook my head. "I'm not very good."

"You are good enough to have characters come alive in your mind, and that is no small thing," Milda said. "I wonder how you must feel to know that these characters belong to you, and to you only. How it must be when they visit your imagination in hopes that you might bring them to life for the rest of the world."

I glanced up. "By writing them on paper?"

"Yes." Milda handed me my story. "You brought these characters alive for me, and now they are my friends too. But until I read your words, they never existed. You were born for books, Audra. To read them, to create them, and to save them."

A short silence followed while I stared at my papers and thought of all that Milda had said. I didn't know if she was right, that I was born for books, but I certainly was coming to love them. Perhaps one day I would create a Lithuanian book that could be shared all over the country, a story that would do for others what Milda's books had done for me.

Until then, I had other work to do.

"I want to deliver books again," I said. "Please, Milda."

Now her smile faded. "It's not safe. There has been a greater Cossack presence in town this month. I cannot stop those who come into my shop to buy them, but to deliver one . . ."

"If people are going to get the books anyway, let's do it the safest way possible for everyone. Let me deliver them."

She sighed. "All right. Get your father's bag. No one should pay any attention to that. Perhaps it's time to start again."

I couldn't have raced up the ladder fast enough.

At first, she let me take only one or two at a time, simple deliveries around the village, and never to anyone's home. Instead, I'd leave the books at prearranged drop sites, at the base of an overgrown gravestone or behind a loose rock in a stone wall, or inside the hollow of a tree. I never knew who came to pick up the books and I never asked. I didn't want to know, just as I didn't want them to know my name.

But we were still left with the problem of a diminishing supply of books. Milda's collection was half what it had been when I first met her.

"Is there no word from Ben or Lukas?" I asked.

"None," Milda said. "Let's hope it means they've been busy."

"Then why aren't they asking for my help? Autumn is passing fast and soon it will be too cold for smuggling."

"We hope so!" Milda saw my surprised reaction and added, "We want ice on the soldiers' noses if they go out, deep snow they must trudge through on their patrols. We want freezing rain that makes them so miserable that they stay in their barracks, or near the public fires in the villages."

"But if we smuggle, then there's ice on our noses, or freezing rain on our clothes!"

Milda grinned. "Aren't we lucky to be stronger than the soldiers?"

"We can't wait for winter. Another month and your books will be gone!" Almost without thinking, I added, "If

Ben won't bring the books, I'll go to Prussia and get them myself."

Milda drew back, her eyes wide with alarm. "You have no idea how dangerous a border crossing can be, Audra. The soldiers know where our books come from, so they watch the Prussian border with the eyes of an eagle, always listening carefully for the smuggler's footsteps or following his tracks. No one may ever have the talent for it that your father did, not even Ben. Let's be patient awhile longer. More books will come." Milda set her hands on her lap and let out a sigh. "I do have one more request. It was for a prayer book, the one with the green fabric binding. There is one last copy below. Will you get it?"

Of course I would. I lifted the hidden stairs and raced down the ladder to find the book. I didn't need Milda to describe it for me any longer. I could read the titles well enough now to know what I was grabbing. I held up a candle and passed it from book to book, looking for a match for the letters forming inside my head.

Except I didn't find it. Or rather, before I found it, I came across the book I had delivered to Milda after my parents' arrest, the one with the aged black leather binding and the lock on the end. I pulled it off the shelf and sat down on the stool, using the candle to better examine the lock.

When I'd given it to Milda, she'd asked for the key to the book, and Lukas had even shaken out the bedsheet to be sure it hadn't fallen inside. There was no key. But the package had traveled some distance in my arms, being used as a pillow, breaking my fall when I'd jumped into the ravine, and nearly toppling with me into the river. If there had been a key, I easily could have lost it. And I'd never find it again. Which meant this book would never be opened, not unless I broke the lock, and I couldn't stand the thought of doing that.

I turned it to its side, but if there had ever been a title, it had worn away. I couldn't even tell what the book was about.

"What's taking so long?" Milda called.

I replaced the book on the shelf and then continued to examine the other titles until I found the one Milda had requested. When I brought it back up the ladder, I found her waiting with a crocheted quilt and some ribbon.

"What's this book for?" I asked.

Milda smiled. "It's a wedding gift. The book is the gift; the quilt is the disguise!"

I giggled and helped her wrap the quilt around the book, then tie it off with the ribbon. "Where should I deliver the gift?"

Milda glanced back at the clock hanging from her wall. "The wedding will soon begin at the church. Go there and follow the wedding party to the reception. Have a fun evening and enjoy the celebrations, but"—she added as I began to run off—"stay away from the Cossacks. They've been good to let us keep our traditions so far, but we must always be careful."

"I will!" I kissed Milda on the cheek and ran out the door with the package in my arms. I'd never been to a wedding before, which was exciting enough, but the idea of delivering a book to the new couple about to begin their lives together made it even better.

I made it to the church just in time to see the bride entering with a wreath of rue around her head. I paused there and swallowed a lump in my throat. I imagined I could almost hear my father's voice calling me, "Little Rue, come inside, it's getting dark!"

"Little Rue," he'd say before bedtime. "Remember that I love you."

And what would he say now? "Little Rue, I am waiting to come home. Bring me home soon."

"I can't, Papa," I mumbled beneath my breath. "I'm sorry. I'm so sorry."

Then I walked the rest of the way to the church, ducking inside to see the bride already kneeling at the altar beside her groom. The wreath of rue had been replaced with other flowers now, because the bride would be a married woman and rue was symbolic of childhood.

Maybe similarly, I was Little Rue no longer. No longer the innocent child I had once been. And that was a good thing, because I had proven myself strong enough now for so much more.

When the priest pronounced them married, the groom placed a ring on his wife's finger, kissed her, then led her right past me outside the church and across the road near a barn where the evening's celebration would continue. It had been decorated with candles and ribbons and lace, and with all the colors of the harvest.

At first, I stood back to watch the families perform their rituals to protect the new couple in their life together. When they'd finished, trays of bread were brought out along with wine and bowls with salt for everyone to eat. It wasn't particularly tasty—I felt my face scrunch as I tasted the salt—but a woman nearby explained the symbolism. Bread represented the hard work of building a family, salt was for the tears the couple would shed, and the wine was for their celebrations.

"What a lucky coincidence, meeting you here!" I jumped and saw Lukas had snuck up behind me yet again.

I smirked at him. "The last time you surprised me like that, I nearly broke you in half with a stick."

"Nearly," he said. "But thankfully, not entirely in half. Would you like to dance?"

I realized I was still holding the quilt with the book inside. I'd wanted to present it to the bride and groom myself, but that seemed absurd, given that other gifts had simply been left on a table near the side of the party.

I walked with Lukas to set the quilt down, but by then, bowls of grain had been brought out to toss at the bride and groom, symbolic of our wishes for the couple to have a rich and successful life together, full of bounteous harvests.

I tossed one handful forward, then felt a splatter of grain on me.

"Sorry," Lukas said with a wink. "I missed."

I grabbed another handful and threw it directly in his face, then grinned. "So did I!"

Lukas reached for his next handful, but the music had abruptly stopped playing and the clopping sound of horses could be heard on the road behind us.

Lukas leaned out, then the muscles of his face tightened, and through clenched teeth, he said, "We have to go *now*."

I set down the bowl of grain and began to follow him away from the road. But we'd only taken a few steps that way before more Cossack soldiers appeared ahead of us too, and this group was holding torches.

Why were they holding torches?

"Everyone remain where you are," a man said from behind me. I didn't need to turn around to recognize the voice of Officer Rusakov. He added, "We're going to do a search. And you all had better hope that we don't find anything suspicious."

TWENTY

Despite Officer Rusakov's orders, Lukas and I absolutely could not remain where we were. If these soldiers performed even a basic search of the gifts, they would find the book. Surely many guests here had seen me arrive with Milda's quilt. It would only take one guest to point me out.

Without calling attention to himself, Lukas slowly sank behind a large wooden barrel and directed me to do the same. I shook my head, worried that I'd be spotted. Rusakov called for his soldiers to gather around and receive their orders, and the instant he did, Lukas grabbed my hand and yanked me down.

"In this job, you don't hesitate," he hissed. "When I tell you to do something, you do it!"

I wanted to argue and tell him that I had enough sense to take care of myself, but I also knew that if he hadn't pulled me down here, I'd still be standing up in full view of the soldiers.

Lukas craned his head in the direction he intended for us to go and then began crawling. We weren't taking the nearest exit—there were too many open spaces we'd have to cross. Instead, we were crawling toward the barn.

I'd thought there was a chance of some of the wedding guests stopping us from leaving. After all, if they were in harm's way, why shouldn't we be with them too? But they merely stepped forward or backward as needed to allow us to pass.

Or maybe they were only vaguely aware of us. The soldiers had begun their search, and it was one designed to destroy. Behind me, I saw the flutter of feathers being torn from the pillows the couple had received as gifts, and the crash of a pot on the ground as another gift was tossed heedlessly.

We had barely crossed inside the barn when I heard the thud on the ground. The book.

"What is this?" Rusakov called to his comrades. "What have we here?"

The partygoers had become absolutely silent, not a single person moving. Lukas pulled me to my feet, gesturing that we needed to run out the other end of the barn. But I couldn't, not yet.

"Who gave this book to the bride and groom?" Officer Rusakov shouted. "Confess and save the others from your punishment!"

I took a deep breath and started to turn, but Lukas pulled me back, sharply shaking his head at me.

I shook my head back at him, desperately trying to communicate my thoughts. He had heard Rusakov as well as I did. Someone was going to be punished for that book and everyone out there was innocent. I couldn't just stand here and let that happen.

"You have until the count of five," Rusakov said. "*Adeen, dva . . .*"

Lukas tried to tug me away, but I yanked my hand back. He leaned toward my ear and whispered, "Everyone here will be punished anyway. Trust me."

"*Tree, chityri.*" Rusakov hesitated, then, "*Pyat'.*" When still nobody confessed to giving the book, he said, "Search the village. If you find a second book, this town will burn." Then he added, "Starting with that barn."

This time, I didn't need to be pulled. Lukas and I ran for our lives as torches were thrown inside the barn, the dry straw beneath our feet immediately bursting into flames. We raced through the other side and kept going until we had entered the nearest patch of trees. From there, I sank to my knees, sobbing. "That's our fault, Lukas."

"That's the fault of the Cossack occupiers and the foolish laws of their tsar," he corrected. "We can still help. I know some of the homes that have books. We must get as many out as we can, before the Cossacks get there."

I stood again, ready to follow him anywhere. "Show me."

TWENTY-ONE

We crept three roads past where the soldiers were searching, and even then, Lukas told me to be extra careful when crossing from one house to the other. We visited the first house together, knocking on the door. When an older gentleman answered, Lukas said, "They're searching homes."

The gentleman immediately nodded, thanked us in Lithuanian, then shut the door.

"He didn't understand the problem!" I said as we hurried to the next house.

"He understood," Lukas said. "But he was already prepared to hide his own books. He doesn't need our help."

No one answered at the second door, so we walked inside a small, single-room home. Lukas said, "Search everywhere the Cossacks would, but we only have two minutes. Hurry!"

There were few furnishings. Against one wall was a thin straw mattress on a rope bed frame, a spinning wheel, and a trunk for clothing. I lifted the mattress to check its weight, but it felt too light to hold any books within its seams. Next, I searched the trunk, and sure enough, at the bottom was the same Lithuanian prayer book I had just given to the new couple. I snatched it into my arms, then turned to see where Lukas had pulled a small pile of Lithuanian newspapers from beneath a stack of wood. He tossed them in the fireplace and lit a match.

I gripped the book in my hands. "You won't—"

"Burn the book?" Lukas shook his head. "The newspapers are one thing, but I'll never burn a book. That's what *they* do. Take that one with us. We'll find a better place to hide it and return it when this is over."

Lukas directed me to the next home while he crossed the road to check the homes there. Word of what the Cossacks were doing must have begun to spread through the town, because I'd only knocked once when a woman opened the door with a stack of eight or nine books and thrust them into my arms. "Take them and go!" she cried.

Lukas had been given a small stack of books, too, and said, "Give your books to me and I'll take them into the forest. You go and collect more books. Meet me where we were before. I'll hide them there."

I gave him my books, then ran another few roads ahead, always conscious of the shouted orders of the Cossacks in the homes not far behind me, fully aware that I could run right into them at any moment. Families in the first three homes I checked either assured me they had no books or that they were properly hidden, and the fourth home was empty, so I entered it to do a search, like before. I found a thin book in the back room and was just standing to leave when the door burst open with an announcement in Russian that a search for illegal items was to be undertaken.

I quickly stuffed the book between my shirt and skirt, then retied my apron tighter, hoping it would hold the weight of the book. It might, if I didn't move too much. I was still working at the knot when the Cossack entered the room.

"*Stoy!*" he said. "Did you not hear me?"

He had shouted so loud, I'd heard it vibrate through my heart. He'd interpret my silence as hiding something, which I absolutely was.

So I turned to him and placed a hand in cupping shape behind my ear, then shook my head, suggesting to him that I hadn't heard him because I *could not* hear.

His eyes narrowed and he asked my name in Russian. I squinted back and shook my head again. He swept one arm at me, knocking me to the ground and insulting my intelligence. I thought that was rather stupid of him instead, to have believed the inability to hear was somehow linked to one's intelligence. He could hear fine and didn't appear any smarter than the common pig.

I kept my place on the ground while he finished

searching the bedroom. I knew he wouldn't find anything in there, because I'd already removed the book . . . if there was only one book.

Except there wasn't. When he returned to the main room, in his arms was a tall stack of Lithuanian books. He crossed to the fireplace and began stirring the embers of the fire that must have cooked a supper recently.

"No," I mouthed. "Not the books."

And no, it wasn't the books. When the fire had rekindled, he grabbed the unburnt end of a fiery stick, pushed past me to enter the bedroom, then dropped the stick in the center of the bed. At first I thought the stick would burn itself out, but within seconds, the quilt lit and began to blacken, then the fire spread. The soldier eyed me until he was certain it had taken hold, then frowned, picked up the books again, and carried them out the door.

The instant he left, I ran to the bed and folded up the unburnt edges of the quilt in hopes of smothering the fire, but it had already spread to the mattress beneath. I dashed over to the pump at the kitchen sink, filling a bucket of water and dumping it on the fire to douse the flames.

Then I opened the door and peered out. Other officers were on this road by now, but when their attention turned elsewhere, I darted from the home and ran until I couldn't see them anymore. If only I could have gotten far enough away to no longer hear what they were doing. One by one behind me, I heard the *whoosh* of flames as homes were lit on fire, preceded by the shouts of soldiers calling to one another the numbers of illegal books they had found in the homes.

"*Tree.*" Three.

"*Vosim.*" Eight.

"*Nul.*" None. The soldier laughed.

No books had been in that home. The soldier merely wanted to burn it.

Up ahead, I saw Lukas with another stack of books in his arms, racing up the hillside toward the forest. I started to follow him, when a young girl darted from her home with a single book. "Will you hide this?"

I nodded, but as I turned to follow Lukas, I crashed directly into a soldier who was emerging from another home. I fell on my backside, both books landing in my lap.

With a snarl, he grabbed my arm and hefted me off the ground, but once my feet were planted, I gave him a fierce kick on the shin, hard enough that I might have broken a toe to do it. He dropped my arm, allowing me to squirm out of his grip and run. He called after me, that when he caught me again I'd pay for this, but he didn't chase me. Instead, when I looked back, he was picking up the books I'd saved and was walking away with them.

The books I'd meant to save.

The books I hadn't saved.

My heart shattered.

A few meters ahead, Lukas was motioning me toward him, and when I caught up, he led the way into the forest. Others from the village had gathered here as well, and from behind the trees, sobbing women and children and stoic men with crushed hearts watched as a dozen or more homes went up in flames. Just as mine had.

"How many books did we save?" I mumbled to Lukas.

"Not enough." He pointed to a pile of thirty or forty books, then looked up at me. "Come with me. There's something you need to see."

TWENTY-TWO

I trudged behind Lukas deep enough inside the forest that we wouldn't be seen from the village but close enough to its border that we still got glimpses of the horror. I saw roaring flames with their light filtered against the layers of trees; I choked on the pungent odor of smoke as homes were destroyed. But was it only the homes?

Many of the villagers who hadn't escaped into the forest had been herded into the square, and there I saw another fire in the center of the road.

Burning no buildings this time, no homes. But I knew what this fire was.

Books.

This fire smelled different from other kinds of fires. I knew it was different because it wasn't only ink and paper being consumed by the flames, but also the characters themselves, and their worlds and feelings and stories. Did they cry out for themselves, begging to be saved? I believed so, for I was certain I could hear them calling to me.

A sudden panic sent a shudder through me. "Lukas, why are they—"

He put a finger to his lips, then led us closer to the village square. There, the fire burned bright, its flames crackling with a hunger for more fuel, greedy in its destruction.

Each lick of a flame took knowledge from us. It consumed our ideas and our stories, and what little freedom we thought we had claimed for ourselves with our smuggling.

They were burning our books, and with them, I felt like holes were being burned into my heart. How could they do this? How could they attach such venom to words on paper?

I followed Lukas to the crest of a hill overlooking the square. Fifty or sixty people were gathered around the bonfire—forced to stand there by the ten Cossack soldiers patrolling the road behind them. The townsfolk had their heads hung low, unable to look at the fire and unwilling to challenge the soldiers. Occasionally I saw a woman or child raise a hand to wipe a tear from their face.

Officer Rusakov ordered the villagers to make way for him, and when he pushed through, he picked up a book that had fallen from the stack and threw it back onto the fire. I recognized it as the same alphabet book that Lukas had given me. Maybe my copy of it, or maybe someone else's; I didn't know, and it didn't matter. A piece of me seemed to die as the book was swallowed up in the flames. Perhaps no other book in that stack was a greater threat to this man and the tsar he served so well.

For that book was where it all began. Those simple letters became words that became our identity. That book was all we had to save our future; I saw that now more than ever before. If we were forced to speak a language that was not our own, then how long could we hold to thoughts that were our own? That was why I had to smuggle. If we failed to deliver books, then the collapse of Lithuania was only a generation away.

Surely this had been the tsar's intention ever since the press ban began—not to rob the older generation of their traditions, but merely to wait out their lives. And in their place, to raise a new generation, people my age, who didn't know our traditions had ever existed.

That's why they had to burn the alphabet books.

Officer Rusakov turned his back to the flames, and the people nearest to him instinctively stepped back. He began walking a circle around the fire, shouting, "You peasants, you fools! Why do you insist on clinging to that which is past, that which is dead? You are Russians now. Accept that and we will have peace."

He picked up another book, then held it up for the group to see. "Why must you pray in an illegal language? Do you think your God will not listen if your prayers are spoken in my language?" Then that book also went into the fire.

He lifted a third book, holding it against the firelight to read the title, then said, "What need do you have for Lithuanian history now? There is no Lithuania. There is nothing here but Russia."

An older man stepped forward from the group and spoke in Lithuanian. "No, Officer Rusakov. We are not Russian; we are not one of you. We are Lithuanians, and long after you have been called back home, we will still be here."

Rusakov smirked. "Some of these people, perhaps. But you will not." With a distinct tilt of his head, two other soldiers grabbed the man, forced him to his knees, and whacked him across his back with the butt of a rifle. I sucked in a breath, then stood, ready to walk down the hill and defend the man as best as I could.

"No, Audra." Lukas grabbed my arm and pulled me down behind the bushes with him. "You can't save him."

By the time I looked at him again, two soldiers were dragging the man away. Above the gasps and cries of the crowd, Officer Rusakov said, "This is what happens to those who defy the Russian Empire! Everyone, go home. You have twenty seconds to leave the square or you'll join this man in prison!"

It took less time than that for the square to empty, including the soldiers who were prodding people down the roads, continuing to harass and frighten them. Rusakov picked up another book and opened it, shaking his head as he ran his finger down the page; then it was dumped onto the fire as well along with the remaining books. As soon as he'd finished, he shouted out an order that everyone had better get inside their homes and remain there for the night. When calls for help came back to him, he abandoned the fire and went to see what the new trouble was.

Or really, to create even more trouble than what had already been done.

I immediately turned to Lukas. "I'm going down there to save what I can."

"Are you mad? No, you aren't."

"I'm not asking for your permission."

"And you're not getting it. If someone sees you—"

"If I'm going to smuggle books, shouldn't I also save them? There are ones on the edge of the fire that may only be singed."

Lukas sighed. "All right, but I'll go with you and keep watch. When I say run, we run. Agreed?"

I nodded, and this time I led the way down the hill with Lukas immediately checking the different roads leading into the square. By the time he whispered that everything seemed safe, I'd already slid four books away from the fire. I couldn't read the titles in the firelight, but that didn't matter. Every book had suddenly become a life I could save, something that breathed out ideas as unique to the world as every person was unique.

Right on top of the stack where Rusakov had dumped the last of the books sat a thick book that hadn't started burning yet, but it soon would. I leaned over the fire as far as I dared and reached for the book, but when I did, a breath of flame licked my arm. I yanked my arm back with a cry, unsure of how bad the burn was, but my skin was already screaming with pain.

"Someone's coming." Lukas ran toward me, scooped up the saved books in his arms, then said, "Let's go!"

I still had the rescued book from the top of the pile, and I hoped whatever it was would be worth the pain in my arm. There was no time for us to run back up the hill, so instead, Lukas pulled me behind a cobbler's shop. He glanced down at my burned arm. "Oh no, Audra. Does it hurt?"

My arm felt as if it were still on fire, but I couldn't do anything about that here, nor did I get the chance to answer Lukas's question. Instead, Rusakov must have returned to the square. In his deep voice, he said to the other soldiers with him, "Wait here until it's burned down to ashes, then get some peasants to clean it up. If anyone else tries to challenge you, shoot them and make sure this village knows why we had to do it."

They didn't *have to* do it. They had chosen to do all of this, to ruin a wedding, to search the homes of peaceful people, and then to destroy them for the crime of wanting their own language, their own lives. I hated that Rusakov saw himself as any kind of a hero for what he had done here tonight.

"Hurry with this job," Rusakov added as he began to leave the square. "I'm going for one more arrest—we know where all these books are coming from."

Milda.

I turned to Lukas, locking eyes with him in silent desperation. Milda was going to be arrested!

Lukas cocked his head, suggesting that we should take another route away from the square, and I followed directly on his heels, forgetting my burn. Forgetting everything but the need to warn Milda before the soldiers got to her.

If they did, I was certain her fate would end up just as it had for my parents. Arrested, possibly sentenced to Siberia. Leaving me alone again.

I would not let that happen.

TWENTY-THREE

We were almost within sight of Milda's home when Roze rounded the corner, nearly crashing into us. Tears streamed down her face as soon as she saw me.

"Audra, I was looking for you!"

"Is it Milda?"

Roze folded her hand into mine. "Yes, she told me to sneak out and find you, to warn you to stay away. I escaped through the shed out back, but they almost saw me."

Lukas was still carrying the books I'd saved from the fire. I turned to him. "We've got to help Milda."

"No!" Roze tugged at my arm. "Milda wants us to save her books!"

"She's right," Lukas said. "If they find the books, then they'll have all the evidence they need against Milda."

"They must already have evidence against her—that's why they are there! Lukas, we all care about the books, but this is Milda's life!"

Lukas exhaled deeply, leaving lines of worry across his forehead. "You're right too. Any ideas for Milda?"

My hand had been absently fingering the items in my father's satchel while I'd been speaking. My fingers passed over one of my father's tricks, and my stomach began to twist. I had an idea. A dangerous, terrible, almost-certain-to-fail idea.

Almost certain to fail. Which meant I had some small chance of succeeding. It would have to be enough.

Starting with Lukas. If he knew my plan, he'd never let me do it. I turned to him. "If Roze helps me get Milda out of the house, can you get the books out of the secret school?"

His eyes narrowed. "What are you going to do?"

I smiled as if it were nothing so big, as if the idea weren't making my hands shake and my stomach feel sick. "Just a little magic. I'll meet you in the forest as soon as we get Milda."

I hoped. One of the tricks was something I'd never done before, though I'd seen my father do it many times.

Lukas nodded and ran off toward the back of Milda's home. Once he'd left, I said to Roze, "How many officers are inside?"

"Two."

"You snuck out, can you sneak back in?"

"Probably." Now she looked as nervous as I felt.

"Go in, and when the two soldiers are distracted, you've got to get Milda out the same way you left. I can only give you a couple of minutes, so you'll need to move fast." I looked in her eyes, seeing them fill with tears. "Roze, can you do this?"

She nodded, though her voice quivered when she squeaked out the words "I can." She looked as if she wished the ground would swallow her up rather than have to carry out my plan, and I completely understood. I was just as terrified.

"Go," I said. "Hurry!"

She ran off in the opposite direction as Lukas had gone, and when I was alone on the street, I walked to the front of Milda's home and slipped my father's magic ring over my forefinger. Papa wore it on his pinky finger, but it was too big for me there. I put three small cups facing downward on the flat end of the rail of the fence in front of Milda's home. Next, I pulled out his disappearing sheet. It was only a length of fabric with three bars running through a seam at the top. I hooked the three bars together to form one solid bar that held the fabric at its full width. That was the part of the trick I'd never done before, and I genuinely didn't know if I could do it, but I laid it at my feet anyway.

I hoped Roze was in place to rescue Milda, because I was about to begin.

Until becoming a book smuggler, I'd rarely spoken at all, and even when I did, it was always in the softest voice I could manage. But now I needed a loud voice if I was to get the attention of the soldiers inside. It felt like I was screaming to them, but I didn't think I was. I tried to sound friendly when I shouted out, "Cossack officers, if you're looking for book smugglers, I know where they are!"

That brought one officer out to the front of the home. I needed both of them. If an officer was left inside to guard Milda, my plan wouldn't work.

He said, "You're just a little girl. Go away or we'll arrest you as well!"

I forced myself to smile, though it surely looked stiff and unnatural . . . and suspicious. My heart was pounding so loud in my ears it was all I could hear—could he hear it too? So I spoke even louder to cover up my terror. "I'm a girl who can do magic. So I propose a game. Tell me where I've hidden the coin beneath these three cups and I'll answer all your questions far better than the old woman inside."

He shifted his rifle into his other hand, making sure I saw it. "I have better ways to make you answer my questions, girl."

I swallowed that threat down with another smile. "So you think I can outsmart you with a simple magic trick?"

The second officer ducked his head outside. "What's this?"

The first man pointed to me. "She's offering to trade information for a bit of magic."

The second officer grinned. "I have a daughter about your age who once saw a magician perform on the streets of Kaunas. She's been fascinated with magic ever since."

She had almost certainly seen my father. I hoped he would be proud of me now. Not my courage, for if he knew how badly my legs were shaking, he'd know I had none. But perhaps of my skills as a magician.

In my left hand, I raised a coin. "Watch this carefully and tell me where it is when I'm finished." Then I set it on the railing of the fence and covered it with the center cup. With my eyes on the men, I began switching the places of the cups. The railing was narrow enough that sometimes almost half of the cup crossed past the edge of the beam, which worked out well for me. I knew the soldiers were watching for the coin to drop to the ground, but it wouldn't. I felt when the coin dropped and immediately caught on my father's magic ring—my father's magnetic ring. I folded it inside my palm and continued stirring the cups around.

When I'd finished, I said, "Guess correctly the first time and I'll answer every question you have. Guess correctly the second time and I'll answer three questions. But if you don't guess it, I will leave without answering any questions, agreed?"

They grunted, certain they would guess the correct cup. The first officer pointed to the center cup. I lifted it, and naturally the coin wasn't there.

"Idiot!" his companion said, then pointed to the cup last in line. I lifted it, too, and now came the trickiest part—replacing the coin in my palm to make it look as if it had been there all along.

I said, "Thank you for playing, but the coin is here."

I lifted the third cup with all the fingers of my right hand, dropping the coin to the railing as I did, and there it was when the soldiers saw it.

But the first man said, "You'll still answer our questions, girl."

Which I'd expected would happen. So I backed up. "One more trick first. Watch what happens when I lift this."

I raised the disappearing cloth. The idea was to replace one person with another while the cloth was lifted, but I didn't have that luxury. Instead, I hooked the bar over the top of the branch of an overhanging tree, then immediately turned to run. I figured it'd give me only a few seconds' start, but that would have to be enough.

Except that the instant I turned, I bumped directly into a third soldier who'd come up behind me.

Rusakov.

He grabbed my arm and, without a word, dragged me with him through the cloth, then up the stairs into Milda's home, dropping me on the wood floor near her fireplace. The other two officers had run in ahead of us and now looked at each other, silently asking where Milda was. Then I saw the expression exchanged between them, an unspoken agreement to say nothing to Rusakov about how an old woman escaped while they were distracted by a magic trick.

If they would say nothing, neither would I. But I did have to defend myself.

"It was only a little fun," I began. "Just a few tricks."

"No trick can save you now." Rusakov crouched low and said, "Everything that has happened tonight is your fault, a consequence of your crimes. Yet one question remains. Will you at least save yourself?"

I lowered my eyes. He was right: That was the only question that mattered now. Milda was gone, Lukas was emptying out the books from beneath this very room. But would I do what was necessary to save myself?

TWENTY-FOUR

I was told to stand again, and when I did, Officer Rusakov walked a full circle around me. "Two days," he said. "Were you not told to meet me in two days?"

"Only if I had names for you," I said, my fists clenched tight in hopes that would give me courage. "Which I didn't."

Rusakov wasn't impressed. "We both know that is a lie, and a poorly told lie at that. I can see in your face that you know a great many names. Those who hide illegal books, those who teach from them. Those who smuggle them. Aside from your own name, of course . . . Miss Zikaris."

He saw my burned arm and clutched it with his hand, then squeezed until tears flowed down my cheeks. "How will you carry books with a terrible burn like that?"

I remained silent. I wanted to say that it didn't matter how I carried them, only that I would continue to do so as long as I had any strength for it.

But I didn't say that, because it would almost certainly prompt Rusakov to guarantee I was no longer able to carry books, and I didn't want to know what that would mean for me. Besides that, I barely could speak with the way he was twisting my burned arm.

"Sir . . ." one of the officers in the room murmured.

Rusakov released my arm but pointed outside. "I was told you'd arrested a smuggler in this home, an old woman? Perhaps one of you should go find her before I ask how this girl beside me was able to trick you both?"

The more senior of the Cossacks immediately trotted out the door, probably hoping Rusakov would target the other man left behind for having made such a critical error.

Or that he would target me instead.

I clutched my arm to my chest, somehow able to breathe again, though my tears continued to fall.

"Do you know why this was necessary?" he asked. "To punish this town as we have?"

"Because you're cruel and take pleasure in our pain?" That's what I wanted to say, but I didn't. Just as I rarely said anything that I really wanted to say, and never spoke if silence was enough. I merely held the words inside me, to protect them from what others might do or think.

I wondered if my failure to speak was like an unread book, full of ideas that ought to be read, but living out its life in silence. The book had no control over who read its pages, but I did have control of myself. I had to speak up for what I believed in.

"The people here are innocent," I whispered.

"No, they're not. You are a smuggler, child, so surely you know how extensive the crime is. A few of you carry the illegal books over the borders, others hide them, others teach from them. One crime is the same as the other, and all must be shut down." He crouched in front of me, piercing me with his cruel eyes. I fully expected to begin wilting in the heat of his stare and looked away in hopes of preserving the little courage I had left.

He sniffed. "You probably think that this has been a bad night, but that once morning comes, things will look brighter, and then your smuggling can continue as before. If so, then you are wrong, Miss Zikaris. Before we leave this town, we will have destroyed every illegal word and action here. And then we will move to the next town, and the next. Everywhere you smugglers go, I will follow, and I will bring fire and punishment with me. Do you believe me?"

I didn't answer, I couldn't.

"Look at me!" he demanded. I forced myself to obey him, and he repeated, "Do you believe me?"

Slowly I nodded, and I meant it. Books were important—I understood that now. Words were important and they had power and force, but not enough to overcome the Russian Empire or the size of their armies. We were attempting to stop a raging river with a thin barrier of ink and paper. We never had any chance of winning.

Rusakov stood again, hovering over me. As before, I felt his eyes looking down on me the way I'd feel the heat of the sun on my head. But I didn't look up. I didn't want him to see how afraid I was.

Rusakov grunted. "Your criminal parents clearly failed to teach you proper manners, Miss Zikaris. Do you not respect my authority? Do you not respect the law?"

"The law is wrong," I said. The words had forced themselves out, unable to be contained any longer. And once unleashed, they continued to erupt from me, angry and determined. "What you've done here tonight is wrong, and I will not pretend to respect it."

He smirked at me, obviously amused by my boldness, but not by my message. "You are the reason for tonight's demonstration here. I know you are the one who brought the book to that wedding tonight. Did you get it from this home?"

"No." I got it from a secret hiding place *beneath* this home, which in my mind was an entirely different place.

"Then where did it come from?"

"You searched this entire village for books tonight. I know how many you found, how many you *burned*. Why do you care about a single book given as a gift? Shut down one source and a dozen more will pop up in its place with fifty more book carriers determined to do their job."

He nodded. "If that is true, then we must put our boots down on the people with greater harshness than we have already done. If you refuse to tell me the source for the book you carried as a gift tonight, I may have to continue burning this village. I cannot take the chance of having missed a source."

I looked Rusakov in the eyes and steadied my voice enough to say, "Please don't do that. The people here are good and are just trying to make a life for themselves."

"Then let them live. Where did you get that book?"

If he thought I was incapable of telling a good lie, then he was mistaken. What else had my father devoted his life to but telling a good lie, whether as a street magician or a carrier, or even with the lies he had told me, to make me believe his life was as simple as he pretended it was? I had learned well.

"I brought it directly over the border from Prussia," I said to Rusakov. "I've hidden my stash in the forest, above the village square. The woman who lives in this home gave me a blanket to deliver to the wedding as a gift, only a blanket. I added one of my own smuggled books to the gift. She didn't know."

"Go and find those books," Rusakov ordered the Cossack who still remained in the home, then turned back to me. "And you'd better hope they find some. Otherwise I'll know you are lying, and we'll start again with the questions. I will not be so merciful to you the next time."

I sent out a silent prayer that Lukas had left the books where I'd last seen them, and more important, that he'd be far away from them before the officers arrived. I desperately hoped he would be. Because if not, they'd see the scars from where he'd been whipped and realize he'd been caught smuggling before. And this time, his punishment wouldn't end with a simple whipping.

Nor would mine. Rusakov took my arm and led me outside, handing me over to a soldier guarding a prison wagon. "Put her inside," he said. "We're not finished with her yet." I started to move forward, but he grabbed my father's bag and lifted it from my shoulder. "And this is surely illegal too. Put it on the burn pile."

"No!" I cried, clutching for it, and failing. The door to the prison wagon slammed shut in my face, and I saw my father's bag, the last piece of him I'd ever have, being carried away.

CHAPTER
TWENTY-FIVE

A wave of terror flushed through me once the prison wagon began to move. Surely they wouldn't send a child to an actual prison!

Did they think of me as a child? My crimes had certainly equaled even those of the adult smugglers, so they owed me no mercy.

But I hoped they would grant it.

Did Lukas know they were taking me away, or Milda? Were they able to get the books out of Milda's home? Would it be burned, too, like so many others? Or perhaps the entire town would be on fire before morning.

I cried for the first hour of the ride, until I had no more tears. Until my eyes were so swollen that they felt thick and heavy. After that, I lay on my side in the wagon, my arms wrapped tight around myself, existing in that middle place between sleep and wake where nightmares happened, until the wagon finally stopped.

I sat up just as the door opened, and there was Rusakov again. For a brief moment, he seemed to soften as he noticed my tearstained cheeks and reddened eyes. Then his expression hardened again as he reached in and dragged me from the wagon.

We had passed through an archway with iron doors that slammed shut behind us, and now I was in a courtyard in front of a large building constructed of massive stone blocks, with a few barred windows and Russian flags everywhere standing as a reminder of who was in charge.

With his hand gripping my left arm, Rusakov led me through a main set of doors, though I wasn't taken to a cell as I'd expected. Instead, I was thrown into a room near the entrance, one without a single window and with a door that was locked from the outside. There was no furniture, but I sat on the floor and tried not to let my imagination run away from me.

Instead, I reminded myself that I had to be strong, and I *was* strong enough for this, wasn't I? Back on the farm with my family, I'd been kicked once by a horse, and another time dropped a hammer on my foot while practicing one of my father's tricks. I'd accidentally cut my arm once with a scythe—the same arm that was burned now, in fact—which I was also strong enough to endure. But if they were going to torture me for information, I didn't know if I could withstand it. I didn't know if I was strong enough for that.

The problem was that I had little choice otherwise. If this was only about the books, as awful as it would be to see them destroyed, I wouldn't give my life for them. But it wasn't the books. I knew names of carriers, those who distributed books within the country, and those who bought them. How many people had come through Milda's shop pretending to buy some little item so they could obtain the book they really wanted? I'd already decided I would not voluntarily turn anyone in, but could the information be forced out of me? How much torture could I stand before the names would fall from my lips, even knowing that by doing so, I would subject them to the same torment?

Hours passed before the handle of the door in my little locked room turned and Rusakov walked in carrying a metal box. Two other soldiers accompanied him, one with a little round table and the other with a single chair. A chair for Rusakov. I wouldn't get one. I'd never felt smaller in my life.

It wasn't because of the table and chair. I feared what was in the box, what might have taken them hours to pull together to elicit a confession from me.

By now, I was exhausted. Surely it was morning or maybe even later, and I'd barely slept ten minutes together here in this room. I was famished and terrified, and I doubted the strength of my will. Rusakov didn't need to torture me any further. Not if he knew how much he already had.

"Leave us alone," Rusakov ordered the two soldiers in the room with him. They obeyed, locking the door behind them. I wasn't going anywhere. Neither was Rusakov.

I crossed my legs and sat on the floor, completely unsure of what to expect.

Rusakov withdrew a paper from a pocket in his uniform and unfolded it, then pretended to read it. Pretended, I knew, because obviously he would have already read it, already known what was written on the paper, but he wanted to worry me further with what it might say.

And it was working. My heart pounded so hard against my chest that each beat had begun to hurt. I couldn't see how it didn't break the bones there.

Finally, he looked up from the paper. "These are the sentencing orders for Henri and Lina Zikaris, both convicted of smuggling across our borders and within our borders."

Rather than making me feel afraid, which was surely his intention, I became angry at hearing my parents' names. "Did you send them to Siberia?"

"Their pleas for mercy weren't for themselves—that should make you proud. They only pled for you. The last they saw of you was as you ran into a patch of woods with a dozen of my men on your heels. They begged to know if you were safe, if their punishment could wait until they had the chance to arrange for your care."

"Where are my parents?" I said, angrier than before.

"How interesting that they seemed to care more about your well-being than you care for theirs. If you really loved them, you would have saved them. They would have done that for you."

"Where are—"

"I signed the order myself to send them to Siberia, as I warned you I would." My eyes closed as Rusakov confirmed the worst of my suspicions, but he wasn't finished. "They are lucky, you know. Not many years ago, they would have walked to Siberia in chains, across ice and snow, a journey that might have taken three years, if they survived it. Most didn't. Now we put them on trains for as far as they can take them. When the rails end, your parents' work will begin, building more railways, extending the reach of the Russian Empire. They must work hard, for our prison guards have little tolerance for laziness. Can your mother endure a log being attached to her leg by chains for the next twenty years? How many beatings can your father survive? I hope that will not be their fate."

"How long is their sentence?" I asked.

He shrugged. "Doesn't matter. Once they've completed their term of punishment, they will almost certainly remain in Siberia . . . how would they ever find passage home?"

With my head hanging down, I asked, "Am I now in the same prison where my parents were taken after their arrest?" I wondered how closely I was following in their footsteps, how long until I was given the same sentence as them, or if I had any chance at all of leaving this room.

In answer, Officer Rusakov picked up the box from the table beside him and slid it across the floor toward me. In paint on one side was written the name *H Zikaris*. After some hesitation I opened the box and saw a pipe and a deck of cards, items I recognized as having belonged to my father. Below them was a rose brooch and a crocheted handkerchief, my mother's. At the bottom was a key. I'd never seen that before.

"Why are you showing this to me?" I asked.

"In hopes of reminding you of how much you have lost." Rusakov leaned lower to stare at me. "If you truly miss them, then I will send you to Siberia to join them. Yes, it's true that you may not survive the trip, just as your parents may not have survived it—I'd hate for you to go all that way and find yourself alone there, with nothing but ice and chains and convicted criminals for company. You will be assigned the same work as the adults. If you think carrying a sack full of books is heavy, wait until you are given a railroad tie to drag by yourself for a kilometer through knee-deep snow."

I didn't want that. I didn't want any part of going to Siberia. Much as I missed my parents, I knew they wouldn't want me to join them there either. *If*, as Rusakov said, they had even survived the trip.

I glanced up. "You want the name of that boy who you think is smuggling books. Why?"

"He is giving me a great deal of trouble, and it must stop. I believe he is working for a smuggler named Ben Kagan. Do you know that man?"

My eyes darted and I pressed my lips together, determined not to say a word, not to reveal a single thing.

But Rusakov leaned forward, resting his elbows on his knees and clasping his hands together. "Don't think of them as people. Think of them as your pathway to freedom. When I have what I want from you, I will put you in a wagon that will take you anywhere in the Russian Empire that you wish to go, even back to your land on that little hillside if you like. You can start a new life there, an honest life, a law-abiding life, loyal to the tsar." He shrugged. "Or I will put you on the next train to Siberia. You do not seem properly dressed for the trip. I hope that will not be a problem."

I closed my eyes, pouring all my strength into holding my emotions together, into keeping myself from dissolving into a thousand pieces. I genuinely did not know what to do.

Rusakov reached into the pocket of his uniform and withdrew a single piece of paper and a pen. "Shall we begin?"

TWENTY-SIX

Lukas and Ben weren't just *people* to me. Nor were Milda and Roze and the priest and everyone else I'd met along the way—names Rusakov would surely demand if I cracked and gave him Lukas's name.

These *people* were my friends. And they had opened my eyes to a world I'd never known existed, a world built of letters that made words that made magic—real magic—come alive in my mind.

I would have to pay a terrible price for that magic now.

Sensing my inner turmoil, Rusakov left the paper and pen on the table, then stood and said, "I'll be back for you in one hour. I expect to see names of these criminals on that paper when I return."

And he left. It struck me as odd that he hadn't asked if I had any ability to write. He must have assumed I could. And I could. Maybe I wouldn't spell everything correctly or write it in the prettiest handwriting, but I could write. I had written, was still writing, creating my own magic on paper. I could certainly do a bit of that writing now. But what to say?

Officer Rusakov had left me the box with my parents' things. I riffled through the contents, sniffed the handkerchief that still smelled like my mother and the pipe that carried me back home again to evenings with my father in front of the fire. But it was the small key at the bottom that made me most curious. It must have some importance or my parents wouldn't have carried it with them. I didn't know if it had been with my father or mother but I supposed it didn't matter. The key was yet another secret they had kept from me. I slipped it into my apron pocket and then sat in the chair in front of the paper, hoping if I stared at it long enough, the answer for what I was supposed to do would magically appear.

The longer I stared, the heavier my eyes became. Finally, I scrawled a name on the paper, and hoped I'd made the right choice, then fell asleep.

I woke up when I heard the key turn in the lock outside my room, then Rusakov marched in and snatched the paper from beneath my wrist. I sat up straight, trying to orient myself again and to appear more alert than I actually was.

But almost instantly, Rusakov pounded his fists on the table, then leaned down to look at me. "Do you think this is a joke?"

My heart began to race. "No, sir."

He pushed the paper toward my face. "I asked for the name of that boy."

"You asked for the name of criminals. The only one I know by name is you . . . sir. Lithuania should be a free country. You and the other soldiers occupy it illegally."

He ripped the paper into strips, though I still saw the various letters of his name waft in pieces to the floor. "You will get your wish to see your parents again. You will be on the next train bound to Siberia, with nothing on your back but the clothes you now wear, and nothing in your belly but your last meal before coming here, all of which are more than you deserve. I will make an example of you, show the other peasants that there will be no mercy given to those who violate the orders of the tsar."

I had not expected any mercy, but even the thought that I might see my parents again failed to give me any comfort. An icy shudder shot through me. Siberia sounded like a big place, a terrible place. There were no guarantees I'd find my parents, even if they were still alive. Even if I arrived there alive.

"Do you think you've saved your friends, that they will be safe now that you have refused to name them? I will find them, Miss Zikaris. I will see that they get what they deserve, as will you. Nothing you have done here should cause you any pride."

"No, but I believe my parents would be proud, and that is enough." My voice sounded stronger than I felt.

He frowned at me, doing a far better job of holding in his temper than I was of holding in mine, then knocked for the door to be opened and slammed it shut behind him.

I wished I could have felt some measure of victory at what I'd said and done, that I could dismiss my fears knowing that at least there had been a purpose in my actions.

But I couldn't. In the end, I sank into a corner of my small room, knowing that when the door opened again, no matter what Rusakov's orders were, I was doomed.

And worse still, knowing that I had just assured the same fate for the two people in the world I loved the most. I hoped that what I'd said to Rusakov had been correct, that my parents would be proud of my decision. If they weren't, then at least I hoped that, one day, my parents would forgive me.

I doubted the day would ever come that I might forgive myself for failing to save them.

CHAPTER
TWENTY-SEVEN

I wasn't sure how many hours passed before I heard voices on the other side of the door. They seemed to be discussing me, though there was nothing of sympathy or concern. My life, my future, were simply part of the day's business.

"... you have a young girl in there for transfer to the train station," the voice said. "I'm here to collect her."

To collect me. Was there anything more I needed to know about what was about to happen?

Whoever was standing guard unlocked the door. I'd hoped to see a friendly face when the door opened, or at least someone who looked like he'd accept a bribe, or be swayed by a girl who could pour out some tears at a vital moment—which I absolutely could. Instead, it was a stern-faced guard who frowned at me and only said, "Let's go."

My stomach was already in knots, and I hadn't thought it could get any worse, but I'd been wrong about that too. I stood on unsteady feet, exhausted, half-starved, and certain the walk from here to the prison wagon would be the last time I'd see the world without looking through bars.

The door of the wagon was held open for me and I climbed in, sitting alone near the back. Just before closing the door, the guard said, "You must keep track of your own things on the way there." Then he tossed in my father's shoulder bag.

My father's shoulder bag that was supposed to have been thrown into a burn pile back in Venska! How was this possible? My heart began racing with anticipation.

Even if the bag had escaped the fire, surely it was a violation of rules to give a prisoner their possessions during a transport. It would be far too likely that the prisoner had items that could be useful for escape.

Such as I did, if I could be clever enough.

This guard must have been bribed. Had Ben done that? He must have, because I couldn't imagine anyone else working such a miracle. I wondered what Ben might have placed inside the bag to help me escape.

I waited for the door to shut before I darted for the bag, but once it was in my hands, I immediately began digging through it. Almost instantly, my hopes were dashed for an easy escape. Ben had ensured that I received this bag, but how was it supposed to help? All that I saw in here was what had been in here before. My father's stack of cards, some cups, a bag of pops—

Pops!

If they had another name, I didn't know it. I'd named them when I was very young by the sound they made. Thrown against a hard object, the pop would make an exploding sound, loud enough to make me wince each time. My mother hated them because they spooked our cow, but they had always entertained me.

Now they might save my life.

I threw the first one against the solid side wall of the prison wagon. Its *pop* echoed like a small cannon in this little metal space. That should get the driver's attention.

It did. The wagon stopped. I threw another on the cobblestone road beneath me, and had another in my fist when the driver came running around. "Did you see anything?"

"I think we're under fire," I cried, and if he wanted to interpret my nervousness as panic, then that was perfectly fine.

"That's not gunfire." But the driver withdrew a pistol anyway and began waving it around wildly with his back toward me. As he did, I threw a third pop on a stone near his feet. He jumped, then quickly unlocked my door and dragged me out. "Come with me."

By then I had a fourth pop ready, my last one, and while he pushed me ahead of him to run away, I tried to throw the final pop, but instead, it slipped from my fingers. The mistake couldn't have worked out better for me. The driver stepped on it and it gave a small explosion beneath his foot. He jumped in the air, then shoved me to the ground in his hurry to run for his life.

When he raced in one direction, I ran in the other. I heard him call after me, but I rounded the first corner I saw, my senses on high alert for any possible hiding place. I knew he'd follow me.

Distraction. That was always the key for success. You could do any trick out in the open as long as you got the audience to look in the wrong place.

I needed a good distraction.

At the next bend, someone had left laundry hanging from a line. I yanked a dress off the lines and pulled it over my head as I ran, placing the shoulder bag beneath the new dress, then joined a group of kids my age gathered for a game of marbles. Pushing into their center, I said, "Did you see which way that girl ran?"

"What girl?" someone asked.

I pointed down the street. "I think she went that way, running faster than I've ever seen anyone go. Did any of you see her?"

The kids stood, all of them craning their heads to get a look at this girl whose legs apparently moved at the speed of lightning.

And just in time, for the driver who had been chasing me

ran by, and noticed the group of us. I stayed to the rear of the group with my head down as he asked, "Have any of you seen a girl run by?"

"That way!" a boy said, and all the kids pointed in the same direction I'd suggested to them with another boy near me adding, "She was faster than anyone we've ever seen."

By the time they turned around, I had left the group. I returned the dress, then looked toward the forests. I wasn't entirely sure where I was, though I knew how long it had taken to drive me here, so I had a guess for how long it would take to return to Milda's home. If Milda's home was still there at all.

TWENTY-EIGHT

I didn't dare walk in the daytime. If it wasn't dangerous enough to be a smuggler, I was now an official fugitive of the Russian Empire. Unless there was no other choice, I wouldn't risk showing my face in daylight.

Instead, I traveled by dark, guided only by the moonlight, or the stars if the moon had yet to rise. The autumn weather was rapidly becoming colder and the nights were much too quiet, but it was safer this way. I might trip over a fallen branch or accidentally step into a pond—and I did both several times—but that was better than being spotted by a patrol of Cossacks, all of whom I assumed had been told to watch out for me.

The first night was the worst, an echo of the beginning of summer just after my parents' arrest, how terrified I'd been, how certain I was that my next step would surely be my last. I'd known nothing of the larger world, nothing even about the package I'd been carrying in my arms.

I vaguely wondered what had happened to that book.

I couldn't imagine that Milda had given it to anyone. Considering that it was still locked, who would want it?

And I had the key for it now, I was sure of it. But the key without the book was no more good to me than the locked book without a key. The one needed the other.

By the second night of walking, the burn on my arm had begun to fade, though the memories of how I got the burn never would. I had plenty to drink from the river that accompanied my trek but little to eat other than the occasional wild berry patch or evening primrose that my mother used to find in the forests for salads. Hunger became my constant companion.

And with every step, I longed to know if Milda was safe, to know what had become of Venska following the night of burning, as I would always think of it. And to see if any of her books had survived that night. Those were the questions that made me put one foot in front of the other hour after hour.

By the third night, I felt half-starved and beyond exhausted, for I never slept well while hiding in the daytime. To keep myself awake, I began thinking of Lukas's stories, of the snake and bear, of Rue and her father, and the boy. By now, I understood who all of them were.

Rue was me, but she was also all Lithuanians.

The snake was meant to represent the Russians, who wanted our land for themselves and who would trick us, threaten us, or even injure us to obtain it.

I was fairly sure that the bear was the smugglers, or maybe it was simply Ben, and Lukas was obviously the boy. The boy who had told his truth to a talking frog and no one else.

A frog that didn't exist.

Which probably meant that Lukas had never told anyone the truth about where he had come from. I wondered if his parents had been book smugglers, like mine. Or maybe they were simply smugglers. If so, it was no wonder he had been sensitive about being called a thief.

I decided that when the time was right, I'd ask him more about his life. Maybe it wouldn't be the same as confessing to a nonexistent talking frog, but I hoped he'd talk to me.

When it became light enough that I had to hide, between naps and small forages for food, I read from my father's notebook, or pulled out the paper and pencil that had been in the shoulder bag and worked on my story, writing my ideas for what Rue might do to help the boy and the bear drive the snake out of the land. For in his retelling, Lukas seemed to have forgotten the reason why he began telling me the story in the first place. It was because Rue was a girl who could do magic.

And so would I.

Late the following night, I stepped back into the village of Venska, Milda's town. It was eerily quiet here. I'd arrived too early for the farmers or the bakers, and in the stillness of the air, I could easily catch the bitter smell of the fires that had torn through here. I didn't go down any of the side roads to see the damage for myself, but it appeared that the towns-folk had begun rebuilding the homes of those in need.

The homes would repair easily enough, but it was the people here I worried about. Safely inside their newly repaired homes, would they want their books back? Surely not. Surely the Russians had proven that the price for own-ing a book was too high to pay a second time.

Which meant as far as this village was concerned, book smuggling had probably been ended for good. It infuriated me to think that Rusakov might have won here.

Milda's home had been burned too. Not all of it, but too much to ever be reclaimed. Her wood roof was entirely gone, and all of her store and its contents. The walls of her home were made of brick, so they had survived, but from where I stood, there didn't appear to be anything inside worth saving.

I was too tired and hungry to cry for all that she had lost, but my heart hurt as much as if I had. Milda had been pun-ished for something that should never have been a crime. I hoped she was all right. Desperate to see her again, I leaned against a tree near the front of her home to wait for the town to awaken.

Or, more hopefully, to watch for any sign of Milda. Surely she was still here, somewhere, watching for me to return.

But when the sun began to rise, her house remained as dark as ever. Gradually, the town came to life again, but Milda's home did not. She wasn't there.

She must have been captured. Of course she would have been. Milda didn't move fast and she wasn't used to evading soldiers. Even if she had escaped, she wouldn't be here watching for me to return, for she likely didn't believe I ever would.

I finally took a chance and entered Milda's home. I didn't dare call her name, or rather, I was terrified to call her name and have the silence answer me.

Indeed, at the front of the home, there was nothing but ash and a few items recognizable to me only because I'd seen them so often before. I wouldn't have known what they were otherwise.

The fire must have cooled as it went to the back of her house. Surprisingly, a storage trunk remained there, and a traveling cloak, though its bright colors had been dimmed by smoke and ash. The hidden staircase was scorched but not burned through. Was it possible it had survived? If so, that must be where Milda was!

I lifted the lowest stair, then peered down below, wishing it weren't so dark. But I needed to look. I lit a candle, then descended the ladder, and my heart sank when I saw Milda's shelves. As I'd feared, they were completely bare, including the locked book I'd brought here from my parents.

I hoped the shelves were empty because Lukas had successfully rescued all the books, but I worried that the soldiers had gotten here first.

I explored the rest of the secret storeroom, searching for anything to offer me hope, though I couldn't begin to imagine what that could possibly be. How could I ever find hope in such an empty place, knowing what had been here once, what these rooms had meant to so many people?

What they'd meant to me.

When I had first come into this room, I had been a girl with no knowledge of books, other than understanding that they existed. And now, books had become my life. I couldn't imagine going a day without them, without the worlds they opened up to me.

The books were gone now, and this town had been taught a lesson it would never forget.

From there, I wandered into the secret school, which was even more empty. No chalk tablets, no displays on the walls. No books. Their absence felt like ghosts wandering around me, almost real, almost here.

But not. Suddenly I froze.

Footsteps creaked on the floorboards overhead. They weren't loud and even, like a soldier's might have been. These were softer, and more cautious. If only that were enough to tell me whether the person upstairs was a friend.

I crept back toward the ladder, and when I was almost there, the staircase lifted and a voice called down, "Audra?"

I squinted. "Roze?"

"Yes! I was watching for you to return. Milda said there was a plan to help you escape, and as soon as I heard what happened to Officer Rusakov, I knew the plan had worked."

My eyes narrowed. "What happened to Rusakov?"

"You don't know? Yesterday he came through the town and gathered his things, and I overheard him tell the other officers here that he had been reassigned. But then I also noticed he'd been stripped of his badges, so we think that maybe he wasn't reassigned, maybe he was released, and maybe it's because of the fires here in town, that he'd gone too far." She finished by taking a deep breath.

I tilted my head. It couldn't be true. "You're sure that he's gone? He won't be back?"

"We think he's not a soldier anymore. No, he won't be back, Audra."

I still couldn't believe Rusakov was gone. Not just gone from this town, but no longer a threat to us. Obviously, any of the soldiers could put us in danger, but Rusakov was especially cruel. I wanted to dance with happiness, and perhaps felt a little satisfaction that I might have played a role in getting rid of him.

Roze sighed deeply. "I'm glad you came back here. Milda said you would."

"Milda's still alive?" My heart leapt with excitement and I couldn't get my questions out fast enough. "Where is she? Is she safe? What happened to the books?"

Roze paused. "Will you come up? I'll tell you everything else that happened that night."

I climbed back up the ladder and saw Roze sitting on the floor beside the open staircase, her hands folded in her lap.

After shutting the secret entrance, I said, "Let's start with the books. If the Cossacks didn't take them, then where are they?"

Roze said, "Isn't it obvious? Lukas got the books out. I don't know how he did it so fast, but he did it. Then the next morning, the people whose books had been burned found Milda and begged her for more books. We gave out every single book that Lukas had saved."

I couldn't help but smile. "They wanted more? After all that happened to them, they wanted more books?"

"They needed the books and would have taken more if we'd had them. So that's what we're doing."

My ears perked up. "Getting more books? Where is Milda? And Lukas and Ben?"

Roze got to her feet and motioned for me to follow her. "Lukas has been hiding, hoping to find you before you came into town. But since you somehow made it past him, I'll take you to him and he can answer the rest of your questions."

"Definitely." I started to go with her, then said, "But first, is there anything to eat?"

Roze grinned. "Anything left here is a little overcooked, but I've been bringing food to Lukas from my home since the fire. I'm sure he'll have some to share."

He'd better have. I was excited to see Lukas again, though I'd never admit it to him. Nor would I ever admit that, just this once, I was a hundred times more excited to get something to eat.

TWENTY-NINE

Lukas had created a shelter for himself in an old hunter's cabin deep in the woods, though he explained that he only went there to sleep. Even then, I could tell from the dark circles beneath his eyes that he wasn't sleeping well. How could he? If the cabin were ever searched, he'd surely be trapped.

Still, he looked as happy and relieved to see me as I was him, and better yet, Roze added to his small stash of food with some bread she had brought from home. My mouth was already full when she hugged me goodbye and wished us luck on our next adventure. Whatever it would be, I didn't care. I only wanted to eat and was halfway through my third piece of bread before I remembered to ask about Ben and Milda.

"Are they far away?" I asked. "Are they safe?"

"Yes and yes," he answered. "But we're not going to see them."

"We have to! Roze told me they need more books—"

"Yes, they do, and we're going to provide them. I was supposed to leave tomorrow, so your timing is excellent!" Lukas grinned when he saw my confusion. "That's my assignment, to cross the border into Prussia and meet a printer who should be ready with an order of books. I've got a wagon that will take us most of the way, though we'll have to be extra careful since we'll have to stay on the roads. You can wait here, or—"

"I'm coming with you."

He smiled like he'd already known that would be my answer. "Ben won't be happy about this."

I'd already assumed that and, with a shrug, I said, "Ben doesn't like me, I understand that. But I've done a good job of smuggling so far—"

"Wait." Lukas held up a hand to cut me off. "Audra, Ben doesn't try to stop you from smuggling because he dislikes you. He tries to stop you because he cares. And because he thinks one day, you'll be among the best. He wants to keep you alive until you're old enough to prove to everyone how amazing you are."

"I'm almost the same age as you," I said.

"Yes, but Ben knows I'm going to do this whether he lets me or not. And so will you, I know that. But if anything bad happens to you, he'll blame me."

My brows furrowed. "It won't be your fault."

213

"Let's hope not." Lukas grinned again. "Because the true reason I'm bringing you along is so that you can make sure nothing bad happens to me!"

For the remainder of the day and through the night, Lukas and I were so tired that we switched off keeping watch while the other slept. Lukas took longer watches than me, though he wasn't supposed to, but I was too exhausted to fight him on it. When I awoke early the next morning, Lukas was just finishing hitching up our small wagon, and we started the long ride to the border. As we rode, he started to teach me about smuggling over the border.

"They don't worry too much about who leaves the country," Lukas began. "A well-told lie, and a simple check of our papers, and then we'll be on our way."

"I have no papers," I reminded him.

Lukas only glanced sideways at me, hesitating as he quickly composed a new plan. "Who needs papers, then? We'll go another route, a perfect rehearsal for when we come back in with the books—something they worry about a great deal. Each of us will take as many as we can carry, and we'll have to go on foot, the safest route."

"But we have this wagon!" I protested. I'd walked so much in the last few days, I wasn't eager to do so again.

"It's a fine wagon, but we can only use it on the roads, where the soldiers are; even on horseback, we're too visible.

Of course, on foot, we're still likely to look suspicious. It's best if no one sees us at all."

A shiver ran through me. "Tell me about it."

Lukas lowered his voice, which only made me more nervous, as if someone might overhear us. "There are three layers of border security. The first is the most difficult. For the first two kilometers along the entire border with Prussia, the soldiers station themselves close enough to be within sight and hearing distance of one another. Within the next five kilometers, the soldiers are still on patrol, only the line is thinner. Past that for at least three kilometers, the soldiers are on horseback, looking for anyone who somehow got through the first two lines."

I shook my head. "Ten kilometers of border security? Impossible! How could anyone get past all that?"

Lukas looked over at me. "That's our job to figure out, each time we cross, because each time, it will be different."

I took a deep breath, hoping a little air would help me feel up to the challenge. Then I sighed. That hadn't helped at all. "What else do I need to know?"

"Ben believes that if we're spotted, it's better to surrender immediately. If we run, they're allowed to shoot."

"But if I'm caught, they'll hang me." Until saying the words, I hadn't believed it could happen. I did now.

"Then if you remember nothing else that I teach you, it's

not to be caught." Lukas's nervous laugh quickly turned serious. "Truly, Audra. You don't have to do this. If you are caught—"

"How often are book smugglers caught?" I asked.

"More often than we would like," Lukas said. "But we're bringing in over a thousand different titles each year, and we hope to double that within another few years. The more we give to people, the more they want. They're starving for information. They need us."

"Hmm." I'd been thinking about my version of Rue's story and the ideas Lukas was giving me without even realizing it.

"What are you thinking about?" Lukas asked.

"Nothing very interesting."

"I hardly believe that."

I wasn't going to tell him, but he was waiting so patiently for me to say something, I finally said, "I've begun to write."

"Really? What are you writing about?"

"I'm only practicing my letters."

"Milda hinted that these letters you've been practicing are randomly arranging themselves into a wonderful story."

"It's just practice, Lukas." Which was certainly true. My story was evolving and growing, and beginning to feel like it had a life of its own. But it was also far from perfect and almost nothing like I had first imagined it inside my head. Worst of all, I had no idea how the story should end.

That night we slept one at a time in the back of the wagon, taking turns to be at watch for any passersby, which allowed me a better rest than I'd had when on my own. And while I was on watch, I dug into my shoulder bag to work on my story. But when I went to pull out my papers, my father's notebook came with it.

Now that I'd had more practice, it was becoming easier to read it. Most of his entries were descriptions of tricks I already knew how to perform, or notes he made to remind himself how to perform the tricks better. That was useful.

Tonight, with the smallest bit of candlelight possible, I thumbed through the pages of my father's notebook, finding words here or there that I knew and sounding my way through several more, studying his art and trying to match it to his descriptions, figuring out the meaning of his instructions as best I could. Nearer the end, I turned the page to something that wasn't a design, but a recipe.

My eyes widened and I sat up straight, wondering if this actually worked, or whether it was simply something my father intended to test some day. I had to know, and there was only one way to find out. I'd need to make the recipe myself.

I didn't tell Lukas about the recipe as we rode the next morning, but it was constantly on my mind. So I only vaguely listened when he showed me the various sites along the way, explaining how the land itself could help a smuggler move about, from the thick trunk of an oak tree to the bushy branches of a willow plant, to the steep slope leading to our many rivers—all these places could save our lives, if used properly. By the end of our third night of riding, he was only repeating what he'd already told me a hundred times already. Or so I believed.

"Trees are good in an emergency, but only if you can remain opposite a soldier who is trying to find you, and if you don't make a sound—nearly impossible on the forest floor. And soldiers are rarely alone anyway, so if one doesn't see you, another will. It's better to get flat upon the ground, preferably buried in the ferns or grasses. Then you become part of the shadows. I've lain there in the darkness so close to a soldier's boot that I could describe the tread on it, and wasn't caught."

Then, several kilometers later, Lukas said, "The worse the weather, the better the opportunity to smuggle. When the soldiers don't want to go out, we do."

Milda had already explained that much to me, though I hardly relished the idea of smuggling through a blizzard or downpour. Which brought up another question, this one something I hadn't considered already.

"How do I keep the books from being ruined by the weather?"

"You won't carry them in the open. Ben taught me how to bury them in a canvas sack, so that if you're crossing a wider river, such as we'll do on this first mission, you can load them into a wood barrel while you cross. He always stores a few in the area. The barrel will help you keep your head above water, no matter how deep or wide the river is."

And so our conversations went until Lukas finally pulled the wagon into a barn that he described as having a "friendly owner," then added, "We'll walk the rest of the way."

"How far?" I tried to sound positive, but the truth was, I was dreading this walk more than I'd dreaded anything in my life. A stiff wind had been blowing all day. As uncomfortable as it had been riding in the wagon, it would be worse on foot.

"We'll be there before you know it!" Lukas said cheerfully.

"How far?"

He shrugged. "Six or seven hours of walking, I suppose. And you'd better get used to it, because we won't take this wagon back with us. As I said before, there's too great a chance of us being noticed and searched."

I sighed. "Let's get going, then."

His prediction was wrong, or maybe it only felt to me like we had walked twice as long as that. For the last hour, my feet seemed to be made of bricks, and I could hardly move my numb fingers. I put one hand on my stomach, wondering whether the pit inside was due to nerves or to hunger.

"It could be worse," Lukas observed. "The wind isn't as bad here."

Which meant I could hear myself think above the sound of the wind, and all I could think about was how we were supposed to cross the Neman River as it became visible in the distance. This river marked the border of Lithuania and Prussia, but it was much wider than I'd expected. At my best, I'd have trouble throwing a rock across it, and it looked deep enough to have a powerful current.

I didn't care how many books were on the other side of the border. I was certain this was an impossible challenge. My stomach twisted. "I can't cross that alone!"

"We have to, Audra. They watch the bridges too carefully."

"My father used to have papers for his work as a street magician," I said. "He used the bridge. So if we could get papers—"

"Your father could travel because of his work. What excuse would you have? And while I'm sure he left legally, if he was bringing books back with him, I doubt he came back on the bridge, not unless he had some magical way of hiding them."

My shoulders fell. "So we can't use the bridge?"

"I could." Lukas tilted his head toward the pack on his back. "I have forged papers that I used once when crossing with Ben. But I still wouldn't dare return on the bridge, and you have no papers at all."

I groaned. If I were going to make a habit of this, I would need papers. Crossing a cold river at night just once should be enough for a lifetime.

We were in a forested patch looking at the patrol of Cossacks ahead, with more soldiers than I could count in such low light. This must be the first layer of border security, with men standing close enough to see and hear one another. Which meant we must have already crossed the other two thinner layers, without even realizing it. That had to be good news!

"There are many farms along the river, so the soldiers pay little attention to anyone moving westward," Lukas said. "It's when we try to come east again that they ask about our business."

From our relative safety inside the thick trees, I studied the line of soldiers. They stood in their assigned places, looking from side to side and then forward again, and occasionally calling out to one another, all while maintaining their forward stances. We'd never get past them!

"How far ahead can they see?" I asked. In other words, at what distance inside Prussia could they see us coming?

"Depends on the area," Lukas replied. "But you should assume that if you can see the border, the guards can see you. It's always better to be safer than you think you need to be."

"Safer?" I nearly choked on that word. "Nothing about this feels safe."

"Correction," Lukas said. "Nothing about this *is* safe. Never forget that."

I surely never would. But that wasn't enough to make me back out now, not after coming all this way. I merely looked at him and asked, "When do we go?"

Lukas studied the movements of the soldiers a moment longer, then finally said, "It will be easier than you think, I promise. How about we cross now?"

CHAPTER
THIRTY

I didn't understand why Lukas thought it would be easy to sneak out of Lithuania beneath the steady watch of the soldiers. It seemed incredibly difficult to me.

Lukas and I crept down the slope toward the river, sneaking past the soldiers on our hands and knees, aware of the crunch of each dry autumn leaf, the crack of every fallen twig, or the scattering of a startled bird or squirrel at our approach. By the time we stopped at the bank of the river, my hands had tiny cuts on them and my knees were raw, and we hadn't yet begun the difficult part of the journey.

Difficult, and dangerous. After we passed the approach to the bridge, Lukas led us beneath the planks as they rose overhead. I understood it was our best place to hide, but the soldiers were directly above us. One slip, one roll of a rock beneath our feet, and they would hear us.

Once we reached the river's edge, Lukas silently pointed to the undergirding of the bridge. At first, I thought only wood beams were there, hardly enough to get a solid grip, but when I looked closer, I saw a rope that extended from one side of the bridge to another, directly under the feet of the soldiers.

I shook my head, but even as I protested, Lukas took hold of the rope with his hands and legs, then began pulling himself, hand over hand, above the river.

Overhead, one soldier shouted an order to the others to do a sweep of the area, which surely included checking the shores of the river. I had to go. Immediately, I copied what Lukas had done, wrapping my legs around the rope and moving hand over hand across the water. If I looked upward through the slats of the bridge, I saw the boots of the soldiers, heard them discussing their luck at being on duty after the cold wind had died down, and closed my eyes when their weight shifted and grit fell onto my face.

The rope lowered with our combined weight, but we remained in the shadows of the bridge. When Lukas finished crossing, the rope bounced higher and I was closer to the soldiers than before. If they looked down, they would easily see me. I was terrified.

Once on the other side, Lukas grabbed my arm and pulled me low, which was hardly necessary. I had no intention of standing tall and offering the soldiers a target.

"We're in Prussia now, so they won't shoot," he said.

"They have no way of knowing which side of the border we belong to, so they won't risk a war. But if they suspect we've crossed, they'll be more watchful for us trying to come back."

My ears perked up. "Trying? Why didn't you say we would *succeed* in coming back?"

Lukas only grinned, then tilted his head in the direction he wanted me to follow him.

From there, we trekked through the night, and the city of Tilsit came into view by early morning. Along the way, Lukas pointed out various places where it was safe to rest or to load sacks to smuggle back into Lithuania. "This territory has been claimed by Germany," Lukas explained, "and so it's still not our own land, as it should be. But Germany likes anything that makes life more difficult for Russia. They're usually quite happy to overlook their own smuggling laws on this side of the border."

I giggled and let Lukas take me on a tour of the town, though it wasn't much of a tour. Half the time, I thought he only decided which road to lead me down when I was already on it ahead of him. Then he'd point to various landmarks and buildings and make up stories about them that couldn't possibly be true, not unless fairies had built the bakeries and trolls had paved the roads. At least the stories kept me awake until the print shop was finally open.

Lukas greeted the printer by name. We were told that Ben had paid for the order already, but he was glad that two of us had come, for there were several books to be carried.

"*Several* books?" Lukas glanced sideways at me. "That's too many. Only one of us is carrying the books back."

That didn't make sense to me. I wouldn't trudge along beside him while he did all the work. So I shook my head. "If you can carry them, so can I."

He nodded at the printer to give us a moment alone, then pulled me to a corner of the room and frowned.

"I'll take half the books," I said. "I'm strong enough."

Lukas sighed. "You don't understand, Audra. I'm the only one going back. You're staying here."

"What?" Pressure began building inside me. "You tricked me into crossing the border?"

"I had to! If I'd told you that I was getting you out of Lithuania for good, what would you have done?"

"The same thing I'll do now—refuse to listen! I'll make my own decisions. I don't need your help, or Ben's—"

"Do you know what Ben risked, what Ben *paid* in bribes to get that shoulder bag to you in the prison? And now you'll thank him by ignoring his orders?"

"I'll thank him by helping with the cause he still risks his life for!"

"I don't mean to interrupt," the printer said, wheeling out a cart piled high with what had to be thirty or forty books. "But Ben actually has more books waiting here than he might have remembered. I can't continue to store them. Our police tend to look the other way when we print illegal books, but if things are getting so dangerous over there that a young girl's life is in danger, then I don't want that trouble following me here. You'll take these books or I'll have to dispose of them."

Lukas had been eyeing the books, his jaw falling open as the printer spoke. Finally, he mumbled, "I can't carry all of these."

"No," I said, smugger than I ought to have been. "You can't. Not if you're crossing alone."

Lukas sighed. "Just this once, Audra. And when Ben yells at you for returning with me, I'm going to tell him that I tried to stop you."

"I'm going to tell him a few things as well."

We loaded the books into four canvas sacks the printer gave to us, carrying one over each shoulder as we left the shop. But we hadn't gone far before I knew I was going to have trouble hauling them all the way back into Lithuania.

Testing the weight again, I told Lukas, "I'm worried that I'll fall into the river and ruin these books."

"And drown," Lukas said with a wink.

I didn't see why he would wink. I could swim well enough, but not if I had to keep hold of a pile of wet books.

"We're not going back on the rope," Lukas continued.

"The books would make our shoulder packs hang too low and we would easily be seen."

"Then how?" My eyes widened. "Ben wasn't serious about the barrels?"

Lukas pressed his brow low. "Ben is serious about everything, Audra. You know that."

By then, we had arrived at a barn that Lukas said was owned by an elderly Lithuanian couple. "They've devoted their lives to helping with book carrying on this side of the border," he explained. "Good folks."

From inside an empty stall, Lukas rolled out two wooden barrels, each the size of a small traveling trunk. Either end had a rope handle attached. I shook my head.

"We'll still drown."

"Not if you hold on." He opened the lid and began setting his books inside. "The lid will keep the water out, and the barrels will float, so don't let go of the handle. We'll enter the river in a quiet place and you must be sure to exit in a quiet place, the sooner the better so that we can find each other again. But even if it means we exit a kilometer or two apart, stay in the river tonight until the area feels safe."

"Tonight? When it's dark . . . of course when it's dark." I arched an eyebrow. "What should we do until then?"

He pointed to the upper loft. "We sleep. And if we're

lucky, when we wake up, there'll be a raging rainstorm. That'll triple our chances of a safe crossing!"

"And get us soaked!"

Lukas chuckled. "Trust me, we're going to get soaked tonight. I'd rather be soaked than be seen."

With a frown, I asked, "Tell me the truth. Do we really have any chance of getting back safely?"

Lukas leaned against the barn wall and considered his answer for a moment, then finally said, "In the story of Rue, who is it that is constantly giving her trouble?"

I'd have preferred that he gave me a direct answer, but since that clearly wasn't going to happen, with a sigh, I said, "The snake gives her trouble."

"Yes, and I'll grant you, it's a dangerous thing to have a snake for one's enemy. Snakes are fast and they strike hard, often killing their prey. You may not see or hear the snake coming until it's too late, and if you are not careful when you fight back, with a single turn of its body, in an instant, you might be its victim."

Now my sigh became a groan. "Thanks for telling me that, Lukas. But the soldiers ahead of us—"

"No, this story is about Rue and the snake! We're not thinking of the soldiers right now. You see, although Rue understood the danger of fighting against a snake, she also knew that she had all the advantages. The snake is confined to the ground, able to see only the smallest piece of its world. But Rue can stand taller and higher, and she can see more than the snake even knows exists. She can see how much better her land might be if she could rid it of the snake. The snake has no hands for working, no feet for walking and running, but Rue does. All she needs is a plan."

I looked down at my father's satchel, thinking of the recipe I'd found inside his notebook. I needed a plan too.

"We should get some sleep while we can." Lukas finished sealing the lid on his barrel and reached for my load of books, but I pulled them away.

"Maybe later. Perhaps while I'm waiting to sleep, I can read, just a little."

It wasn't just a little. I chose a book of fairy tales, stories not so different from those of Rue and the snake, with words I wouldn't have been able to read at all a few months ago. Now I flew through them. That night, I devoured one story after another, of heroism, bravery, and nobility, often finding myself looking through the eyes of the characters as if I were the warrior, or the princess, or the trickster. I read until I couldn't force my eyes to stay open any longer, until they ached from all they were absorbing. Even then, I shook my head, hoping for one more line, one more page.

I loved the feel of the paper between my fingers, the smell of the ink. Every word was a symphony, singing to me of other lands, of other people, of places where new ideas were encouraged, not made illegal.

Not here.

I shook my head again and forced myself to continue reading. Hopefully something in one of these books would tell me what to do when I was about to cross a border so dangerous that it very well might cost me my life.

CHAPTER
THIRTY-ONE

We only slept until midafternoon, and when I awoke, Lukas bought us some sausages to eat while we made the trek back to the border, hauling the barrels in our arms. My shoulders already ached from the effort, but we couldn't drag them. They'd leave tracks.

"How often do you do border crossings?" I asked Lukas.

"Twice."

My eyes narrowed. "Twice a week, or twice a month?"

"No, twice—this is my second time. I crossed for the first time last month."

I nearly dropped the barrel I was carrying. "You've only done this once before now?"

"That's what 'this is my second time' means, Audra."

"You don't know the safe places, the border guards to avoid or who can be bribed. I thought I was going with someone who'd done this enough to teach me what to do, not someone who was making up everything as he went along!"

Clearly irritated, with a huff he stopped walking and stared at me. "Every smuggling job is making things up. What works the first time might get you arrested the second time. So here's what I can teach you: The safe place is where the border guards aren't. Avoid all of them, attempt bribery as a last resort to being shot. And whatever you can do to get those books into the hands of other Lithuanians and stay alive in the process is the right thing! And, I should remind you, Ben wanted you left behind. I was supposed to be making this return trip alone!"

He was right about that, and probably right about everything else too. I mumbled an apology and while he took a breath to calm himself down, I said, "So we'll keep going, yes?"

A beat passed. Then, "Yes."

"Are these books expensive?" I'd seen how little Milda charged for the books that left her place, often nothing at all. But someone had to be paying for the printing.

"The church helps as much as it can," Lukas said as he munched on one end of his sausage. "And there are Lithuanians here in Prussia who are living in exile. They donate a great deal of money to aid in our work."

He walked at my side for several minutes more before he said, "I'm not as good at smuggling as I used to be."

I stopped again. "What? Lukas, you're very good at it!"

"No, not since I was whipped for it. The choices I make now are too safe, which makes them too predictable. That's why I wanted to do this border crossing, to prove to myself that I still can. But the truth is, I wanted you to come back with me. I'm sure I'll need your help."

After all he'd done for me, I was more than eager to return the favor. I had plenty to prove to myself too. "How can I help?"

"You're good at this because you think differently than the rest of us. If the logical thing is to turn right, you turn left and then suddenly it makes sense. I'm not here to teach you, Audra. You need to teach me."

I held his words in my mind until we entered the woods on the Prussian side of the border and found our place to enter the river. From here, we could see the border guards on the other side already gathering for the night, just as Lukas had said. At least until it got darker, they were close enough to see one another and certainly they could hear one another.

Lukas was wrong about the way I made decisions—it wasn't that I had a different logic than everyone else. It was that I had a different motive. From what I could tell, the object of most smugglers was to avoid, deny, and hide.

Mine was, as always, to distract. To put in plain view what I wanted to be seen, and turn attention away from what shouldn't be seen. In this case, Lukas and myself.

I looked over at Lukas. "Give me your barrel!"

He did. I opened it and set my books inside next to his, along with my father's shoulder bag and everything else I had with me, then sealed it up again.

"This won't float as well, Audra. It's heavier now."

"But it will float, right?" When he nodded, I said, "Now give me your coat."

He removed it and I carried it with me down to the edge of the river next to the tall rock we had passed earlier. I draped the coat over the rock, then set my empty barrel to the side of it, laying one sleeve of the coat on the barrel, as if a hand were holding it.

"We need something round, for a head!" Lukas whispered, catching on. As quietly as possible, he explored the area, coming back with a rock roughly the size and shape of a human head, and also with some grasses for the hair.

By now it was dark enough to build our rock person, and when we finished and viewed it from a distance, it had a fair resemblance to a human, albeit one who never moved at all.

"You're rather brilliant, you know," Lukas commented. "Now what?"

"Now we float together," I said. "You hold one handle of the barrel and I'll hold the other. I'll keep watch for guards while you scout a good location to go to land. When we both agree, we leave the river." I gave him the barrel, then said, "Go get in the water downriver and wait for me to float past you. Then grab my hand."

He grinned and began moving downriver. "I think I know what you're doing."

"Be sure to grab my hand, Lukas."

But he only nodded and disappeared into the brush. Meanwhile, I began making noise—not so much as to be obvious but certainly enough to ensure I was being heard. I pounded the lid of the barrel with my fist, then when I heard voices calling from the other side of the river, I went silent, except for a large rock that I threw upriver, one that splashed in with a loud *kerplunk*.

The voices turned to shouted orders. I caught enough Russian words to know that they were being directed to investigate the sound, well upriver from where Lukas and I would be. Then I quietly slipped into the water.

Instantly, my breath lodged in my throat. It was so much colder than I had imagined, chilling me to my core. I tried to move my limbs, but they were already freezing up. I couldn't allow that—if I didn't move, I would drown.

I floated that way downriver for about ten seconds before Lukas grabbed my hand. Although I'd been watching for him, I hadn't noticed him in the thick brush bending into the water, and at first, the branches and leaves scratched at my face and tangled in my hair. But as he drifted with me into the current, I wished to be back among the brush again. More soldiers were moving down the river, trying to monitor a tall coat-wearing rock that might attempt an illegal crossing at any minute. If they looked carefully enough at the water beside them, they would see us.

We continued floating for another minute until we had passed the soldiers, then began fighting the current to make our way across the river. If I hadn't been cold enough, I swallowed plenty of icy water, and now I really was chilled from the inside out. My mind cycled between three separate thoughts: Don't get caught. Don't stop swimming. And whatever you do, don't let go of the barrel.

Lukas was nearer to the Lithuanian shore and finally began making firmer tugs toward land. I followed his lead until I was able to touch the muddy bottom, then we remained crouched low in the water, listening for the sounds of any soldiers.

When we agreed it was safe, Lukas nodded, and we rolled the barrel onto land, giving it a chance to drain off as much water as possible before we continued walking. Then we emerged from the water, keeping low while we squeezed excess water from our clothes. The night air turned my clothes icy and my teeth chattered nonstop, but nothing could be done about that now. We had to keep moving.

Lukas pried open the barrel and we took turns grabbing books and stuffing them inside the sacks we'd each wear over our shoulders. Mine was dry and Lukas had rolled his tight, so although there were some wet patches, the books should be all right. We covered the sacks with some sticks poking out the top to look like gathered firewood. It wasn't much for a disguise, so if we were caught, it would only take the soldiers a few seconds to realize who we were.

And it was entirely possible that we would be caught. After all, we hadn't yet passed through even the first layer of border security.

With everything packed, Lukas began to slip the barrel under the bushes, but I motioned for him to pull it out again. After all, it still had some use for us . . . farther downriver. I placed a few rocks inside it to give it some weight, then sealed it again and sent it on its way. If the barrel was spotted by soldiers, they'd follow it downriver, expecting smugglers to be attached to it. And leave us free to move forward.

My idea must have had some success, for we saw the evidence of Cossack soldiers who had been here only moments before on the first line of defense—their tracks, a cigarette butt still smoking. Not far away was a small wooden building with a Russian flag flying overhead and a pair of boots outside, so I suspected it was where the border soldiers slept. But it seemed empty now, and hopefully would stay that way for a while.

After another two kilometers, we reached the edge of the forest and had to cross a wide cornfield before the next patch of woods. It was still dark but the moon was bright in the sky. So we flattened ourselves on the ground and pushed our sacks in front of us as we crawled through tall green stalks that made for a thick cover, and warmed me a bit. But I was also fighting a sneeze the entire time, finally suppressing one into my sleeve.

Once we reached the next patch of woods, we got a look at each other in the moonlight and nearly burst out laughing. Lukas's hair was filled with burrs and was wildly tousled in every direction. His clothing was filthy and still damp, and his face had a scratch from some sort of thorn. I was sure I looked no better. Maybe it helped to make us look like the children of a peasant farmer, out in a desperate attempt to sell food.

Maybe it made us look like book smugglers who'd crossed a river and then crawled through a field.

We broke off a few overripe ears of corn, robbing a pig of its feed, but at least not a family of their supper. We stuffed them at the top of our sacks for cover—much better than the twigs had been—then Lukas nodded at me and we continued our walk through the woods. After another hour, Lukas held up two fingers, signaling that we had passed the second level of security. That was good, but we still had the third level to go.

Every step that crunched beneath my feet seemed to ring out like an alarm, for hoarfrost had blanketed the fields overnight. Maybe Lukas and I were covered in the frost, too, which seemed quite likely, cold as I was.

We traveled in near silence for endless kilometers, always on alert, ducking at any sound that could possibly signal a soldier was nearby. Each time we paused, after we were sure it was safe, Lukas and I would signal each other to move on.

By the time we finally emerged from the woods, the morning sun was low in the sky. It was a welcome bit of warmth, though the light was hardly a friend to us. We wouldn't get away with crawling or sneaking around any longer. Border guards at this level would be on horseback, with better visibility than those on foot and more speed to chase us.

I looked at Lukas and we seemed to exchange the same thought. We couldn't hide. We simply had to do our best to stay out of the way of the soldiers, and if that was impossible, then we'd test ourselves by playing out our roles as children of a peasant farmer.

Playing the most dangerous game of our lives.

THIRTY-TWO

I had time to reflect as I walked beside Lukas that morning, time to think about who I'd been and who I now was. In all my life, I'd never felt as strong as I did following this first border crossing, nor had I ever understood more that my life *mattered* as I did now.

I thought of my name, Audra. In Lithuanian, it meant "storm."

Before today, it had never felt like the proper name for me. Rather, I'd have expected that I should be named for a mouse, or a soft breeze, or named for the moment after a whisper, when no one is quite sure whether you've spoken at all.

But now I had grown into my name. I was the storm.

I redoubled my grip on the sacks slung over my shoulder, bracing myself against the wind coming at me, and continued down the path.

I'd come this far. No matter what was ahead, I could not stop now.

I *wouldn't* stop now.

And I understood, more than ever before, that the lives that depended upon me to succeed wanted to breathe in the air of a free country and exhale words spoken in our own language. I no longer worked for myself, or for my family. I had become a smuggler in the service of Lithuania.

Lithuania as it should be.

Free.

THIRTY-THREE

Lukas and I passed through the final ring of border guards without seeing a single person, and by mid-morning caught a ride with a friendly trader who said he'd take us as far as Šiauliai, near where Lukas said we'd meet Ben.

"Why don't we deliver these books first?" I asked.

"I don't know the priest. He'll be less suspicious if the books come directly from Ben."

So we rode in the back of the wagon, both of us sleeping flat on our backs, too exhausted to care whether we looked ridiculous, whether we were headed in the right direction, whether we could trust this trader. I only woke up when Lukas shook my arm, saying, "We're here, Audra. We need to go."

I groaned but rolled out of the wagon and onto my feet. The sun had shifted in the sky, though I wasn't sure how far we'd gone or exactly what time it was. At least my clothes were dry and I was warm again.

"We'll walk the rest of the way," Lukas told me after the trader had left. He couldn't be serious!

I picked up my two sacks of books. "How far?"

It probably wasn't far, but no matter how he answered, it would seem like half a world away. After all the walking I'd done lately, my legs were tired, my boots had holes in them, and I would've really preferred if the trader had just taken us all the way to wherever Ben was.

Lukas and I turned down a dirt road marked only by wagon wheels that had crossed it from time to time, though even the road was overgrown with thick grasses. I took comfort from that. This wasn't a place where many people had gone before, which meant it wasn't a place the soldiers would have much interest in.

"What do you know of the Hill of Crosses?" Lukas asked as we walked.

"Nothing." Which was true in the most literal sense. I'd never heard of it and could only guess that its name had some religious significance.

"I read a book on it," Lukas said. "About sixty years ago, there was an uprising here—"

"The one that ended with all our books being banned?"

Lukas chuckled. "No, *that* uprising was thirty years ago. But every generation has to try to prove itself against the Russian Empire, I suppose. And every uprising fails sooner or later, including the one sixty years ago. That fight happened on the same hill where we're now headed, and it became a major battle. So many fighters were killed that most families couldn't find the bodies of their loved ones. With no other way to mourn their loss, one family placed a cross on the site of the battle. And then another did it, and another. I heard that by now, there are over a hundred crosses."

"In honor of the dead?"

Lukas shook his head. "Yes, but it's so much more now. The crosses are a reminder of the people who belong to this country, those who have fought to preserve it. It's in honor of all Lithuanians."

"Like you?" I turned to him. "Were you born here in Lithuania, Lukas?"

He stepped backward. "Of course."

"Where?"

He hesitated, then slowly shook his head. "It doesn't matter."

"Do your parents know where you are?" When he didn't answer, I added, "Don't you miss them?"

"I do miss my mother," he murmured.

So he had a mother, somewhere. I said, "Go see her! To have my family back again, I would give up anything!"

"Even me?" I immediately fell silent as Lukas kicked at the ground, then said, "Would you even give me up, Audra? That's what Officer Rusakov wanted from you, wasn't it?"

I paused far too long as an ache worked its way through my chest, finally managing to say, "If you know that, then you also know I refused his offer."

"I do know that. But why didn't you tell me he'd made the offer? Don't you think that's something I'd want to know?"

"I didn't tell you . . ." I had to say the rest, had to make myself say the words, no matter how difficult it was. "I couldn't tell you until I knew what I'd decided."

He clicked his tongue and looked away, then after what felt like hours, said, "I know how hard that decision must have been."

"Knowing that I'll never see my parents again is awful, but if I turned you over to Rusakov, then I'd be the cause of whatever he did to you—imprisonment, or Siberia, or hanging—and I couldn't live with that. Also . . ." I cleared my throat. "I've never had a friend before, but I'm fairly sure turning you in would make me the worst friend ever."

Despite the seriousness of our conversation, he smiled. "Yes, I believe it would. I'm sorry you had to make such a decision. I can't tell you if it was right or wrong, but I am glad I'm still here."

By then, we had reached the hill of crosses, illuminated by a bright moon in the sky. The land was relatively flat all around, so although the hill wasn't particularly high, its very presence felt significant. And just as Lukas had described, at least a hundred crosses had been planted into the ground, some made of wood, others of metal, some ornate and elegant, others equally beautiful in their simplicity.

Lukas wandered at my side until he noticed a few old sticks that had fallen from a nearby tree. He broke off the ends of two of them to make a simple cross, then tied it with some twine from his pocket.

"Here," he said, placing it in my hands. "For your parents and all they fought for."

"Thank you." I walked back to the hill and laid my cross on the beam of another large wooden cross. "I believe if my parents knew what I was doing, they'd be proud."

"You'll have to tell them all about it," Lukas replied. "*When* you see them again."

He gave my hand a squeeze, and I realized how sad I would be if I couldn't do this work anymore, because it would mean I would no longer see him, likely ever again. The smuggling mattered, but my friendship with Lukas mattered as well.

"They're here!" a familiar voice called.

I turned to see Milda waving at us, with no disguise. Just Milda in a striped skirt with a white shirt and apron, a red vest, and with her gray hair in a netted cap. I stared back at her without waving, trying to convince myself it really was Milda. A . . . *normal* version of the woman I was used to seeing, which wasn't normal at all. She was standing in front of an empty wagon, feeding one of the horses.

I ran down the hill and threw my arms around her, though when we separated, she put her hands on my shoulders. "Ben won't be happy to see you."

"Indeed I am not," he grunted, walking up behind us, his face in a deep frown.

I'd already expected that from him, so I merely hugged him, too, even though his arms remained stiffly at his side. "You saved me, Ben. You got me out of that prison."

Once I'd released him, Ben scrunched his face and threw out a dismissive hand. "Nah, you saved yourself. A foolish girl like you, I knew you'd come up with a wilder scheme than I ever could to get yourself back to us. I only needed to give you the right tools."

"You didn't know it would work, though. What if I couldn't figure it out?"

He turned to me and his expression became serious. "I won't always be there to save you or teach you. Lukas won't always be there to keep an eye on you. At some point, Audra, you were going to have to learn to look out for yourself, and you did."

"That's why you can trust me to be here now."

"She was good at the border," Lukas said, offering me a hand into the back of the wagon. I gave him my books first, then climbed in with him. "Really good, and not just at the border, but everywhere she smuggles. Certainly better than I was when I started out."

If Lukas never paid me another compliment in my life, I figured that was about the nicest thing he could have said, and I beamed with pride.

"Where are we going?" I asked.

"My place." Ben coughed as he climbed into the driver's seat beside Milda. A deep cough that concerned me, though he'd only scold me if I pointed it out. "It isn't much for a home, but the Cossacks don't seem to know about it, so as far as I'm concerned, it's a castle."

We drove for a half hour to a small hut in a tiny patch of woods, which I supposed was about as far from everything as a person could get. Ben was right to describe it in such humble terms. The walls were made of logs that had been stacked and mudded together, and I expected the thatch roof likely collapsed with each new snowfall. But it had a small rock chimney and smoke was coming from it, and even from out here, I smelled something delicious.

"We kept a stew warm for you," Milda said. "As we have every night, hoping you would arrive safely."

She dished up bowls of stew for both Lukas and me, then offered one to Ben, who said he wasn't hungry. He definitely wasn't feeling well. Even if I were on my deathbed, I'd still never refuse one of Milda's meals.

While we ate, Milda sat across from me and said, "I still

haven't decided whether to thank you or scold you. You traded yourself as a prisoner for me."

"I did the right thing, Milda," I said, then lowered my eyes. "But only because I almost did the wrong thing. Officer Rusakov wanted me to give up Lukas to him, and maybe Ben as well. So he was always planning to arrest me that night, because he was sure I'd give him the names. I hoped he'd be so consumed with the thought of arresting me that he'd forget about you."

My confession clearly came as a surprise to Milda and Ben, both who turned their attention to Lukas for his reaction. But with a kind smile at me, Lukas said, "Audra and I already settled this." He finished with a wink, a reminder that suggested he understood, and that there was nothing to forgive.

With those few words, Milda's expression warmed again and she said, "Well, in that case, I think you both need a double serving of supper."

While I ate, I looked at Ben. "So what happens now?"

Ben coughed again. "The same thing that Lukas was supposed to take care of before. You're leaving Lithuania and this time we'll send Milda with you."

I'd already anticipated that answer, but more than ever, I didn't want to leave. Not now, when I was finally figuring out how to do this work. "No, Ben, I can still help!"

He shook his head. "They know who you are, they've seen what you can do. If you are caught again, this time they probably won't even send you to Siberia. They'll hold a public hanging, prove to the people that everyone who breaks the law will be punished, no matter who it is."

"They wouldn't hang someone as young as me," I said, realizing my hand had inadvertently gone to my neck.

"They have before, and they will again if necessary. Until you're older, you're finished with smuggling."

"I just need to be smarter about it, like you are. You can teach me, you can show me what to do!"

Ben waved away that idea. "You haven't survived so far because of anything I've taught you. You survive on your instincts, your bag of magic tricks, and your foolish hope that there will ever be an end to this. I can't teach you to be smart, or weed the foolishness out of you—that's just who you are."

My cheeks warmed. "Then trust who I am. Let me keep smuggling."

"Your parents would agree with me, Audra. They would say—"

"My parents aren't here anymore, isn't that your whole point?"

"Then I'll act as your father, and I'm telling you—"

"You are not my father, Ben. You are not in charge of me!" I realized I was yelling, but I didn't care. For once, I needed Ben to hear me. "My parents left me alone and now I have to make my own decisions. I don't care if you want me to continue smuggling or not. I will do it because that's what I've decided!"

Ben opened his mouth, then closed it and stared at me. After he had calmed himself, he shook his head. "No, you will not. First chance we get, Lukas and I are taking you and Milda out of Lithuania."

I slammed my spoon down on the table, then threw back my chair and stomped outside. They let me stay there until my temper had cooled off, and when I walked back inside, Milda only pointed to a bedroll that had been laid open on the floor near the fire. "That's for you," she said. "Take a few days to rest and I'm sure you'll begin to see that Ben is right."

With some reluctance, I thanked her and lay down to sleep. But it didn't come easily to me. All I could think about as I finally closed my eyes was that I already knew that Ben was right. The smartest thing to do was to leave the country and get to where it was safe.

And despite that, I intended to stay. There were still more books to be carried, more shelves to be filled. I couldn't give up now.

CHAPTER

THIRTY-FOUR

The few days they wanted me to rest became a long week of waiting for Ben, who had come down with a cold that seemed to be getting worse each day. But when I asked about his health, he only brushed me aside and said, "You won't use my little cough as an excuse to stay here. Lukas and I are going to fill the order for the priest and then take you back where you belong. Milda won't be far behind, though she has some deliveries of her own to handle on the way out of the country."

"She's willing to give up book smuggling?" I asked.

"She has to, for the same reasons that you do," Ben said. "No more arguing."

If we weren't going to argue, then we weren't going to speak, for I couldn't do one and not the other. When Ben was finally well enough to travel, I rode in the back of the wagon with Lukas, rather than up front beside him, in protest, which he said was all the better because then I could keep watch for Cossacks. By late afternoon, we arrived in

Kražiai, and made our delivery of books to a dark-haired priest who met us at the doors of a large and beautiful white church with tall windows on all sides and a tower on the front. After ushering us inside and inspecting our titles, he put money in Ben's hand, then gave him a paper, saying, "Here are the orders for our next books."

"Already?" I asked.

"Already," the priest echoed. "The people here have been waiting weeks in hopes of getting these books. They will be so delighted to finally have them. So when can you return?"

I swallowed hard. It didn't appear that I'd be allowed to come back again. But where Ben could hear, I said, "The sooner the better, no?"

The priest gestured around him. "This church has stood for over one hundred years, outlasting war and fire and the ravages of nature. But it faces a new enemy now, a tsar who insists we believe in his God. At first, he politely invited us to abandon this place and gather in his own cathedrals. When we refused, he tried to lure us away through rewards and bribery. Now, when all else fails, he intends to force us out." The priest took a deep breath. "The soldiers among us have new orders, to destroy our churches and our relics. If they cannot remove the people from the church, they will simply remove the church and the people will have nowhere else to go for worship. One day soon, they will come for this place. The only weapon I have to stop them is a people who feel powerful enough to stand between a Cossack soldier and the doors of this building. And how do I make them feel powerful?"

"You give them books," I whispered.

He leaned forward, resting his arms on his knees. "I know the risks you are taking, and I beg your forgiveness for continuing to ask more of you, but despite how young you are—or maybe because of how young you are—you are finding ways past the soldiers. Maybe they see you but don't believe a girl your age could commit such serious crimes. Or maybe they never see you because a girl your age is more clever than they wish to believe. Either way, I have books here today that I did not have last night, and I hope that I can tell my people to expect more soon. Will you bring them?"

Ben said, "Stop filling her head with this talk. She . . ." He paused for a coughing spasm, one that continued on even after the priest helped him into the pew of a church.

"You're ill." The priest stood and offered a hand for support, but Ben brushed it away.

"Nonsense. I've got an order to fill."

"*We've* got an order to fill," Lukas said. "Audra and I can do it, Ben."

"Let them do it," the priest said. "Your cough will betray yourself and everyone around you in an instant."

Ben started to protest, but even that ended in a coughing fit. The priest helped him to his feet and promised to find Ben a bed where he could rest, but Ben looked at Lukas and me long enough to say, "I don't have a good feeling about this trip. Wait for me to recover and I'll do it."

"Get some rest, Ben," Lukas said. "We'll be back soon."

As we began to walk away, I asked, "What do you think he means, that he doesn't have a good feeling about this trip?"

Lukas shrugged. "I think he's angry about being left behind, and angry that you are going out yet again."

"Well, if we're going, let's go," I said. Though if I was being honest, I didn't have a good feeling about it either. Which was ridiculous—there was no reason to be any more worried this time than any other time. But I was worried.

Before we left, the priest insisted on sending us with as much food as we could carry, which unfortunately wouldn't be enough for the entire journey. I appreciated it anyway. Ben also gave us some money for the printer and a list of other places we needed to visit to collect orders.

"Will we have to return with all these books?" I asked Lukas.

"As many as possible," Lukas said, the answer I already knew he'd give.

It should have only taken us a day or two to collect the orders, but at each stop, we met someone who begged us to make one more stop for someone else who was running out of books. Our stack of orders was growing fast.

"We'll never fill them all," I told him.

But Lukas only grinned at me. "Maybe not, and isn't that wonderful?"

I supposed it was, and so over the next week, I made a point of working harder and faster during the waking hours and spending every moment before I fell asleep trying to figure out how we might transport so many books.

The first snowfall of the season came the night before Lukas and I were planning to cross the border, and proved to be a great disappointment. There wasn't enough snow to keep the soldiers inside their huts, but what little had fallen would easily mark our footprints.

"Distraction," Lukas said. "That's what you're always saying. So how can we use the snow for distraction?"

I glanced over at him. "What if it's not about distraction, but rather, creating the scene that we want them to see?"

His eyes narrowed. "What do you mean?"

I took a deep breath. "Where is the nearest camp of soldiers?"

We wouldn't look for just any camp, but rather one with bunkers where the soldiers might be sleeping overnight. We'd passed one on our last smuggling route and I remembered seeing a pair of boots left outside, likely so no one would track dirt into the bunkers. It took us awhile to find the same bunker as before, but it seemed perfect. Tonight, there were four pairs of boots outside.

Which meant there were at least four soldiers inside. I would not forget that.

Lukas shook his head. "If they see a missing pair of boots, they'll be able to warn the others what we've done. They'll know the tracks we've made are fakes!"

"They'll know some of the tracks are fakes, but not necessarily which are ours and which are theirs. This is a good plan, Lukas!"

He grunted. "You say it's a good plan because you'll be in hiding while I go up to steal them."

"And if you don't get caught, then it's an excellent plan! Better hurry—we don't know when they'll be coming out."

He cast me a skeptical look, then slowly rose to his feet and crept toward the bunker. This plan really could work, but it wasn't as simple as I'd made it sound and we both knew it. Lukas's boots were left back here with me, so if he ended up having to run at the last minute, he'd be doing it in only socks. He needed to slip on one pair of boots and then carry back a second pair for me, returning in the exact same prints he'd made on the way there.

Lukas was nearly to the bunker now, and he had begun to crouch down to pick up the first pair of boots when the door opened. He darted behind the bunker with wild eyes on me, certain he was already caught.

I was anxious too. His footprints were clearly visible, including those leading to where he was now, and there was nothing I could do to help him from here. My mind raced through the few items still left in my father's shoulder bag, but nothing would be of any use, not for something like this.

Two soldiers walked outside, obviously on orders to check on the horses, for they were grumbling loudly about it.

In Russian, one said, "Why are we always picked for the worst jobs? I have half a mind to refuse the order next time and see what happens."

His companion said, "What happens is the commander will leave you with half a mind, by the time your punishment is finished. You check on the horses, I'll check the area for any activity."

While the first man walked away from the bunker, the second one stepped in front of it. If he turned around, he'd see Lukas.

I signaled to Lukas to begin moving, which he did, and fortunately, the soldier was too busy searching in the distance to look directly beneath his feet for Lukas's footprints.

The soldier continued to walk around the back of the bunker, which would force Lukas to the same side of the bunker as the soldier who was checking on the horses. That man had finished now and was on his way back up the hill, saying, "The horses are fine. Where are you?"

By then, I had scooped enough snow into my palm to form a loosely packed snowball. I threw it as high as I could into the air and at a slight angle, hoping it would land directly on the soldier's head.

My aim was off and instead it landed in the branches of a tree near the soldier, creating enough of an impact to shake a much larger dusting of snow down on him. If Lukas were not still in danger, I would have giggled to see it. But he still was.

The soldier cursed and brushed at his face, giving Lukas the chance to cross to the front of the bunker, shove his feet into a large pair of boots and pick up another, then dart crossways into the woods to hide.

The second soldier had come around the bunker by then and began laughing at his companion, who wasn't at all amused.

"I've got snow down my uniform," he said. "Even the Lithuanian birds are against us."

"Come, let's go inside and let you change. We'll be on patrol soon and you'll be better off if you're dry."

He led his companion inside, brushing off snow from his shoulders as he did. Neither of them looked at where the pile of boots had been and noticed the two missing pairs.

Once it was safe, Lukas made his way to me. I put on one of the pairs, then we trekked away from the bunker, covering our former tracks until the new fallen snow had covered the oldest tracks.

"That was the worst plan ever," Lukas said.

"We can discuss that after we're across the border." I grinned and began leading the way, relatively unconcerned about the tracks we were leaving behind, and trying not to think about the many hazards that still awaited us.

THIRTY-FIVE

As before, it wasn't difficult to leave the country, and with Lukas and me walking about in boots that left Cossack prints, I wasn't worried about being followed. We removed the oversized boots for our own shoes to cross the rope over the Neman River—otherwise I don't know how I'd have kept my feet wrapped on the rope line.

"These are . . . heavy boots," Lukas said as he crossed. He'd tied the boots together and slung them over his neck, and it seemed they were cutting off his air. Not his wisest move.

I wasn't doing much better. My boots were slung over one shoulder, making it hard to lift that arm every time I needed to slide along the rope. Not my wisest move either.

Or, I supposed, when one was crossing on an icy rope over a cold river to avoid soldiers who were prepared to shoot us on sight, wisdom and foolishness lost all usual meanings. Fortunately, we did cross it, resting for a while on the opposite bank while I massaged my shoulder and Lukas simply breathed. As soon as we saw the shadows of soldiers beginning to patrol across the river, it was time to walk on.

We reached Tilsit shortly after dawn, and though I looked forward to sleeping, I was also eager to see the printer again and put in the order for books. To our surprise, he merely glanced at the titles and said, "You carriers are providing me a fine living. Are you sure this is all you want for today?"

I smiled at him. "Lower your prices and we'll order more titles."

He chuckled. "Maybe I'll raise my prices. Where else will you go for books?" He laughed at himself and said, "I am a fair man, and my prices are generous because I wish to see Russia as far from my doorstep as possible. It would be worth it to me to never earn another ruble again if those soldiers were gone. But I warn you, some of these titles will make the tsar angrier with you than usual."

Lukas smiled. "I hope so. When will these books be ready?"

The printer looked over his list again. "I'll need a week. That should give you time to figure out how you're going to bring all of these back with you."

"Where should we stay in the meantime?" I wondered aloud.

"That reminds me," the printer said. "I have a note for you." He passed a paper over to me, something that might have seemed a small thing for anyone else, but I received it with a swell of pride. Only a few months ago, I wouldn't have been able to read this paper, but he'd given it to me assuming I could read it, and now I could.

I unfolded it and immediately said to Lukas, "It's from Milda! How did she—"

"She gave me that only yesterday, when she came in with a book order of her own," the printer said.

Summarizing the note, I said, "Ben sent her over here, too, only she intends to stay. She's found a little place to live a few streets away from here and has asked us to come."

That was a relief, especially since I hadn't had a decent bite to eat in days and we both knew Milda was sure to have food ready for us. When we arrived, she was just pulling out some potato pancakes, as if she'd been expecting us. I never did understand Milda's instincts for knowing when guests were coming to eat, but her timing was almost always perfect.

"After you're finished, I'll show you around," Milda said. "I've only arrived two days ago myself, so I've hardly had time to settle in, but this place was available immediately, so I took it. Perhaps you've already noticed the extra coffins in the back room."

Lukas's head popped up and our eyes met, not sure whether to be amused or horrified. He said, "Milda, is this an—"

"Undertaker's home, or it was, before the undertaker himself died. There was no one to take over his business."

A shiver crawled up my spine. "Is he still . . . here?"

"His body, or his soul?" Milda asked the question like either possibility could be true. But before I could reply, she said, "He had a proper burial, so let's hope his soul went with him. The other coffins are empty. Don't worry, I checked."

Of course she did.

She continued to describe the home to us, saying, "I'd like to convert the parlor into some sort of shop. I'll begin by selling off those extra coffins. Everyone needs one eventually! Or I could remake them into beds. Do you suppose . . ."

She puttered about, telling us her plans to expand the little home and make it a place of rest for smugglers—before their deaths and not after, she was careful to point out—and to use the shop to raise funds to purchase more books for those in Lithuania who could not afford them.

But my mind was already elsewhere, on how to get all the books we had ordered back into the country. We had twice the number of books to carry as we'd brought across the border before, and the river water was so icy cold by now, I dreaded having to cross that way.

There had to be an answer.

And while Milda pulled out the ingredients to bake bread, I remembered the second issue on my mind. I reached into the shoulder bag for my father's journal and opened it to the last page of notes he'd made, the page with the recipe. I said, "Milda, do you think you could help me get a few things?"

She glanced up, midway through sifting a cup of flour. "Such as?"

"Two of them are the same cooking items you have there, sugar and baking soda. And I need some cotton fabric, if you can spare any. The final item is harder: saltpeter."

Milda arched a brow. "Saltpeter?"

"Surely some of the farmers in this area will have it. Maybe if we ask nicely."

"Saltpeter?" she repeated, more suspicious than before. "What are you making?"

"My father's final trick before he was arrested. Milda, if this works, it could save our lives one day."

"Well, I'm in favor of that." Milda sighed. "All right, then I will find you some saltpeter."

It took her three days, but finally she located a farmer who made saltpeter from his cow's manure and sold it as a powder to blacksmiths for creating gunpowder. Milda clearly hadn't known that was the use for saltpeter when I'd first asked her for it.

She held the bag of it close to her chest and looked down at me. "Promise me that you aren't making gunpowder. No weapons."

"What I'm making isn't a weapon, I promise you. It shouldn't harm anyone."

She caught my word choice. "Shouldn't?"

I held out my hands for the saltpeter. "Please trust me, Milda."

With a sigh, she gave me the bag but said, "If my new home explodes because of this, I will be angry with you, Audra."

"It won't explode," Lukas assured her, then when her back was turned, he whispered to me, "Will it explode?"

I shrugged. I genuinely hoped not, but hope was all I had.

We waited until Milda had gone to bed for the night, then cooked the ingredients on her stovetop. It resembled a soft dough when it was ready, and we rolled the dough into a tube shape inside some of Milda's cotton fabric, then poked a little stick inside the center of it.

By morning, when everything was dry, we pulled out the stick and inserted the laces from the soldiers' boots that we had stolen, to use as a fuse, cut the tube into pieces, then wrapped everything up tight with Milda's extra stockings, though we didn't intend to tell her about that. She wouldn't be happy about the sacrifice of her stockings.

"Only four," Lukas mumbled. "Do you think it will be enough?"

"There's no way to know," I said. "Honestly, I wish we had many more, but until we know if they work, I suppose it doesn't matter. We'll just have to put them to good use and pray they work when we light them."

"They've got to work," Lukas said with a smile. "But for now, they are the four most beautiful smoke bombs I've ever seen."

"I think they're the only smoke bombs you've ever seen." With a smile, I handed him half the pile. "Two for you and two for me. May we use them well."

He drew in a deep breath. "I don't see how these will help us get across the border."

My grin widened. "These aren't for the border. I have a different plan for that."

THIRTY-SIX

By the time our books were ready, Lukas and I were well rested and eager to test our plan.

"If this works, we might be able to do this over and over again!" Lukas said.

"Let's just try it once, then decide."

I wasn't sure which of us had the more difficult job for crossing. Because he had papers, Lukas would drive our wagon over the bridge. And if the border guards asked, he'd have a good excuse to be traveling.

To deliver a body for burial.

That was my role.

I'd be inside the coffin wearing Milda's old woman makeup, which would give me a corpse-like appearance. And I'd be lying on top of a blanket covering all the ordered books. We'd drilled small air holes into the sides of the coffin, so although I wouldn't be breathing comfortably, I would be able to breathe.

"I thought your last idea was horrible," Lukas said, slowly shaking his head. "This is so much worse, Audra."

"Just get me out of the coffin as soon as it's safe," I said with a shudder. Every time I remembered what I was about to do, my gut twisted worse than usual. I hoped this idea would not be a predictor of how this trip would go.

"You'll deliver these books, then come directly back here, yes?" Milda asked.

"Unless they need my help." A good excuse, I figured.

"*I* need your help," Milda said. "There is so much good we can do over here, and your parents would want you where it's safe. That's why they sent you to me."

I paused, knowing she was right, even if I hated the idea of leaving the adventure of smuggling behind. But I did have to go back today, for there was one very important item I still hoped to find. "Do you remember the locked book I brought you? After the fire, it wasn't in your home anymore."

Milda frowned. "Oh, my sweet child, I don't know where it is."

Tears filled my eyes, which was ridiculous, because only a few months ago I'd hated the book, resented it for all that it had cost me. I'd been indifferent to it, I had forgotten it, and now that it was gone . . . I wanted more than anything to see if my key might open it.

"Could they have burned it?" I asked.

Milda didn't answer, because maybe she couldn't. Or

maybe she couldn't bear to tell me the truth. If they had burned it, then I didn't want her to answer.

Milda kissed me on the forehead, then waved goodbye as Lukas helped me into the coffin. We'd tried to pad the lining, but I still felt the books unevenly layered beneath me. At least they were bound in cloth so the discomfort wasn't unbearable.

Lukas covered me in burial cloth, including my face, which was what the soldiers would expect if they decided to inspect the coffin. I turned my head toward an air hole, though with a cloth over my face, I didn't get much fresh air. But it made me feel better to know it was there.

"Don't die in there," Lukas said, his idea of a joke.

I answered, "Don't die out there." Not a joke.

Minutes later, we rode away. I passed the time trying to add to the story I'd been writing, guessing the spelling of words as they drifted through my mind, making plans for my future with Milda after I returned to Tilsit, thinking of Lukas and how he'd become such a dear friend to me. Thinking of myself and how much I'd changed over the last few months.

Thinking of anything but where I was, and how much was at stake, and hoping Lukas could pull off his role at the border.

I knew exactly when we reached the border, because even from inside the coffin, I heard the shouted orders of the soldiers to stop.

Lukas obeyed and in Russian told the soldiers he had papers and was transporting a body for burial.

"Into Lithuania?"

"Her family's cemetery plots are here."

"We need to see the body."

"Sir, that would be disrespectful."

"We need to see the body," the soldier repeated, and heavy footsteps made their way to me.

I turned my head forward, closed my eyes, and tried to appear . . . well, dead. I waited until the last possible second to suck in a breath of air and hoped I wouldn't have to hold it for long.

Milda had done my makeup to drain my face of color and to make my eyes and cheeks appear sunken in. But I'd also been sweating a little while in this tight space and I wondered if the makeup had begun to run. If they lifted the thin sheet over my face, they might notice. Even the slightest flutter of my eyelid might give me away, and I wasn't sure if I could control that.

Relax. I had to relax.

The coffin lid shifted and it was hard not to breathe in the rush of cool, fresh air. I felt the weight of eyes studying me, wondering whether to lift the fabric.

"She seems to be young," a soldier said to Lukas. "How did she die?"

"Typhus."

The coffin lid slammed closed and instantly both soldiers were yelling at Lukas and I think one might have hit him with the butt of his rifle.

"Do you want to give us disease?" another man asked.

"No, sirs, of course not. I just didn't think to tell you. You'll forgive me. I haven't had much education."

"Yet you speak excellent Russian. Where did you learn it?"

Lukas hesitated a few seconds longer than he should have before finding his lie. "I used to work in the home of a Russian family."

My ears perked up. Was that a lie or not? Something about it rang truer than when I'd heard him lie before.

"How long ago did you work there?" a soldier asked. "Because I thought you looked familiar."

That worried me. The last thing Lukas needed was to be recognized by anyone, for any reason.

"Whatever my past, now I work with the sick and diseased," Lukas continued, obviously hinting that he had been around many typhus patients. Or more specifically, hinting that it was possible he might be a typhus patient himself one day.

That, I knew, was a lie. And it sounded different to my ears from his claim of having once worked in a Russian home. My curiosity about Lukas's past was beginning to burn inside me.

"On your way," the soldier ordered. "Begone."

I smiled and finally began to breathe again. At least that had gone well. Hopefully in a wagon, the rest of the soldiers would assume we had already passed inspection, but that wasn't certain yet.

We still had a long way to go.

THIRTY-SEVEN

Somewhere during the ride, I must have fallen asleep, because my eyes flew open as soon as the wagon jerked to a stop. At first I panicked, realizing I didn't know why we had stopped, or where we were.

I listened for any voices but heard none, including Lukas's. Was he still out there?

I fought the temptation to push at the coffin lid and free myself, though I desperately wanted to. With so much silence around me, I was feeling trapped and like I couldn't get a decent breath. I turned my head and sucked in what air I could from the small drill hole. I wished I could tell whether it was still light outside.

What was happening out there?

Then the wagon beneath me shook a little, feeling the same way as when the soldiers had climbed in to check on me. If it was them, I had to appear dead, had to make them believe.

I'd just turned my face upward again and closed my eyes when the coffin lid shifted, then was pulled open. It was dark outside, which was a relief. Had sunlight glared down on me, even through closed eyes, I likely would have flinched at so much brightness.

But no one spoke and I couldn't peek. I had to wait, to be as patient as the dead always were.

Then a hand touched my shoulder and shook it. "Audra, are you—"

Recognizing Lukas's voice, my eyes popped open, and I drew in a breath. He pulled the fabric off my face, and I saw him staring down at me, his concerned expression slowly relaxing.

"You looked so believable, I was worried. Truly worried."

"*You* were worried? Why did you have to be so quiet? You couldn't have told me it was you before you opened the lid? Help me out of this box, please!"

"I didn't think to warn you it was me," he said, grabbing my arms to help lift me. "And we do need to be quiet. We're quite a way past the border security, but we still might see patrols coming through the forests. You ought to wash that makeup off. If a patrol does come through, you won't have time to get back into the coffin and I don't think we'll be able to explain why you look like that without convincing them that the dead have risen."

"That's not funny, Lukas." But I laughed anyway and so did he.

He pointed off to his left. "There is a stream where you can wash. I'll check on the books."

I jumped from the wagon and hurried toward the stream, eager to have a clean face again. I dipped my hands into the cold water and brushed it over my face, then dipped my hands in once again and scrubbed harder with my fingers. If our luck continued this way, then the worst was over.

But in the same instant I completed that thought, I regretted it. Our luck had run out.

I slowly lowered my hands, sucking in a breath that I could not release. Directly across the stream was a man dressed in peasant clothing with a rifle in his hands, staring at me with a dark expression that sent a chill up my spine.

"What's a girl like you doing out here on such a cold night? And what's all that paint on your face?"

I didn't say a word. I didn't even remember how to speak.

"Stand up and come with me. We've already found your friend."

We. Then it wasn't only him, and they already had Lukas.

My heart sank. Lukas had been my one hope to get out of this trouble, but sure enough, when I got to the crest of the hill, he was seated in the back of the wagon on top of the coffin, his arms tied behind him and a gag around his mouth. A woman with a second rifle was standing watch over

Lukas. She was similarly dressed to the man who had captured me and had matted brown hair sticking out from her head scarf. Her eyes flicked between the man and me, growing colder with each look.

"We were hired to transport that coffin," I said. "Nothing more."

"Yes, but I'm looking at the paint on your face and I'm thinking maybe you were *in* that coffin before stopping here. And if you were, then I already know why. One smuggler can always recognize another, isn't that right?"

"We're a brother and sister—"

He whistled. "Too bad. Your friend there just claimed you were cousins. You two should get your lies straight for next time, if there is a next time. Get into the wagon."

Lukas looked at me apologetically while I climbed in and sat on the coffin, reminding myself that at least here, we were protecting the books. The man followed me with a length of rope provided to him by the woman who I guessed was his wife.

He tied one end to my left wrist and then began wrapping the rope around me. I inhaled to expand my chest and widened my arms as much as I dared, hoping he wouldn't notice. While he wound the rope, he said, "We were there at the border when your friend spoke with the Cossack officers. They said he looked familiar, and my wife thought he did too. Your friend said he used to work in the home of a Russian landowner, but so did my wife. Except she truly was a servant there." He turned to Lukas. "She was one of *your* servants, boy. You are one of *them*."

I looked over at Lukas for confirmation of what she had said, or a denial, but he was looking down, refusing to acknowledge them or me. Which was probably its own confession.

By then, the man had finished winding the rope around me, and now he knotted it on my right hand. I slowly exhaled but kept my arms widened.

"Come morning, we'll take you both back to those same Cossacks, offer you in trade for our son, who they arrested a week ago. They'll get back one of their own, and we'll get our own back."

"They won't honor the trade," I said. "They'll take us, then arrest the two of you as well."

"Look who knows so much about the Cossacks," his wife said with a wicked grin. "Maybe we should ask what it is she smuggles."

He held up a lantern and stared directly into my eyes. "Medicines? Drinks? Food? Books?" My eyes must have widened because he smiled and turned back to his wife. "They're book smugglers."

"Books. Absolutely worthless," his wife said.

"That's what they must be hiding in the coffin." The man rubbed his hand over his beard. "We'll take this before we turn them in tomorrow. We could use this too."

"Please let us go," I said. "I promise that you will receive no reward for our capture—we're not that valuable. And you risk being caught yourselves."

The man rapped Lukas on the back of his head. "You might not be valuable, but this is their boy and they'll want him back. All the blame for the books in the coffin will rest with you. *Rest in peace* with you, I should say." He laughed at his joke, but his wife didn't seem to understand it and Lukas and I weren't playing along. So he added, "You'll fit in nicely with the Cossack plans. We overheard them talking about a demonstration in a couple of days, as punishment for that town's love of books."

"What town?" I asked.

"Kražiai."

My heart sank. That was the last place we had been, where the priest had warned us of rumors of trouble. But they weren't rumors. It was going to happen two days from now, and there was nothing we could do to help them, or to stop it from happening.

At this point, I wasn't even sure we could save ourselves.

THIRTY-EIGHT

After double-checking the knots on my hands and Lukas's, the man jumped from the wagon and began a muttered conversation with his wife. I kept my head down but listened carefully, trying to pick out any useful words.

There wasn't much. She was tired and wanted to sleep, but he insisted they had to keep watch over us. I took that as a signal that we should look as nonthreatening as possible, so I nodded off, closing my eyes. I hoped Lukas did the same.

He must have, for in a louder voice, the man said, "They'll sleep through the night. You and I can trade off checking on them."

"You can check on them," she said. "I'll be useless tomorrow if I don't sleep too." I heard her footsteps pad away from the wagon and shuffling sounds as she prepared a bed for herself in the back of their own wagon.

The man seemed to be walking around our wagon, a slow constant circle that was beginning to irritate me. I was cold and uncomfortable in this position in which I was faking sleep, and I had to keep my arms out so the rope looked tight. Meanwhile, I thought it was possible that Lukas actually was sleeping. I heard his light snoring.

After what might've been a hundred rounds, the man sat on the back of our wagon. With one eye, I peeked at him, saw him facing away from us but resting his arm on the far side of the coffin where we sat. Twenty minutes later, he was resting his head there. After another twenty minutes, he was snoring too.

I slowly raised my head and was pleased to see Lukas do the same. He shook his head at me and shrugged as if to say there was nothing he could do to escape. But I sat up straight to make my body as lean as possible, pulled my arms in tight to myself, and the rope went slack. Both of my wrists were still tied, but if I was quiet enough and patient in my movements, I could escape this rope.

This was another trick of my father's, borrowed from a young magician who was quickly garnering fame for his escape acts. My father used to tell my mother that if he could perfect the same escape tricks, perhaps he'd become famous too.

I didn't know any of the special tricks he had for untying knots, but I did know enough to keep my arms close to my body as I wiggled to loosen the rope. When it had gathered at my waist, I quietly stood and let the rope fall.

The wagon creaked when I did and the man stopped snoring. I froze in place and waited breathlessly until he started again, then I stepped out of the first loop of rope to fall at my feet, making the rest of the rope even more slack, and in less than a minute, all that remained was my tied hands. With so much rope now available, I had no trouble bringing them around front where I could untie them with my fingers and teeth.

Lukas had been slowly shifting his body to face away from me so that I wouldn't have to move much in order to untie his ropes. Once I did, we gestured to each other about the best way to escape.

I pointed to the coffin, silently asking what we were supposed to do about our books. Lukas shook his head, pointing the direction he wanted us to run.

But I couldn't accept any escape that left these books behind. Not when we had worked so hard to get the books this far, and when so many people had given us what little money they had for them.

So I pointed to the man's rifle. Lukas shook his head, but I gestured to him to get into the driver's seat. He had better do it, for I was going to do my part of the plan whether Lukas was ready or not.

He rolled his eyes and I was fairly sure he whispered a prayer to save himself from me, or our captors . . . or mostly from me. But he did climb into the driver's seat and lift the reins.

I crept toward the man, whose rifle was lying beneath one hand as he slept. I started to pull it free, but he stirred and redoubled his grip. I turned to look at Lukas again to ask what I should do and he mouthed the words "Hold on."

I wound the rope that had tied us around a post of the wagon. That would keep me in the wagon bed. With my other hand, I grabbed a handle of the coffin, and I closed my eyes. The instant I did, Lukas shook the reins to rush the horses forward. They bolted as if fire were at their hooves. The man awoke, but I kicked him with one leg and he rolled off the edge of the wagon, landing facedown on the ground. Working against the momentum of our ride, I tried to position myself as much as possible behind the coffin, and it was a good thing I did because the man fired off a shot toward us, and I heard it pierce one side of the coffin.

"Keep going!" I cried.

"Obviously!" Lukas's attention was on keeping our wagon balanced until we got back on the road, but once we did, he only rode us faster.

We had to expect the man and his wife would follow us, but by the time they hitched their horse to their little cart, we would have a good lead on them.

I climbed into the seat beside Lukas and said, "We've got to get to Kražiai."

"Agreed. We've got to warn them."

We rode as fast as we dared to push the horses, and when they began showing signs of exhaustion, we pulled off the road to wait out the night and to catch our own breaths. Luckily, by then the snow had melted so our tracks weren't as visible as they might have been a few days ago. Still, the ground was wet, so we couldn't trust that we were totally safe yet, and even if we could, my heart was pounding far too fast to consider relaxing.

While Lukas tended to the horses, I crept back as near as I dared to the road, watching for any signs of the man and his wife. But though I waited for almost half an hour, I never did see them. Either they had taken a different route, or they had given up.

I finally returned to Lukas, who was sitting on the edge of the wagon, just where the man had been before we rolled him out. But Lukas's shoulders were slumped and when he looked up at me, he merely said, "I never heard them coming toward me, not until it was too late. Maybe for once I should save you instead of it always being the other way around."

"The first time we met, you saved me," I said. "And we escaped together. I couldn't have done that alone."

He gave me a half smile, then slumped again. "It might not have mattered if the soldiers hadn't recognized me at the border, or thought they did. Just when I thought I'd escaped my past, it comes back to me again."

I sat beside him. "Why would they have recognized you? Did you work for that Russian family, Lukas? Or . . . are you *in* that Russian family?"

He shrugged. "My mother is Lithuanian and my father is Russian. I was born here, raised with other Lithuanian boys and girls, but when I turned twelve, my father demanded I end all friendships with anyone who wasn't entirely Russian. 'I'm not entirely Russian,' I told him. 'Should I not be a friend to myself?' Despite what he'd said, I didn't end those friendships. I refused. One night I couldn't get home because of a snowstorm and my best friend, a boy named Otto, let me stay with him. His parents always read to him before bedtime, though I didn't know then that it was from an illegal book. I just sat with them and listened to the story. They were only halfway through it when Cossacks burst into the room and took Otto's father away. They dragged him into the square and were about to whip him. I ran after the soldiers and tried to stop it, then realized the officer in charge was my own father."

I drew in a breath. "That must have been awful."

"He told me to go home, but I refused. I asked him why they were doing this over a book, but he wouldn't answer and only said that Otto's father was getting the punishment he deserved. I stood between them and said I would not allow the whipping to happen."

"Surely that ended it." I couldn't imagine any father would refuse his own child something so important.

"'Back down right now, or you'll get the same.'" Lukas glanced over at me. "That's what my father said. I refused that, too, so he had one of his men grab me and drag me away. I escaped him and ran, just ran as fast as I could. The soldier I'd escaped was chasing me, but someone reached out from the shadows, grabbed my arm, and pulled me into hiding with him, whispering that if I stayed quiet, I'd be safe. That was Ben, almost a year ago." Lukas sighed. "I haven't been home since then. I don't even know if my home is still there. You'll understand why when you hear my father's name."

"Rusakov," I whispered, putting together the pieces. "Your father is Officer Rusakov. That's why you had to hide when he was inspecting wagons on the road, and why you wanted to stay in the forest when they were burning the town. You didn't want him to see you."

"My father isn't evil," Lukas said. "But he is wrong. Wrong about Lithuania, wrong about books, and wrong about the way to enforce the horrible laws. Until he changes his mind, I won't go home."

I put my hand over his, and we sat there in silence for a very long time, until finally Lukas sighed. "If the horses are rested, we should get on the road again. We have to get to Kražiai before the soldiers do."

THIRTY-NINE

By midafternoon we arrived in the town of Kražiai with illegal books hidden inside a coffin, which now felt far too ominous. We had expected to be the first to give the warning that soldiers were on their way, but it was obvious from the moment we arrived that the warning had already come. It was as if the entire pulse of the town had changed.

Unlike on our previous visit, no one came from their homes to greet us, or in from the fields or markets. We'd passed several public places on our way there, and no one was in any of them. Maybe they were huddled in their homes.

Huddled. Hiding.

Planning. Praying.

They knew what was coming.

We had barely driven to the door of the church when Ben came out, waving his arms as if to shoo us away. "Now? Why did you two have to come now?"

"We had to warn everyone—"

"They're warned. Can't you tell? Now go."

"We have their books," Lukas said.

Ben eyed the coffin in the back of our wagon and seemed to understand. "Let's unload them and get you two away from here as quickly as possible." Then he glared at me. "You should have stayed back with Milda. Why don't you ever do as you're told?"

"Tell me something I can obey, and I will." I wasn't in the mood to be scolded by him, not after all we'd been through to get here.

Ben directed us to drive around to the back of the church, where the priest was already waiting at the door. He said, "Get inside before someone sees you."

We followed him inside as he directed a few men to go out and tend to our horses and to get the coffin. I couldn't see how anyone heard him above the bustle of noise and activity inside the church, but his request was obeyed.

"What is everyone doing?" Lukas asked.

From where he stood, it must have looked like the people were dismantling their own church, but I stood a little deeper inside the nave and realized they were passing items belonging to the church to others waiting outside, attempting to rescue them.

A woman I had seen here on our last trip pointed at us. "They're book carriers! They can help us get these treasures to safety."

"No," Ben said, cutting in front of me. "That is not their job."

"Soldiers have arrived!" a man called from a position near a window. "Call everyone inside!" I wasn't sure where he was stationed, but he must have had a view out front, because four men immediately brushed past us to get to the front of the church, where our wagon had just been. Each man held a pitchfork in his hands like it was a rifle. The main doors were opened barely long enough for me to look out and see a line of Cossack soldiers coming up the hill.

The priest said, "On orders from the governor in this region, this church is supposed to be burned. He believes that if we have nowhere to worship our God, we will be forced into worshipping their God."

A woman standing near us said, "We won't let them burn this church. But if they do, we must get everything out. Please help us."

"You've gotten out everything that you can," Ben said, stifling a cough. "Now please, for the last time, listen to me and get as far from this place as possible."

"And let the Cossacks win again?" she asked, to echoes of agreement from the people around her.

"They will win," Ben said. "No matter how many of you are here, it won't matter. They will win."

"Can't we help them?" I asked. "She's right, we are smugglers. We can—"

Ben pointed out the window. "What orders do you think those soldiers were given? To back down and let the people have a victory against the tsar? No, they are just waiting for more soldiers to arrive and then one side or the other will start a fight that will only end one way, and that is with dead Lithuanians in the street and a church burned to its foundation. Your work is to deliver books."

"Our work is to do everything we can to free Lithuania! Words are never enough of a weapon. We must help these people fight!"

"No, Audra! For every man we bring to a fight, they can bring ten. For every weapon we can forge out of sickles and sticks and pitchforks, they have rifles and pistols and swords. The only weapon we have is who we are, and that is our words, our stories, our culture. If we preserve that, then there is always a chance for freedom, but to preserve that, we must stay alive." He wanted to say more, I knew he did, but his next words were drowned out by a coughing spasm severe enough to force him to lean against a wall for support.

Lukas had a simpler argument. Touching my arm, he said, "Ben is right. Our lives are dedicated to saving the books. Maybe others teach from their books or transport them, and that is their purpose. These people are here to save this church. We've got jobs to do, and so have they."

Reluctantly I began to follow Ben out the back of the church, but we didn't get far before another group of people entered, those who had been outside helping to take objects from the church. "More soldiers are coming," a woman said.

"Then why would you come in here?" Ben growled. "Go back to your homes!"

"That's what I'm telling you," she said. "We can't leave. They've got us surrounded. If we go out there, they'll arrest us."

Lukas looked at me. "You can find us a way out, Audra. You always do. One of your father's tricks, perhaps?"

I shook my head. "There's no trick for something like this. Those soldiers intend to destroy this church, with or without us inside it."

Ben pushed us behind him. "Here's what we're going to do. Lukas, you and Audra go as far to the back of the church as you can, and if shots are fired, I want you both inside that coffin you brought here."

"What are you going to do?" I asked.

Ben coughed, then said, "I'll help these people fight." Before I could respond, he added, "Only me. We have a long night ahead, and no matter how it ends, when news of what's happened here gets out, the anger against Russia will rise more than ever. Which means the need for book carriers will be greater than ever."

Lukas and I started to protest, but Ben ignored us as he continued pushing us toward the back of the church. We'd only taken a few steps before the first shots were fired out in the street.

"Was that them or us?" Lukas asked.

Ben turned back to us, his face grim. "Get inside that coffin and stay there until I come for you, or until it's been silent for an hour. Hear me?"

"We're not hiding like cowards while everyone else fights to defend themselves!" I said.

Ben turned on Lukas, his face reddening with anger. "I've seen these fights before, Lukas, and I know how they end. Get her to safety, now!"

Lukas nodded and grabbed my arm, even as more shots were fired. I yanked it away and stomped ahead of him toward the back of the church, furious.

"Aren't you afraid?" he asked. "Why are you in such a rush to join the fight?"

"Of course I'm afraid!" I said. "Just as I've been afraid nearly every moment since the day my parents were taken away. But every day, I tell myself to push through my fear, because if I do, maybe I will finally carry the book that brings them home, and it never does, *never*. Book smuggling isn't enough, Lukas—isn't that obvious? At some point, we've got to stand on our feet and face the Cossacks and force the Russian Empire out of our land! What if tonight is the night we could have made a difference, the night I could have brought my parents home, but it doesn't happen because I'm hiding inside a coffin instead?" I hesitated as we heard more shots firing above and a loud crash directly overhead, as if the soldiers had already broken into the church. Lowering my voice, I said, "We can help these people. It's the right thing to do and you know it."

Lukas sighed as if he knew he'd lost the argument. "I should have made you stay with Milda, and then I should have stayed too. So what do we do?"

My eyes were on the door that someone had left slightly ajar. Through it, I couldn't see any soldiers, nor were any shots coming from back here. I suspected when the fighting began, anyone who was here joined the others at the front of the church.

I said, "Let's get outside and find a place to see for ourselves what's happening. If there's a way to help, we'll do it. If not, I promise, I'll leave with you and escape into the forest."

Lukas nodded. "That's fair enough." He took a deep breath, gripped the handle of the door, then said, "I told you once that if you began to work with us, there'd be no going back. I wish you hadn't taken me so seriously."

I put a hand on his back and pressed him forward, then with a sigh added, "I wish that too."

CHAPTER
FORTY

As we had hoped, the back of the church was abandoned, and my first thought was to tell the people inside that we had a way out. But before that thought was even finished, Lukas grabbed my arm and yanked me to the ground, just in time, as the soldiers who'd been here returned, grumbling about being assigned watch duty when the real action would happen up front.

For now there was no more shooting, so I hoped what I'd heard earlier were only warning shots intended to scatter the men with pitchforks. Though if those were warnings, I doubted that anyone had left. The men weren't only protecting their church now, they were also protecting their loved ones inside.

Their actions were noble and brave . . . and probably would end in tragedy. And now I had dragged Lukas into the midst of this too. I wished none of us had to be here, but we were. The air felt thick and seemed dark, as if death hovered nearby, waiting for his opportunity to collect more than his share for the day.

Lukas began crawling on his hands and knees away from the soldiers who were still talking about how they would handle this situation if they were in charge. Grateful for the noise they were making among themselves, I followed Lukas until we were far enough away that we could hide in a patch of trees and hope to figure out a way to help.

"If we could draw the soldiers away," I said, "even for a few minutes, we could get the people out."

"Too late," Lukas said, as the instant I'd finished speaking, the front church doors burst open and the people spilled out onto the church lawn, ready to fight.

"They have no weapons," I whispered to Lukas. "They have no chance here."

"Then let's help them escape." Lukas darted forward, silently grabbing the arm of a girl near our age and pulling her toward me. I was directly behind him and took her hand, then motioned to her that we would be crouching low to the ground. She nodded and followed my lead, and I pointed out the patch of trees behind the church where I wanted her to go. The most dangerous part would be the low brick wall that surrounded the church. Her only choice was to slip over it. I hoped she was fast, and even then, I hoped she'd be lucky.

Others around us weren't so lucky. A man running right in front of Lukas was caught with a bullet. A fraction of a second's difference, and it would have been Lukas instead. But he had been encouraging people to get to the ground as well, and directing them in the same way I was.

I turned again to find Lukas, but whatever he had been doing a moment ago, now he was completely still. He was facing me, but staring at something, or someone, directly behind me, his eyes betraying the kind of horror that told me I was in terrible trouble. At first I didn't understand why. Not until Lukas said, "Spare her, Father. Let her go."

"It was never about her. I came to find you." I recognized the voice and closed my eyes, not daring to turn around, nor did I need to. Officer Rusakov was behind me. Lukas's father.

"Do you intend to arrest me?" Lukas stepped closer. "You should. I am a book smuggler, Father. Everything you worked to stop was everything I fought to achieve. I'm still fighting for it."

I shook my head. "Lukas, stop. He—"

"Lukas?" Now Rusakov crossed to where I could see him. He was still in his uniform, but it had been stripped of the decoration he'd worn every other time our paths had crossed. I got the feeling he had come here as a father, not as a soldier. "Lukas is your name now?"

It hadn't occurred to me that Lukas must have had a Russian name before this, but of course he had, and he would have changed it to keep people from knowing his background. That must have been part of the reason why Rusakov had wanted my help.

Lukas didn't answer his father, but Rusakov walked closer to him, almost forgetting me. He said, "You were there that night, when the village of Venska burned. I was sure I saw you with this girl. I tried to get her to reveal your name . . . Lukas . . . so that I could find you."

"If you'd looked for me with the other Lithuanians, you would've found me."

"You are Russian—"

"Half-Russian, and I never even felt that much. I remember once seeing my friends reading a Lithuanian book, and when they realized I'd seen it, they dropped the book and ran from me in fear. From *me*, Father, simply because of the language of the book! I picked it up, determined to understand why those words were so dangerous to the tsar. Do you know what it was? A simple fairy tale of a girl named Rue," Lukas said.

"Perhaps all of Lithuania is a fairy tale! An imagined place that refuses to acknowledge its position in the real world!" Rusakov shouted.

"If Lithuania has a place in the real world, then it deserves its own language, its own culture," I said. "We deserve our own books."

Rusakov gestured to the soldiers and villagers behind us, still fighting. "Then you deserve what will happen to all of you tonight. Freedom is never given as a gift; if you want it, then people will die for it. Why can't you just accept the occupation and live in peace with us?"

But before he could say anything more, a rifle fired into the air and the area went quiet. A soldier nearer to the front of the church shouted, "Enough of this! Go to your knees if you want to live! Stay on your feet and you'll be shot!"

Several people immediately obeyed the order, though more remained on their feet, either still trying to escape, or worse, trying to fight back, using pitchforks against bayonets. It didn't help that those who had knelt were immediately assaulted by the soldiers, their cries for mercy returned with beatings on their backs or heads. One woman had fallen to her knees, her fists clutching the frostbitten grass, praying for a miracle from the God she was trying to defend. But a soldier yanked her to her feet by one arm, told her she was being arrested, and began leading her away. Even then, I saw her lips still moving, still praying.

Other soldiers continued to order the crowd to their knees. But why would they think anyone else would obey now, only to receive that same treatment?

"Get the people out of here," a soldier ordered.

His men began herding those who were still on their feet down the hill away from the church. Halfway down, a woman slipped and might've been trampled if others nearby hadn't stopped to help her up, receiving beatings of their own as repayment for their mercy.

"We've got to help them." Lukas's tone deepened, and then I knew he had been addressing his father. "I'm going to help them and you will not stop me. You know this is wrong."

Rusakov hung his head. "Then go. Do what you must, but remember that I have no more authority among these soldiers. I cannot save you."

"Perhaps having no authority is the first step to saving yourself," Lukas said.

Rusakov nodded grimly, then I grabbed Lukas's arm and we began running down the hill to keep us ahead of where the people were still being forced to march away from the church. As we ran, I glanced back at Lukas. "Tell me you still have some matches left."

He began patting at his pockets and withdrew his matchbox. "Only a couple. Will that be enough?"

No, it wasn't. We had four smoke bombs, and now at best we would only be able to light two of them. I had always counted on using all four.

But two would have to be enough. We rounded a corner where a crooked wooden home offered Lukas some cover to hide. I took the matches from Lukas, then darted to the opposite side of the road, though there wasn't much here to protect me. Lukas would have to do most of the work.

"What is your plan?" Lukas hissed.

I shushed him. The Cossacks were still pushing the people closer to us. I had to concentrate. My timing had to be perfect. I hoped Lukas would know what to do when the right moment came.

That was all I could do, to hope he knew me well enough to guess what was in my head. This wasn't much of a plan, but without Lukas, it had no chance to succeed.

I did nothing while the first dozen people passed us by, each of them so terrified and distressed they didn't even notice we were there. Then I crouched behind a willow tree and lit the first match, cursing under my breath as it was extinguished in the night air. Now at least twenty people had passed us, and the nearest soldier was only seconds away, driving the people forward like cattle. I put my back against the breeze and struck the match closer to my body, then immediately lit the smoke bomb that I had made with the saltpeter, hoping that I had read my father's instructions correctly.

Instantly, thick gray smoke began pouring from it, and I tossed it into the center of the road, already choking on its fumes.

"Fire!" someone yelled.

"Keep going!" a man's voice replied in Russian.

The soldier who had been near us on the road must have stopped just short of the smoke to push others forward. If there was a fire ahead, he obviously had no problem with my people having to face it. At the point of his bayonet, they were forced through the smoke, faces buried against their arms or nuzzled into their shirts or aprons. As soon as I saw each one come through, I'd grab them and pull them off the road with me, then tell them to run. On his side of the road, Lukas did the same.

The smoke didn't last long, not nearly as long as I'd hoped, before the tendrils began to thin. If we had planned better, I'd have had enough matches for the other three smoke bombs we carried. If we had planned this at all, we would have already been running away with the people we'd saved, for I had no idea how visible I'd become.

From behind me, a soldier's arm wrapped around my neck and began dragging me backward, with a voice saying, "You'll pay for that."

I kicked at the ground and beat at his arm, anything to force him to loosen his grip, but nothing worked. Lukas had seen this man take me, I was sure he had, but he wouldn't be able to help me, nor should he. If he tried, he'd only share in whatever punishment I was about to receive.

Before I knew it, the soldier had dragged me across a field and toward a river where I heard other voices somewhere nearby. I couldn't see them, but I knew the other people here were in as much trouble as I was.

The soldier pulled me into the river and threw me under the water, which was icy cold and deeper than it looked. His grip on my arm was like a vise, so I couldn't get away, nor could I stand. I turned my head against the current, hoping to get a few sips of air, but every draw brought more water into my lungs.

Then I understood. That was the soldier's intention. The people they had captured, the ones we had failed to save, they were being drowned here.

And I would be among them.

CHAPTER
FORTY-ONE

When it became clear what was about to happen, I began fighting the soldier more fiercely than ever. More fiercely than I believed I was capable of fighting. Oddly, I didn't feel like myself in that moment, but rather, I felt like Rue, the character from the stories that Lukas had told me all these months. I'd once been timid and fearful, but now I was much more like Rue: strong and confident and forceful. And if she would not give in to this fight, nor would I.

I yanked my father's bag off my shoulder and swung it at the soldier's face. Water had filled the leather satchel now, so the smack against his jaw caused him to stumble, enough that he loosened his grip on my arm. I wrenched free but, in doing so, lost the bag, which floated downstream out of my reach. I dove for it and failed to notice the soldier had lunged for me, grabbing my arm again. This time, his pistol was out.

My gut twisted. I had no defense against that. And with the river more than waist deep, I couldn't fight him off again.

"Back away!" The soldier raised his pistol, even while keeping a hold on me. But his head was up, speaking to someone else, someone ahead of him in the water. Who was it?

Not Lukas. The last I'd seen him, he was on the bank of the river, some ways behind me.

"I said back away!" the soldier repeated.

The voice that answered became muffled against all the water splashing around me, but I did get a few bits of phrases.

". . . would've been your commander."

". . . this is wrong . . ."

". . . I will stop you by force if—"

That was the last I heard before the pistol fired and the soldier released me. Exhausted, half-frozen, and choking on water, I drifted downstream, only vaguely aware of Lukas shouting. Was it my name? It didn't sound like my name.

Seconds later, someone pulled me from the water and dragged me back onto the riverbank, turning me to the side and pounding on my back to force the water from my lungs.

"You're so concerned with saving others you never think to save yourself first." That was Ben's voice. "I'm not letting you die here, so you get some air into your body, Audra, or else. You start breathing, hear me?"

I coughed out water and drew in air with it, beautiful, breathable air. I lay there on my side until Ben's face came into focus, his expression grim.

"There are others downstream who still need help." Ben pointed up the riverbank to some brush that somehow was still holding on to most of its leaves. "Can you get up there to hide until this is over?"

"Where is Lukas?"

"I don't know. He jumped into the river to attack the man who was holding you. That's all I saw before I grabbed you."

Then I had to do more than crawl to a hiding place. I had to find Lukas and make sure he was all right. While Ben went in one direction, I continued coughing out water, then staggered to my feet, bracing myself with anything I could find along the way to keep stumbling forward.

The trouble at the church wasn't over—I heard cries and shouts everywhere around me—but I couldn't think about that. I had to find Lukas.

I rounded the bend in the river and was relieved to see him kneeling on the bank, but not alone. A man lay in front of him and seemed to be bleeding. Lukas had his hands pressed on the wound, I realized.

Wasn't this the officer that had just tried to drown me? Why would he—

No, it wasn't. This was Officer Rusakov, Lukas's father.

The man who had tried to save me. He'd been the one shot by the pistol.

I knelt beside Lukas. His father was alive and conscious, but bleeding from a wound in his leg.

"Let's get him into the forest," I said. "Where we sent the others. I saw people go into a barn there."

Rusakov shook his head. "They won't take me in."

"They will, or we'll smuggle you in," I said. "But we've got to get you somewhere to bind that injury, and we'll all become ill if we stay out here in these wet clothes."

Together we helped Rusakov to his feet, then Lukas braced his father's weight while I kept watch ahead. Slowly we made the trek into the patch of trees where a barn stood as silent as the night should have been.

At first I wondered if anyone was in there—from the outside it looked as abandoned and quiet as before, but when I opened the doors, I saw it filled with people.

Their eyes widened in alarm at seeing Rusakov with us, but Lukas said, "This is my father, and he saved our lives."

They made way for us and let us lay Rusakov on the ground, then a woman came forward and tore at her apron to create a bandage for his leg.

Only then did I look around at who was in this barn with us. We had a little light filtered in through the slats to illuminate our barn, and I welcomed the sight of every person here.

We hadn't saved all these people. Several of them must have escaped here on their own, though I noticed many injuries, some more serious than Lukas's father's. Tears streamed down their faces as they held one another and desperately looked out the barn windows in hopes of seeing even one more person join us.

Ben.

I hoped if there was one more person, it might be Ben.

We waited there for the rest of the night, huddled together for warmth, until in the early morning hours the priest of the church entered the barn with only a small candle to guide him. His face was grim.

"How bad is it?" one man asked.

"At least a hundred and fifty arrests," the priest said. "We'll appeal to the authorities for their release. I hope we'll have some success, given what else happened tonight."

But it wasn't only arrests, or else his face would not seem so pale now, so haunted.

"What else?" Lukas asked.

It took the priest a long time to answer, but as gently as he could, he said, "Some who tried to escape were recaptured and beaten. Another thirty or forty are seriously injured from the initial attack." The priest drew in a deep breath as he looked around our solemn group. "And we have at least six dead, driven to the river and drowned."

The news was met with an eerie silence. No one moved or spoke, and if they cried, it was with silent tears and mouthed words of comfort. But no sounds.

I vaguely realized Lukas's arm was around me, and I leaned my head on his shoulder to cry. I knew we were both thinking the same thing, that Ben had not returned. Would not return.

And he never did return.

It felt like an entire month of silence passed before people began moving again, speaking again. I watched them as if through a fog, as if seeing each person through the same thick smoke that had brought them here in the first place. If only I could have lit the rest of our smoke bombs, or made one that lasted longer. If I'd done just a little more, maybe another ten or twenty or thirty people could have gotten through it. Maybe more people might still be—

"I'm alive because of you."

I looked up to see a woman staring down at me, her plump cheeks and kind smile reminding me of Milda. Tears still creased the corners of her eyes, but I wondered if maybe a little gratitude was mixed in with her sorrow.

The woman took my hand in hers and gave it a firm squeeze. "You, dear girl, I don't know how you did what you did for us, but I'm alive because of it. We all are."

"Thank you," a man behind her echoed. He hoisted a young boy with curly hair into his arms, probably his son. "Thanks from us both."

"And from us," said a girl who was standing with her arm around a woman I hadn't noticed earlier, maybe her mother. "We were among the first you pulled from the smoke."

"Thank you," a voice in back called, then another voice repeated the words, and another. The sun broke through the loft window that morning to warm us, but it was nothing compared to the warmth bursting in my chest. Yes, we had losses, and yes, the night had given us a terrible tragedy. But once again, my people had proved that we would never stop fighting, never stop resisting.

And we would never forget who we were.

The priest stepped toward me and smiled. "You're the book carrier who does magic."

I shook my head, aware that everyone had gone silent, waiting for my answer. Suddenly, I was that shy girl again, the one who never wanted to speak if there was any way to avoid it, the one who was certain she had nothing worthwhile to say.

But I also knew that I'd been wrong before, staying silent when I had something important to say. I couldn't fade into the shadows, nor would I whisper my words to Lukas so that he could say them for me. The words in my mind had to be spoken by me.

"I don't do magic," I said. "I do tricks that my father taught me. That was how he earned money for our family, but that wasn't his purpose in life, nor my mother's. My parents sacrificed everything they had, everything they loved, and maybe even their own lives, for the true magic. It's our books. Our language, our culture, our identities are inscribed in every word. As long as we have our books, we cannot be crushed, we cannot be forgotten. Because of our books, we will not be erased from our own history. We will remember who we are, all that we stand for, and all that we will fight for and continue fighting for until the day we see the last Cossack soldier leave this land. If you want revenge for what they have done here, then tonight gather your family around you by the firelight and read. Learn. Create ideas of your own and spread them to others. It will be proof that we are winning."

I finished speaking to warm embraces and more wishes of thanks, and Lukas leaning over and whispering into my ear that we had better leave while we still could.

I nodded back at him. He was right. This had been the worst of nights, but morning had come, and we had work to do.

FORTY-TWO

When the priest told us it was safe enough to leave the barn, most of the people hurried to their homes, eager to report to their loved ones there about who was safe, and who would not be returning home.

One of the men we had saved was a physician, who had Rusakov carried to his home, where he could tend to the wound more properly.

Lukas and I decided to walk back to the church, to see if anything of it remained after the soldiers had carried out their orders. I must've looked back a thousand times, hoping to see Ben following us, but Lukas finally said, "He won't be there, Audra."

"I know." But knowing didn't make it hurt any less.

A few steps later, Lukas said, "When Ben was gruff with you, or tried to get you to go away all those times, it was only because—"

"He just wanted to keep me safe, I understand."

"It's more than that. I'll show you."

By then, we'd reached the church. The priest was seated on the front steps, looking deeply saddened.

"They'll call what happened last night a massacre," he said. "If there was anger in the country before now—"

"The church is still here," Lukas said.

The priest shrugged. "Yes, but at what price?" For the first time, he seemed to really see us. "You both should get inside where it's warm."

We nodded and walked past him to enter the church, which was empty now. I sat on one bench but rather than sit with me, Lukas excused himself, returning a minute later with a wrapped package that he set on my lap.

From its shape, I already had a good idea of what it might be, but I unwrapped it anyway to see the same locked book I had given to Milda five months ago. Except this time, I had the key, somehow still in my apron pocket.

"Ben had this book?" I asked. "Why would he care?"

"Open it, Audra." While I dug in my apron for the key, Lukas added, "Last night, Ben told me where this book was hidden. He said if he didn't make it back, that I was to give it to you, but only if he didn't make it back."

"Why would that have mattered?" I pushed the key into the lock, though it didn't seem to want to turn.

"He said that if you knew what was inside, he'd never get you to stop smuggling. But if he didn't return, he hoped that once you saw the book, you'd listen to his final request and leave the country, go to where it's safer."

Finally, the key turned and the lock snapped apart. I opened the book and began thumbing through the papers. Page after page was the same, names connected by lines, many of them with pictures drawn beside the names.

These were family records. I kept turning pages, one after another, wondering why Ben would've cared so much about showing this to me.

And knowing in my heart why he did. But I had to see it.

Two-thirds of the way through the book was the last recorded page. Halfway down I read the name "Ben Kagan" and a line across from him with the name of a woman who must have been his wife once.

But for now my eye dipped lower to a drawing of my mother with her name, Lina, below the picture. Across from her was a line with my father's picture, and his name, Henrikas Zikaris.

A line descended from their pictures, but nothing else was there. This book hadn't been updated since my birth, but suddenly the reasons for Ben treating me the way he did became clear. Why he hadn't wanted me to smuggle, why I'd become more headstrong the longer I knew him. Why he wanted to keep me safe.

Ben was my grandfather. He must've known, must have

ached as much as I did to hear what had happened to my mother, his daughter, but he'd never said a word about it.

"Milda is over the border," Lukas said. "She needs someone to stay and help her. You'll still be helping books get into Lithuania, maybe even doing more good there than you could do here."

I nodded. It was the right thing to do now. It's what my parents would've wanted. What Ben wanted. And if I was being honest with myself, I wanted it too.

Then I looked up at Lukas. "You'll come with me, won't you?"

He pressed his lips together. "When my father is well enough to travel, I'll escort him home. I'll go home, Audra, at least for now. My father saved your life in that river, and if it means he's trying to change, well, I've got to give him a chance. Maybe I can do some changing of my own, be a tad less stubborn, break fewer laws . . . that sort of thing."

Tears filled my eyes. "Then once we say goodbye here, I'll never see you again."

Lukas only smiled. "You've been writing your own story about Rue and the boy who lived on her land. How does it end?"

I could answer that question now. "They continued to work and to fight against the snake, never once giving up on their dream that Rue's land would one day belong only to her. And one day, on the day she least suspected it might ever happen . . ."

"The snake left for good," Lukas said. "It had to leave. For Rue had grown so strong, so intelligent, that the snake was no threat to her any longer."

I drew in a slow breath. "What I don't know about my story's ending is if Rue will ever see the boy again."

Lukas smiled, as if the answer was obvious. "Of course she will."

"I need something to write with," I said, glancing down at the heavy book on my lap. "Before I finish that story, I want to complete this one." He must have had a pen ready for he immediately put it into my hand.

And there, below the names of my parents, Henri and Lina, and beneath the name of my grandfather, I wrote A-U-D-R-A.

EPILOGUE

On my final journey toward the border, I spent the hours between sleeping and waking reading from the locked book. Years earlier in his life, Ben must have recorded the full story of his role in the uprising, the catalyst for the ban on our books now.

The uprising had failed—catastrophically failed—and Ben had never gotten over that. He didn't consider himself a hero for the role he had played back then, nor did it matter that they had come so close to gaining freedom. Instead, he felt guilt, wondering if they had never fought, would Lithuania still have its books, its language?

That's why he smuggled, constantly hoping to undo the damage done to our country because of the uprising.

My heart ached for Ben. He had gone to his death believing that the smuggling didn't matter, either, that his defense of the church in Kražiai didn't matter. How wrong he was.

The church never was burned, and after the news of that night spread throughout the country, our relationship with

Russia became worse than ever before. Which meant the demand for books—for knowledge and ideas—became stronger than ever as well.

Russia's hold on us was weakening. Every year we pushed harder for our independence, and every year their laws softened. But not enough to allow us our books. Still not enough. So there was always more work to be done.

From the first day I returned to Milda's home, we devoted every waking moment to preparing books to be smuggled into Lithuania. We raised funds for printing, collected book donations, left books in drop points near the border, and managed the orders that flooded in.

I met dozens of book smugglers, those who continued to risk their lives to carry the books into the country. They were heroic and determined and passionate about their work. Every smuggler who walked through our door lifted my spirits.

But not once did Lukas ever come through that door.

I watched for him every day, and the days of missing him turned to months, which became years. He must have stopped smuggling; perhaps he had even become a respectable person in his father's home. In his Russian father's home.

Milda and I spoke often of Lukas, of our favorite memories of him. The way he laughed, the way his eye turned to food whenever it was nearby. His kindness, his bravery. Milda seemed to have a new story of him every time his name came up in conversation.

Until conversation became too difficult for her. Until she became confined to her bed, unable to speak more than a few words at a time, but with a mind keen on listening to every page I could read to her.

Until one day, when the last words of the book I was reading said, "The end," and I looked up to see Milda's eyes closed, a pleasant smile on her face, having reached the end of her own story.

I had her buried in a church plot as close as I dared get to the border. As close to her home as she could ever be again. Then the entire task of getting books printed fell to me.

And not only books, but I wrote for the newspaper about the power of words and why the fight must continue. My words were true and came straight from my heart, although deep inside, beyond thought and reason, in that place where there were only feelings, I wondered if the fight mattered. I wondered, like Ben, if maybe none of it would ever make a difference. Because how could a nation as small as ours ever defeat an empire?

I got my answer on the one-year anniversary of Milda's death. The year was 1904 and I was now twenty-three years old. I had a wreath of flowers for Milda, but when I went to lay them on the arch of her gravestone, I saw a bouquet of rue already there. Curious, I stopped. Who would have brought these . . . and why? The bouquet wasn't appropriate for remembering a death. They would have come from—

Drawing in a sharp breath, I set my wreath down, then began looking around. "Lukas?" I knew it must be him!

He was standing directly behind me, as grown up as I'd become, more handsome than I remembered, but with the same playful grin as always.

"I haven't seen you in more than ten years and all you bring me are flowers?" I asked, a twinkle in my eye.

Lukas's grin became crooked as it widened. "Those flowers aren't from me, Audra. But I did bring you this. I thought you might want it."

He'd had one arm behind his back and he brought it forward, with my father's shoulder bag in his hand, the one with the tricks that had saved my life and introduced me to real magic.

I reached for it, uncertain of how I'd feel to have it back again, empty now. Empty forevermore. Still, I was glad to have it. There was so little I had for memories of my childhood. I would treasure this like it was gold, like it was everything to me.

"How did you find this again?" I asked.

Lukas shrugged. "It wasn't easy. But if you want to thank me, then I hope Milda taught you to cook. We're definitely hungry."

My brow arched. "We?" When he didn't answer, I added, "Lukas, where did that bouquet of flowers come from?"

He must've been so eager to answer that he began

bouncing on his toes. "I can see I've traveled faster than the news. It's happened, Audra, it's finally happened! The press ban is over! Our books will be legal again. And if our books are no longer a crime, then—"

"Then those who smuggled them are no longer criminals!" My heart leapt. That meant I could return to the land I loved, the place I belonged. I could go home.

If only I had a home there.

Lukas stepped closer to me. "It took my last coin to purchase two train tickets."

Then I understood. I glanced again at the flowers. I had once been nicknamed for these flowers.

"Don't say it." By then, tears had welled in my eyes. "Don't say it if they aren't here."

"Then we'll say it," a woman's voice said. More than ten years later, I knew that voice. I'd heard it every night in my dreams.

"My little Rue, you brought us home. How we've missed you." I knew that voice as well. It had been imprinted onto my heart.

The tears rolled down my cheek as I turned around, then rushed forward with my arms wide open.

"Mama! Papa!"

They looked older than they ought to have, and tired, and their clothes were worn into threads. Yet they were smiling and their eyes shone with excitement and love.

My parents folded me into their embrace and there we cried and laughed and cried some more. After we parted, Lukas was invited in, where I noticed he stared at me with a very different smile on his face.

It would be another fourteen years, a world war, and an occupation by Germany before Lithuania finally gained its freedom. By then, Lukas and I had children of our own, children who were growing up with books in their language, being taught in schools in their language and of their culture. By the time we formally received our independence, Lithuania had long considered itself free.

And always would, no matter what other troubles would come.

So tonight, like every other night, I picked up a book and sat beside Lukas in front of the fireplace of our home. Our children gathered around us for story time. Like every other night, I would read a page, then Lukas, then the children would beg him to tell a story from back when we were book carriers. A true story.

And like every other night, Lukas would begin the same way.

"Well, as you all know, your mother's name, Audra, means 'storm.' And so she is, children. She was a storm that helped bring freedom to all of us."

The work of restoring Lithuania's independence began not in 1918, but rather at the time of the book carriers. With bundles of books and pamphlets on their backs, these warriors were the first to start preparing the ground for independence, the first to propagate the idea that it was imperative to throw off the heavy yoke of Russian oppression.

—Father Julijonas Kasperavicius

ACKNOWLEDGMENTS

This book would be incomplete without a recognition of those who gave me a love of words. Thank you, Mrs. Flores, the first teacher to truly celebrate me as a reader. Thank you, Lorraine, for the challenging word finds and crossword games. Thank you, Mom, for always giving me access to books, no matter what, and to Dad, for the word definition games.

I also wish to honor the *knygnesiai*—the book carriers, who are among the true heroes of Lithuanian history. This work that began with a single priest eventually expanded to include nearly every citizen in the country, either involved in smuggling, transporting, hiding, teaching, or purchasing the illegal books. Over the forty years of the ban, nearly eight million books were published across 1,740 titles. More than three thousand people were arrested in connection with the ban, and approximately 10 percent of the books were seized by authorities. The Kražiai Massacre in November 1893 deepened the Lithuanian resentment against the Russian occupation, and efforts to resist their laws intensified.

Eventually, it became apparent to the Russian Empire that the press ban had been a failure, and in 1904, Tsar Nicolas II revoked the ban. On February 16, 1918, Lithuania officially received its independence. Another seventy-three years of difficulty with Russia followed until 1991, when Lithuania finally regained its independence, which exists today.

Many thanks to my family for their constant support of my writing, especially Jeff, who is the best of men, best of husbands, and my best friend. Thanks also to my agent, Ammi-Joan Paquette, for her enthusiasm and input on this project, and to my editor, Lisa Sandell, for her extraordinary work in the editing of this book, though I never see anything less from her. My gratitude as well to the talented people throughout the Scholastic family, for all the hard work they put into every one of my books. I am deeply indebted to each of you.

And because this is a book celebrating the love of words, my thanks extend to the teachers and librarians who have made it their lives' work to spread words to their students and patrons. You are literally building a better future for us all.

Finally, to readers, I hope you loved this book, and that upon finishing you will look for another book to dive into and love just as much, and then another and another. For who are we all, if not the product of who we love, what we know, and every wonderful word that we have read?

Read *LINES OF COURAGE* from *New York Times* Bestselling Author

JENNIFER A. NIELSEN

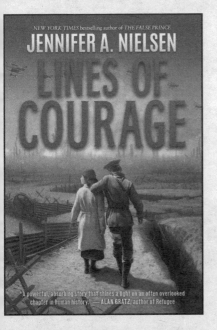

World War I stretches its cruel fingers across Europe, where five young people face the terror of battle, the deprivations of hunger, and all the awful challenges of war.

Felix, from Austria-Hungary, longs for the bravery to resist Jewish deportations.

Kara, from Britain, dreams of earning her Red Cross pin and working as a nurse—or even a doctor.

Juliette, of France, hopes her family can remain knitted together as the war's longest battle stretches on and on.

Elsa, from Germany, hopes her homing pigeon might one day bring her a friend.

And Dimitri, of Russia, wants only to survive the battlefront.

Together, they will discover that friendship and courage can light the way through the most frightening of nights.

In this remarkable exploration of World War I, award-winning author Jennifer A. Nielsen weaves together the extraordinary stories of five children, each of whom holds the key to the others' futures . . . if they are lucky—and brave—enough to find each other.

Read these thrilling stories
from *New York Times* bestselling author
JENNIFER A. NIELSEN

When the Berlin Wall divides her family, Gerta finds herself in a race against time to escape to the West.

When the Nazis occupy Poland, Jewish teenager Chaya decides to fight back…to resist.

When the Russian Cossack soldiers occupying Lithuania arrest Audra's parents, she becomes caught up in the deadly struggle to save her nation.

When one girl fights to save her father from the Nazis, she works with the French resistance and finds herself racing against the clock to crack a crucial code.

When World War I stretches its cruel fingers across Europe, five young people hold the key to one another's futures.